C000132694

I, RICHARD PLANTAGENET

THE PREQUEL: Part One

THE ROAD FROM FOTHERINGHAY

By J.P. REEDMAN

Table of Contents

Chapter One: Prologue

Evening light shudders over the spires and towers of Westminster; in the distance, the bells of abbeys, priories and churches clash endlessly, an endless paean heralding the coming of the dusk. The last slanted shafts of sunlight pierce the ancient glass in the mullioned windows; red pools stretch across the elaborate tiles like spreading blood. They reach, then die, consumed by purpling darkness. The horizon swallows the sun; a thin moon, a fingernail paring, slides out from behind a church tower beyond the palace walls, across the mist-exhaling ribbon on the Thames.

In my apartments, I am alone; so little time have I to gather my own thoughts, to lay aside the cares of kingship, I cherish these few hours, caught in the glimmering, almost mystical hour betwixt day and night. I hold my prayer book in my hand, fingers stroking the well-worn cover. It has always been a comfort to me, inscribed with prayers to my favourite saints, such as the Collect of Ninian, and a prayer asking God to protect me from my enemies.

I have so many enemies, and each day the crown grows heavier on my brow…

My lips twist up in a bitter smile. What fool, drunk with his own important, his own power, said it was good to be King? Rumour, rebellion; all manner of evil has plagued me since I assumed the crown, chosen by the Three Estates, my right soon to be asserted in the document called Titulus Regius. I already feel a hundred years old, worn out with care…I have not yet reached my thirty-second birthday.

Carefully, I open the prayer book, my fingertips light on browning edges; it is old but not ancient, crafted at least fifty years ago for another man, but on this night, I will make it forever my own, a thing of comfort to hold close through the tribulations of my reign.

Turning to a chosen page, I place the open book on my desk, pushing unsealed and unsigned missive aside, and lift one of the quills that lay there. With slow deliberation—I have always been proud of my neat hand, I write in the calendar of October 2—*'Hac die natus erat Ricardus Rex Anglie tertius Apud Foderingay Anno domini mlcccliio.'*

On This Day was Born Richard III King of England at Fotheringhay in the year 1452.

Fotheringhay...Memories flooded over me, of the castle, the little town, the great church that was the burial place of many members of the House of York—my Uncle Edward, who died at Agincourt, my father Richard, killed at Wakefield, my brother Edmund—murdered by Butcher Clifford. I had not visited the place of my birth for several years now. The last time was when my brother King Edward invited the Duke of Albany, brother of the Scots king, to treat with him. My job was to help convince Albany to accept Ned's terms; Albany would get the Scottish crown out of the arrangement and one of Ned's pretty, golden-locked daughters as an additional sweetener. Albany had wanted the crown but not enough, as it turned out, and Ned had never made the move northward that he promised, leaving me to fare to Edinburgh without his backing. I did not remain long but did what I could ere money ran out. At the very least, I took Berwick back for England, where it belonged, undoing the folly of our old foe, Marguerite of Anjou, who had handed it to the Scots in order to obtain their aid.

I lay down the quill, stretching out my legs before me. My back ached from shoulder blade down to my hip; I shifted uneasily, rubbed my right shoulder that was, beneath careful padding, a little higher than the left. My curse. My secret. The strange serpentine formation of my body, so inferior to the titanic form of my dead brother Ned, who was at one time deemed the most handsome man in Europe...

I let my finger trace the gold-painted writing of the page in the prayer book, running over the lists of saints and jottings about the length of the days whilst avoiding the new ink that was still wet, glistening on the vellum like dark, viscous tears.

Yet ever my gaze drew back to what I had just written. Fotheringhay. *Fotheringhay.*

The name struck like an arrow into my soul. It seemed an eternity since I was a child there, a child born to be nothing, the youngest son of a huge brood. The runt of the Duke of York's litter, named for a saint from Chichester and for his royal-blooded father.

My father, whose head should have worn England's crown but instead ended up on Micklegate in York, food for the hungry crows, a mocking paper crown upon his brow.

As my chamber darkened, the candle on the desk dying in a draught, I let my thoughts flow free and immerse myself in the memories of a time long gone past...

Memories of a time of bright hope and of terror and tears that began at Fotheringhay...

Chapter Two

Ursula was dead.

Nurses wept openly in the castle halls, consoling each other with embraces and prayers as they huddled together like birds that clustered on the castle turrets before a storm. I watched them through a crack in the chamber door, perplexed, not understand their grief. How could Ursula be dead? She couldn't be, it must be some terrible mistake. Surely, she was just playing a prank, holding her breath like she always did when she had a temper tantrum over having her hair combed or eating food she did not like!

Ursula was my little sister and but two summers old. We had played together in the nursery—games where I rolled coloured marbles for her pleasure or where we raced my carved wooden horses. Ursula was still clumsy with babyhood, her fingers thick and fat, but I never chided her or made fun when she threw the marbles or lost the races. Sometimes, deliberately, I even let her win a race or keep a marble for her own. But then, suddenly, all had changed. She had started to ail, her throat growing sore and coughs wracking her small body. Her golden curls clung damp to her brow and her eyes grew dull and dark. She became listless and soon, after much whispering, she was taken from the nursery to another room. Doctors in black came, swishing in and out in their long black robes that smelt of strange potions.

And now they said she was dead.

I chewed my lip, fretting.

Suddenly, I heard footsteps coming swiftly down the corridor. Hastily I closed the door and pretended to toy with a tin soldier I'd received on my last name day so that I would not receive a smack for eavesdropping.

Old Annie, the foremost of my nurses, hobbled into the room, blotchy-cheeked, tears streaking down her bristly chin. Her eyes were flame-red with weeping. "Come, little Dickon. Put down your toy and come with me at once. Your Lady Mother the Duchess has arrived. I am ordered to take you to the chapel where they have laid Ursula out, God assoil the wee mite."

Mother was here at Fotheringhay! That thought frightened me nearly as much as this foolish talk of Ursula being dead. I knew something must be amiss if she had returned to the castle. Mother travelled much with my father, Richard, Duke of York, and I seldom saw her save on great occasions. She bore the air of a Queen, proud and distance, and I found myself frequently overawed, perhaps a little afraid.

Annie took my hand and guided me down to the castle chapel. All around members of the household, dressed in mourning black, bowed their heads as we passed. Crossing the windy courtyard, we entered the larger of the two chapels in the castle. Immediately incense and tallow-scents reached into my throat and made me cough. Annie frowned at me, shaking her head. I forced my coughs into silence.

Ursula lay outstretched on an ermine lined pall. She looked even tinier than usual. She wore a white gown beaded with seed pearls, and her face and hands were as white as her dress. Soft coils of dusky gold hair lay on the satin pillow beneath her head. Over her the Rood reared up, Jesus on the Cross, bleeding, guarding her. The priest who gave me lessons even morning said gentle Jesu was especially kind to little children. A strong smell of cinnamon and other spices wafted from her, almost as if she had been bathed in them but below their pungency, there was a more unpleasant fragrance that permeated the room, sickly-sweet, cloying, foul.

My brother George was already in the chapel, staring morosely at the tiles and fidgeting as if he wished he were anywhere else but here. My elder sister Margaret was at his side, weeping freely while pressing a kerchief to her nose.

As I appeared the chapel door with Annie, Margaret glanced at me and beckoned me over to stand at her side. She put away her kerchief and took my hand in her damp, soggy one.

"Meg…" I began plaintively.

"You mustn't speak, Richard," she whispered in my ear, bending her head to me. "Not now. Not today. Be brave."

I shut my mouth and clung more tightly to her hand.

The chapel's nave was already quiet but a deeper hush descended over God's house as a shadow suddenly stretched from the door across the tiles with their patterns of falcons and roses. Glancing to the side, I saw Mother walk slowly into the chapel. Margaret's fingers clamped on mine, almost painfully.

Mother was not a tall woman but her air of majesty made her seem almost a giantess. So too the tall, coned headdress she wore, a dark veil patterned with white gems trailing over her shoulders and down her back. She was rather old, around forty summers, and small lines marred her carefully plucked brow, but her features remained very beautiful, her nose long and tip-tilted like my brother Edward's, and her mouth small, red and bud-like. As she saw Ursula lying upon her pall, she hesitated for a brief moment and bit upon her lip, a habit I, too, have when I am upset. Her ladies-in-waiting clustered at her heels, cooing, fussing and crying; she pushed their solicitous hands away with stern rebukes.

I wanted to go to her, for she was still my mother, even if she was the Duchess of York and unlike the mothers of the peasant children in Fotheringhay, who played with their children in the river and hugged them when they skinned their knees or fell out of trees while playing. We children of York had nurses for our childhood wounds. Yet still I desired, deep in my heart of hearts, to bury myself in her long, flowing skirts. To have her say, "Richard, it will be fine; you need not fear."

She proceeded to the pall, hung with the customary black draperies, and knelt stiffly before it, head bowed in silent prayer. The nurses broke out in renewed fits of weeping, as did we children, but not one tear jewelled our mother's long lashes. The priest came out of the vestry, wreathed by the cloying incense smoke, and droned of the Resurrection.

Before long, George was growing restless, as he always did no matter the gravity of the situation, nudging me and Margaret with his elbow. "I need to piss!" he hissed in my ear.

Margaret cast him an angry glare; her tear-dazzled eyes red as fire. "Don't you understand?" she whispered back. "George, your behaviour is most inappropriate. You will get a birching! I swear I'll flog you myself!"

He scowled. "You and who else? You're just a weak girl!"

I glanced away from their feuding and over to mother's rod-straight back and the doll-like shape of Ursula on the bier. I noticed my sister's lips were blue but other than that she looked as if she was sleeping. Sleeping deeply in an enchanted slumber. Ready to awaken like a faerie princess in an old tale.

I was barely four summers old; I knew no better. I did not understand death's true meaning, its awful finality.

As George's fingers poked my velvet-clad back, I gazed up, wide-eyed, outspoken in my innocence, and said, my voice clear as a bell in the little chapel, "Mother, when will Ursula wake up? I do not like all this weeping, and George is bothering me!"

My punishment was swift and sudden. As my mother turned from the pall, her face rigid, icy, I was swept off my feet by one of the younger nurses and carried bodily out of the chapel and into the dim-lit corridors beyond. I started to kick and struggle, striving to return to the chapel and make amends for whatever I had done wrong, but the woman, a thin, hook-nosed girl called Tibbot, shook me like a ragdoll, making my head wobble. "Shame on you, Master Richard! Shame! What on earth possessed you to say such a thing in the presence of your dear Lady Mother, the Duchess Cecily? You shall stay on your own tonight and have but bread for your dinner while you think on what you've done. Just be glad you're a Dukes son and not my own bairns, or I'd have my hand to you!"

I still did not understand what I'd done that was so wicked but I ceased to fight my gaoler. Resistance would do me no good and might even bring further punishment. I was taken to a disused tower room, musty, a little dusty, with a small bed in one corner and a chamber pot. There was a missal on the stand near the bed; I could not yet read but at least I could hold it and think on my great sin. Whatever it was.

I sat down heavily upon the bed and as the door banged shut behind Tibbot, the self-pitying tears started. I tried to blink them back for boys did not cry. George would pretend he never did, although I knew he howled when he did not get his own way just like a baby. I never dared say so to his face, though; I did not want a thump or a twisted ear.

Alone in the tower room, my place of penance, I cried for my humiliation in front of the household, in front of my Lady Mother. I cried even harder when my mind, mulling my errors suddenly leapt forth lightning-quick and comprehended what I had done. The great awfulness of death, the horror of the void, yawned before me. I remembered the dancing skeletons on Doom Paintings, the scythes that sliced down men and maidens, children and kings. Ursula had looked like she was merely sleeping…but Ursula was never going to wake.

Never.

And my clumsy, unthinking child's words had thrust an added knife of grief into my Mother's breast.

The next day, old Annie and Tibbot, pouch-eyed and sombre, dragged me from my hard, uncomfortable bed, dressed me, scrubbed my face with a rough wet cloth, combed my unruly hair till my head ached. I could barely speak and they glared at me when I tried; I knew I had not yet been forgiven—a greater punishment was coming than a night in solitude without dinner.

I was going to be hauled before *her*.

My Mother the Duchess.

I would have to stand before her and receive chastisement for my foolish ill-doing, my own ignorance. My buttocks began to hurt already as I imagined a caning but that was little compared to the pain needling my heart. Mother would not beat me herself, of course, but the household tutors were often keen to strike bad children in an effort to make them grow into upright adults.

The nurses marched me into her quarters, scented with frankincense and rose-petal pomanders. The tapestries on her bed were cherry-red, threaded with gold, and bore the image of a lady seated on a chair of estate. The draperies were stitched with gilt pineapples, and on the floor, covering the deep blue tiles, were imported rugs from Spain. The walls bore vivid paintings from the Bible—Job and his daughters Jemimah, Keziah and Kerenhappuch, Noah and the Ark, and the near-sacrifice of Isaac by his ages father, Abraham.

Wide-eyed, I stared up at that one, a lump growing in my throat. Isaac was sprawled on a stone altar, hair tangled, face full of terror as his father raised a dagger over his head. I felt like I, too, was a sacrifice, but one God would not spare, for I deserved my punishment.

A curtain was drawn aside from a corridor leading further into the state apartments and my mother walked into the room, alone, her ladies dismissed. She waved an abrupt hand for my nurses to depart, leaving me standing alone before her. In my shame, I could not meet her eyes and stared at the floor where a random ant was trying to navigate the pike on my shoe.

Mother stood before me, radiating grace and authority. Queenliness. I wondered if I should kneel.

"Richard, why do you not look at me?" she asked after a few minutes.

My entire small, skinny body trembled but I forced myself to stare up into her face. Her neat, upturned nose was like my brother Edward's, rather than mine, as was her small, red mouth and her eyes were greenish-brown, the colour of hazelnuts mixed with leaves. Other than her littleness in stature, we were not much alike in aspect. That somehow made my failure as a son even more poignant.

But I refuse to cry, although the urge was there. I was my father's son in that at least. Stubborn.

"Richard..." To my surprise, there was a tiny quaver in her voice. It vanished almost instantly. I thought I saw the hint of tears, then they were swiftly blinked away. Calm, cool nobility reigned again; she was like a church effigy, smooth, white and emotionless. "Richard, I can see that you and your brother and sister have been left to your own devices for too long. The nursemaids have indulged you. George is full of uncouth tricks, Margaret is unruly and you...you speak out of turn as a young boy should never do in the presence of his Lady Mother...and God. Whatever possessed you to speak so at your dead sister's bier?"

I thought of George poking my back with his hot sharp fingers, but I would not tell on him. I was not full of tittle-tattle like a spiteful old beldame who sought to stir the pot and blame all others for her ills.

"I—I do not know, Maman," I said weakly. "I am foolish. I beg forgiveness..."

"Maybe you truly did not understand," Mother murmured, gazing away into the distance, eyes clouding. "Oftimes I forget how young you are—my little problem son."

I cringed at her words. I had heard the nurses say how my birth had hurt mother, how she had been unwell for a long time after and had complained in a letter to Queen Marguerite about the aches and pains that assailed her after bearing a child in old age. I was indeed, it seemed, her 'problem.'

"There is only one thing for it." She clapped her hands together; to my childish ears, the sound was loud as God's thunder, the sound of the unrighteous being smitten. I tensed, ready for the pronouncement of doom—the humiliation of a switch striking my buttocks while George jeered.

What I feared did not come.

"We will remove to Ludlow in the next few months. You will be under my eye and that of your Father more often there, and you will be in the company of your elder brothers. Hopefully, they will prove a good influence on you."

Chapter Three

When the winter snows had passed and the skies were rain-washed blue and the trees budding, my family left Fotheringhay, the only home I had ever known. Huge wooden wains, groaning with our goods—fold-down beds, tapestries, canopies, plate, garments—trundled from the castle gate over the ford in the river. Our chariots, ornate, painted with York Roses and symbols on the Trinity ambled after them, surrounded by stout contingents of Father's men-at-arms.

George bragged how leaving did not bother him one jot—he had lived overseas in Dublin when he was a babe so was well-used to travel. Yet he was the one who griped and groaned as our chariot lurched and rattled along the muddy trackway leading westwards, making him feel ill to his belly. "It's your fault, Richard," he complained, "that we are being sent to Wales."

"Ludlow's not in Wales," said Margaret, who was travelling with us while Mother and her ladies rode in an even more elaborate chariot. Agitatedly, she toyed with her long, golden-brown braid; she was not best pleased to find herself cloistered with two younger brothers on a lengthy journey.

"It lies on the Border in the Marches," George shot back, all superior. "It's considered Wales by many."

Meg rolled her eyes and pushed her braid behind her shoulder as if fearful that a petulant George should try to swing on it. "Be that as it may, I am looking forward to a change…and it will be lovely to see Edward and Edmund again." A crooked smile crossed her lips. "Is that why you are reluctant to go to Ludlow, George? You're fearful of Ned and Edmund smacking you whenever you act the fool?"

"I don't act the fool!" George screamed, fists clenched, face crimson with fury. He had the golden curls and features of the cherubim depicted in illuminated manuscripts and church windows—but when the mood took him, which was all too frequent, my brother could be as foul as Satan himself.

"You cannot take a bit of teasing, can you, George?" mocked Meg, who loved George dearly for reasons known only to her, but who also, spurred on by some girlish folly, enjoyed tormenting him.

I sighed and placed my chin on the wooden ledge of the little window that allowed us light and vision. Outside fields rolled by and village with pointed churches. The day was sunny, the sky cloudless but washed-out, and pale. In the distance, high on its huge motte, Fotheringhay Castle was a yellow-gold blur, sinking into the haze that clung to the horizons. Before its feet, the river Nene coiled, deeper blue than the sky, a snake stretching into infinity.

I thought of Ursula, left behind, sleeping upon her pall for eternity. They had buried her in St Mary and All Saints, which my sire intended as the vault of the York family, rising like a vast lighthouse across the fields that surrounded castle and village, a beacon to all homecoming travellers. Ursula's tomb was marked by just a little stone, next to those of other brothers and sisters who had died before my birth; nearby, more ornate, was the canopied tomb of Edward of Norwich, the second Duke of York, who died fighting at Agincourt. He had no heirs of his body…but he had left my family with a great gift—a claim to the English throne.

Uncomfortably, I stirred on my pillowed seat, wondering where my wanderings would lead me from here. The road bent to the right, a tangled haze of trees thrust up; castle and church sank out of sight.

"Farewell, Ursula," I whispered to the rising wind.

The castle of Ludlow rose on the horizon, scarlet in the light of dawn. Sleepy-eyed, George and I twitched the hanging on our chariot's window aside to gaze upon it as we approached. One of our nurses sleepily fumbled onto the seat beside us, keeping watch to ensure we would not lean out too far and fall onto the road to be trampled by the entourage. Huge mounds in the gloom inside the close confines of the chariot, our other nursemaids were snoring lumps, like whales lying stranded on a beach. Margaret lay beside them, wrapped in a coverlet embroidered with a fetterlock, with just her long braid showing. I saw George's eyes flick to it briefly as if he contemplated pulling it, but then he clearly decided our Father's Marcher stronghold was more interesting than a screaming, blear-eyed sister.

Ludlow Castle was very different from Fotheringhay. It had no motte and the colour of its stones was a dark sombre red. From what we could see from our cramped vantage point, it stood on a great height overlooking a winding river; its highest towers gazing out across the misty-blue vistas of Wales, a land full of fierce men who spoke in a guttural tongue and of giants who hurled stones and ate children. In contrast to the castle's fierce austerity, the townward side was a cheerful place full of tall, timbered houses in black-and-white. The cross-shaped church of St. Lawrence towered over all, its bells booming out a greeting as our entourage entered the town.

The chariots and carts rolled on, trumpets blowing a fanfare to declare our imminent arrival. Through crowds that gathered in the streets, we spied a gate opening in a mighty red tower bristling with archers. "We're at our new home," said George admiringly, his earlier reluctance to go to 'Wales' forgotten.

Once we were in the castle's inner bailey, there was a flurry of activity. Meg woke from her slumber and the nurses flurried to make her look presentable; all three of us were handed down from the dusty carriage amidst another fanfare of brazen trumpets.

I glanced around at the fortress where we would now live— for a while at least. The keep soared on one side, stark and tall, its four heavily-crenellated towers bedecked in flags that bore the emblems of our House. At the entrance to the North Wing, the chamberlain and stewards waited to take us to our appointed chambers. A feeling of excitement began to grow within me, bubbling up till it took all of my control not to run wildly into the building beyond. Soon we would see our older brothers, who had their own household at Ludlow. We saw Edward and Edmund all to seldom—usually from Christmas to Twelfth Night, and because they were so much older, they were often involved in adult pursuits forbidden to their younger siblings, who were shipped off to bed, sick on sweetmeats and with angry nurses chuntering in their ears.

A steward guided George and me to the castle nursery; Meg, being older and a girl, was taken elsewhere, probably to Mother, who had retired to her own luxurious chambers. From the moment of our arrival, she had watched our manner and deportment at every turn. "You are sons of the royal blood, never forget that," she told us, as she had many times upon the road. "You must never shame the House of York. Remember, your father, in truth, should be…" She trailed away then, a hard, determined look on her face.

We both knew, even in our youthful innocence, what she was about to say but dared not.

That our Father, Richard Plantagenet, should be King and not old Henry Six, who men said was mad, dribbling like a babe while he knew not the world around him. Henry, with his wicked French queen and a little son near my age that people whispered bad things about. I did not know *what* things, but I'd heard the name 'Somerset' and sniggering amongst the servants when they did not realise I was within hearing…

My sire's claim to the throne was twofold. His primary claim was through Lionel of Clarence, son of Edward III, and his daughter Philippa, who married Edmund Mortimer. Their granddaughter Anne was Father's mother but he had never known her, for she had died at his birth. Our second line of royal descent was through Edmund of Langley, King Edward's second youngest son; *his* son, Richard Earl of Cambridge, was my grandfather. We children were not permitted to talk of our grandfather Cambridge. With others, he had fomented a plot against King Henry V, seeking to depose him and put Edmund Mortimer on the throne. But he had been undone by Mortimer himself and was beheaded at the Bargate in Southampton, his body humbly buried in the chapel of God's House. (I was not supposed to know such unsavoury tales but servants talked. Oh, how they talked!)

"I like it here, after all," said George, peering around the nursery, which was on the top floor of one of the towers. "It's supposed to be haunted though."

"It is?" I inquired hesitantly, in all innocence. "How do you know?"

George's eyes danced with malicious mirth. "Edmund told me last time he visited Fotheringhay. There was a lady named Marion who once lived here. She let her lover into the castle…and he then brought in an army to wrest the fortress from its rightful lord! Full of remorse, she slit her leman's throat and leapt from the tower to her death."

"Which tower?" I said nervously. The shadows in the corners of the room seemed suddenly dark.

"*This* tower!" said George with relish. "Maybe you'll hear her screaming when the wind blows…maybe you'll feel her bony dead hands clutching you under the bedsheets."

"George, don't!" I said, rubbing my arms which had gone goose-pimply.

"*Yaah!*" The door banged open with a loud clatter and I swear George sprang in the air like a startled cat, then began to yowl like one too, as a pair of brawny arms enfolded him and a big hand slapped down over his eyes.

"Quiet now, George, or I'll put a hand over your mouth too to stop that hellish noise. What are you doing, scaring our little brother Dickon with those wild tales?"

It was our brother Edward who stood in the room, holding George fast, with Edmund behind him, grinning in amusement.

George managed to cast off Edward's hand and wriggle free. "Richard's a baby!" he said with spite. "Only a baby would be scared!"

"I am not scared!" I protested, wanting to protect my boyish honour in the presence of my esteemed older brothers. "I swear it, Ned, Edmund."

"I know you are not." Edward released George who scuttled away in the corner, scowling. Ned was like a grownup now, although not yet of age…and he was a *giant*. He was far taller than Father; in fact, taller than anyone I had ever met. His face was handsome, his eyes warm and friendly. They were a greenish-brown, unlike mine, which were a deep grey-blue. He was as unlike me as one could be, yet I felt no jealousy, but instead a deep liking that went beyond brotherhood, an affinity, a desire to…to serve? An aura of greatness clung to Ned, young though he was; he had the marks of heroism, of nobility, just like Sir Gawain or Sir Lancelot.

"You have grown much, Dickon! Don't you think so, Edmund?"

Edmund stepped out of Edward's shadow. I had heard whispers that Edmund was my father's favourite son, even though he was not the eldest. He resembled me than Ned, being far less in height or girth, and blue-eyed; we were our Father's sons, while Ned favoured the Nevilles in the fairness of face. Mother had at one time been called 'the Rose of Raby;' Edward was the 'Rose of Rouen.'

"I can hardly believe it! Our little brother is very nearly a man, is he not?" Edmund ruffled my hair.

"What about me?" yelled George, buzzing around our brothers like an annoying fly. "I have grown too! Tell me—is it nice here? Will we have ponies? Can we go hunting? I saw a forest! Are there wild Welshmen in the woods? Can we hunt them too?"

"Yes, to all," said Edward, "save for hunting wild Welshmen. You're too young for that kind of sport, and they would have you cooked and eaten for breakfast."

"Would they really?" I asked, blinking. The sound of Welsh cannibals in the wood was most alarming.

George swatted me on the side of the head. "Don't be a goose, Richard! He but jests!"

"I'm not a goo…" I made to take a reciprocal swing at George but Edward caught my arm and pulled me gently in his direction.

"Why don't you come with me, Richard? I'll introduce you to all the residents of the castle. To my friends, the Croft brothers. They are training as squires here at Ludlow."

"There was trouble not long ago, though," said Edmund conspiratorially. "One of the masters was behaving in a beastly manner towards the Crofts. He made them take undeserved beatings and humiliated them before the rest of the squires. We had to write to Father to ask him to intercede."

Edward grinned, his white teeth flashing. "Yes. It was a good excuse to write to Father…it meant we could ask him for new green gowns for ourselves at the same time. My old garments were nearly in rags."

"Only because you've outgrown all your clothes," laughed Edmund, prodding Edward's ribs with a finger. "You'll need another set before long by the look of things! Your doublet is almost indecently short!"

"Maybe I will," Ned said, "and perhaps I'll need a bigger steed too, a nice destrier. Do you think Father would grant me one? Now, come on, Richard…" Unexpectedly, he reached down, lifted me up and swung me onto his shoulders. "Let go meet my friend—and then I'll show you the horses and the hounds! Oh, and the mews—some new hawks have just arrived!"

"Ned, what about me?" Two fiery splotches appeared on George's cheeks. He tugged at the edge of Edward's doublet. "I want to come too. I'm older—I have more right to go exploring than baby Dickon!"

Edward and Edmund glanced at each other. They did not seem very enamoured of George's stream of complaints. I hoped they would tell George he couldn't come along, that it was *our* time together, without him creating a fuss—but I knew that would never happen; we were, after all, brothers and he had been separated from them as long as I.

Edmund lifted his hand to beckon George forward; I saw George smiled smugly…and then another figure filled the doorway. In stormed one of our tutors who had journeyed with us from Fotheringhay, his black robes fluttering about his spindly frame like crow's wings. Imperiously he cleared his throat. "My lord George," he said, "I was waiting for you in the schoolroom. Have you forgotten your Lady Mother said were to resume your Latin lessons upon your arrival?"

George made a spluttering noise. "But…but we've only just been shown our chamber! Surely we are allowed a few hours to explore…"

The tutor had stringy grey hair and a beak of a nose, adding to his avian appearance. He leaned over, that beak jutting into George's stunned visage. "Idle pastimes are not fitting for young boys, especially when their Latin is abysmal. Come along, or your gracious sire the Duke will be informed of your behaviour."

George's face purpled but he did not dare argue. No one wanted to offend our Father…or Mother, for that matter. Silently he stalked out of the room, his tutor flapping behind him.

Edward began to laugh as their footsteps dwindled into the distance. "I should not say it…but thank goodness for that!"

Edmund laughed also, and I tentatively began to laugh too. Edward began to bounce me on his shoulders. "Let's away to see those hawks now, shall we?" he asked.

"Yes!" I squealed, and Ned rushed forward clutching my thin legs in his great big hands, and I rode him like a war-horse out into the bailey.

At a window, high above, I thought I caught a glimpse of Mother's huge headdress for a moment, and my happiness dimmed. She would most likely consider our gallivanting unseemly and loutish and worthy of chastisement.

But whoever it was high at that narrow window, and I was never sure, she smiled and turned away.

The days and months that followed were golden; soon they ran into a year and more. The sorrow of Ursula's death faded from my child's mind, and the political machinations of the King's court meant nought to a small boy far from the court at Westminster. In Ludlow, I was with my dear elder brothers, making every day joyous and buffering me against George at his worst—and the town was a bigger, more bustling place than Fotheringhay, and had many more entertainments for young boys to enjoy. Fotheringhay remained in my dreams, however, the castle resembling some stronghold from an Arthurian tale, the church a lantern hovering in the vapours of the Nene. I swore I would return there one day and place white roses on Ursula's simple slab.

Ludlow teemed with all manner of life, butchers, bakers, fishmongers, furriers. Taverns aplenty lined the streets, doors cast open wide beneath painted signs of bulls and bells and mitres; the alewives who worked within would peek out knowingly whenever our little entourage passed, winking at Edward and Edmund on their skittish new horses.

"Why is that maiden staring at our brother?" I innocently asked George one day as we trundled after golden Edward and smiling Edmund on a pair of new ponies we had been given. A plump, round-faced girl with a tumble of auburn curls was standing by the town well. As Ned went by, she leaned back with her bucket on her hip and winked. Ned touched his cap but passed on by.

"Why do you think, Dickon? Oh, well, you are probably too innocent to know," said George with a knowing snort. "But I can assure you, that slattern's no 'maiden'. Don't gawp at her, Richard—she's probably so dirty, you'd catch a malady just from looking at her!"

I had no idea what he meant as she looked reasonably clean to me, but I quickly looked away from the red-headed girl just in case.

The town was dominated by the massive bastions of the castle but just beyond the large expanse of the market square, the church of St Lawrence was another great landmark, its tower visible for miles around, although the timber-framed buildings of the town were starting to encroach upon the churchyard.

After our castle, St Lawrence's was my favourite place in Ludlow and Edward and Edmund frequently took me and George to pray there. The castle had a chapel, of course, round and full of Norman work, but its interior was dark, cramped and old-fashioned, and St Lawrence's church was not only lighter and airier but filled with the symbols honouring the House of York.

Its porch was hexagonal and led into a vast nave that glowed gold—the windows in St John's chapel, associated with the Palmer's Guild, were filled with vivid glass of rich warm hues that gave additional light to the candelabras that burned both day and night, their scent hanging richly in the air. One window bore the image St Catherine and her Wheel, a second brawny St Christopher carrying the Christ-child on his back; a third, high above the altar, showed the Palmers receiving their charter from King Edward the Confessor.

But it was not the ornate painted glass that intrigued George and me most, not even the window in the Lady Chapel showing a Jesse Tree with spreading branches and a myriad of birds and beasts peering through the knotted foliage. It was the wooden misericords we loved, carved by some master craftsman's hands, which bore creatures that could not fail to fascinate young boys, even within the sanctity of the House of God.

Edward and Edmund knew each and every one and delighted in showing them to us. "There is Father's Falcon and Fetterlock," said Edmund, nodding toward one carving. "A proud symbol—*our* symbol. There's a rose over here...the Rose of York, much better I'd say than that Lancastrian Antelope or that insipid Bohun swan!"

"Look—a devil!" George suddenly cried, pointing to a horned demon playing on bagpipes. The monster faced another devil who was carrying a naked woman draped over one shoulder.

"Who is she?" I asked curiously. Despite having not one stitch of clothes, the woman was clutching a drink-measure in one hand.

"An alewife and a cheat...and a harlot, like the one we saw winking at Edward!" said George with no decorum whatsoever, despite being inside a church. From a distance, I saw a black-robed cleric frowning; we were the lord's children and not likely to be evicted from this holy place, but I had no wish to risk a thrashing by having Mother hear that we were disrespectful.

"This is *my* favourite one..." murmured Edward, approaching a carving of a mermaid with flowing hair and a looking-glass in one hand. "Can you guess why?" He gestured to the mermaid's large, pendulous wooden breasts as Edmund elbowed him, suppressing a giggle.

My eyes were round as eggs, I am certain. George burst into laughter. The priests were glaring and a Palmer looked shocked and scuttled into his chapel. I began to laugh, following my brothers' lead, although I had no real idea what I was laughing at.

Edmund pointed at me, and another explosion of laughter shattered the sanctity of the church. "We must leave," said Edward, suddenly serious, although a little smile still tugged at the corner of his mouth, and he pushed George and me forward, using his huge arms to propel us towards the doors.

A priest was striding over the tiles towards us, brow furrowed in displeasure, full of God's righteous wrath, no doubt. "Father, my small brother has been taken ill!" cried Edward, tone dripping with false concern before the priest had a chance to admonish any of us.

George began to titter and Edward slapped him between the shoulder blades, making him cough. "*This* brother!" he said with a nasty grin that only George and I could see. "Can't you hear his laboured breathing, Father? There's an ague going about the castle, alas. A cruel and embarrassing sickness. Poor George will have also shat his hosen…"

"My Lord Edward!" cried the priest, now looking alarmed as well as angry. "Not in God's House!"

Edmund's face was red as he tried to contain his mirth. George opened his mouth to howl a protest, but Edmund grabbed him from Ned and yanked him out the door. I ran after.

Smiling sweetly, his appearance as fair as one of the golden glass angels in the windows, Edward reached to his belt-purse and pulled out a handful of coins. "For the church, Father," he said soothingly, pressing them into the old priest's hands. The priest began to sputter but grabbed at the coins as if he feared Edward was performing some kind of sleight of hand and the coins would vanish into thin air.

"Go." Edward was behind us again, shepherd to a flock of unruly brothers, herding us out of the church porch and into the sunlit streets beyond.

Almost immediately we were stopped even as we set to mounting our steeds. The members of our little entourage parted as if cloven by a sharp blade. A man was striding through their midst, tall, stern, officious, with a feather bobbing in a high crimson hat. On his shoulder gleamed a large silver badge with Father's Falcon and Fetterlock. I had seen him once or twice before; an assistant to the castle constable.

"My Lord Edward, Lord Edmund," he barked above the noise of the streets—the creak of cartwheels, the shouts of marketplace sellers, the barking of dogs and the grunts of beasts destined for the fleshers. He did not sound terribly friendly.

"What now?" murmured Edmund.

"You are all to return to the castle at once," said the man officiously. "There is news. This is the will of her Grace, the Duchess."

Edward and Edmund glanced at each other. For a moment, I thought Edward might grab the constable's man and shake him till he told us his news then and there, but if he felt the urge, he restrained himself. In silence, he swung up on his waiting horse and Edmund did likewise. George and I clambered onto our ponies with our assistant's help and in silence began making our way through the busy town.

George seemed unconcerned and chattered away about the misericords and how one particularly ugly one of a creature called a Blemya had reminded him of Margaret. I said nothing, the brightness of the day was dimmed; all I could think was 'What if the news is bad?'

What if someone was dead?

Dead like Ursula, back in Fotheringhay.

When our party reached the confines of the castle bailey, we were lifted from our ponies and hustled away towards our chambers by the nursemaids. As we reached the top of the steps into the hall-block, I glanced over my shoulder and saw Edmund and Edward in conversation with the steward. Both my brothers wore serious expressions.

"I wonder what has happened?" I whispered to George as we huddled in the nursery, vainly trying to amuse ourselves and relieve our worries by battering the furniture with wooden swords we had been given. "Do you think someone has…died?" I choked on the word.

"Don't know," said George. "Just know our day out with Ned and Edmund was ruined. Not fair." He gave the bedstead a huge crack with his wooden blade.

"Lord George, stop that!" shrieked one of the nurses, her arms windmilling as she swept towards her charge. Her headdress billowed like a huge sail; I thought she might lift off the ground and soar toward my brother.

George began to whine as the nurse's large hand clamped over the hilt of the wooden sword and pried it from his fingers. "You…can't…take my sword!"

"Yes, I can and I will, until you learn to behave yourself, Lord George! What would her Grace the Duchess think to see you smashing up your bed! Such a bad influence on your brother Lord Richard too…"

George shot me an evil glare, as if I was the cause of all his woes, and stuck out his tongue. I ignored him and clutched my wooden sword to my chest. I was afraid George might try to take it now that his weapon had been confiscated.

He had no chance to try, however, for Margaret suddenly burst into the room, her hair neatly braided, and her best gown flowing around her lanky form. "George, Richard…what are you doing? Nurses, get them ready! Why aren't they ready?"

"I was about to try!" said the great big woman who clutched George's sword, her apple-cheeks turning red.

"Well, you aren't doing much of a job, are you?" said Margaret, imperious. "Here, I will help you. Richard…"

I went to her and hastily she pulled off my riding clothes and dressed me all in deep blue from head to toe, then ran her own jewelled comb through my tangled curls. "Your hair, Dickon!" she cried in dismay. "It's like a bird's nest!"

Next to us, I could hear George almost sobbing in pain as the nurse, eager to regain her authority, brushed madly at his equally-tousled locks. "Now, Lord George, none of that!" she shrilled. He had tried to bite her hand.

"What is happening, Meg?" I glanced up at my sister with round, worried eyes.

"It's Father…" she began.

A great trembling gripped my body I knew some evil had befallen. "Is…is he dead?"

She frowned at me as if I'd lost my wits. "Of course not! What would make you say such a horrible thing, Dickon? No, he's on his way to Ludlow, and Mother wants everyone to be presentable for his arrival. From what I hear, he won't be in a very good mood."

"Why?" I asked although I knew I probably would not understand the reason. Father was a very important man in the realm. He'd fought against old King Henry at St Albans when I was small, along with my cousin of Warwick, Dick Neville, and there his bitterest enemy, Somerset, was killed along with the Lancastrian Lords Clifford and Percy. The King and the Duke of Buckingham were injured by arrows, the Duke's face scarred for life. Afterwards, the King and Father managed to heal their rift; Father did not truly hate simple, holy Henry, merely his evil councillors. He was made Protector of the Realm because the King was sickly and often lost his wits, staring blankly out of the window and letting food dribble from his slack mouth. But in truth, Queen Marguerite was in charge rather than Father, and she loathed him because she feared he would displace her son as heir.

Margaret yanked on the laces at the top of my doublet, nearly strangling me. "Why? You'll find out soon enough, Dickon."

The younger members of the York family gathered in the Great Hall of Ludlow. George and I were seated at a table to the left of the high dais; Meg was with Mother's ladies-in-waiting, wearing a red crown and square headdress that made her look very grown-up. Edmund and Edward, clad in emerald-green doublets trimmed by ermine and squirrel, were at the forefront of the young henchmen eagerly waiting to attend the nobility. For them, it was a particularly special occasion, for they would directly serve our Lord Father, the Duke of York.

I glanced around the Great Hall; colourful banners hung from struts in the great wooden roof above, and painted heads, perhaps of my Mortimer ancestors, gazed down at the assembly with ash-dusted eyes. Three long, trefoil windows admitted shafts of pale golden sunlight that lit up the heart of the room, dancing on rich red-brown tiles bearing hunting scenes.

A trumpet sounded in the bailey outside; the noise echoed about inner and outer ward, bouncing from tower to tower and travelling through the town and even beyond the wide, deep River Teme at the foot of castle hill. The guards at the various entrances stood to attention then parted as Mother appeared, a small but regal figure in a delicate butterfly headdress that sparkled with blue gems. Her grown was blue cloth-of-gold; a girdle of golden wires cinched her small waist. Her face looked grim and weary as if she had received bad news. She proceeded to her place on the dais and sat down beneath a vast canopy broidered with Father's Falcon and Fetterlock. A slight wind from the door leading to the solar block rippled the canopy, making the falcon's head bow and move as if preparing to fall upon prey.

I wondered who or what the prey might be.

The trumpets sounded again, even louder than for the arrival of my Mother the Duchess. Everyone in the Hall rose, except for Mother. I peered down the length of the Hall, eager to see my often-absent Father. It was embarrassing to admit that I scarcely recalled his face, for he travelled much and was usually at court away from the family.

The Duke was of middling height and dressed in a rich black gown, the sleeves lined with red sarcenet. A collar of gold spangled with enamelled white roses hung around his neck; a falcon pendant dangled from its apex, shimmering with rich blue and red gems. He wore no hat and the hair curling down past the strong chin was a dusky gold.

Exuding power and authority, he walked briskly across the tiles, and all through the benches people bowed or curtseyed as if he were a King. Which, of course, had fate been kinder he might have been.

With vigorous strides, he mounted the dais and took his place beside Mother. I noticed his mouth was tight, his colour somewhat waxy; he looked uneasy and troubled, with a hint of anger bubbling beneath the surface.

The banquet that followed his arrival had all the expected accoutrements of a feast—bream and eels in sauce, a boar from the wild Welsh forests with sugared apples in its jaws, venison in saffron-tinted pastry, subtleties fashioned into roses, and helpings of candied figs and violets that sweetened the breath.

We children ate heartily and I began to think Margaret had been teasing George and me when she claimed a disaster of sorts had happened, but when I let my gaze wander to the faces of my parents, I could read unease, dismay, anger. It hung over them like a black cloud.

"George…What do you think it is?"

"What do I think what is?" George was gnawing on a large chicken leg with such gusto one would have thought he had not eaten in a month.

"Why are Father and Mother looking daggers at all and sundry?"

"Are they? I hadn't noticed." George reached out and grabbed a handful of marchpane from a silver tray. He shoved the sweets into his mouth; his cheeks were so puffed out he resembled a squirrel ferreting nuts away for the winter.

"Yes! They've hardly eaten! They are supposed to be celebrating *something* but they seem as cheerful as…as tomb effigies. Something bad has happened—in London, in the King's court."

"Something is *always* happening there! Beheadings and fights and the mad old King dribbling…" George slurped on his watered-down wine then started chasing a jellied eel about his trencher with his eating-knife. "Bloody thing—come here, damn you!"

"George!" I tugged on his sleeve. His arm slipped and his knife flicked the eel off his platter and onto the floor, where it slithered along looking nearly alive.

"Richard!" Disgusted, George ripped his arm away. "Stop pestering me, will you? Look what you've made me do, you gormless imp! My eel is fit only for the hounds!"

"But Father…"

"Just stop! Whatever is making Father frown is of no concern of ours—we are only children!"

I sighed, tugged nervously on the ends of my dangling sleeves, which had become a bit damp from gravy George had splashed on the table. I wished I could be like my brother—unconcerned, attending only to my own boyish fancies. But ever, since I had risen from my cradle and had thoughts of the world, my mind churned, day and night, going round and round like a millwheel—what if? What will happen? What will happen to *us?*

The final subtleties were distributed around the feasting tables as part of the last course. These were not, as usual, shaped into insignias of the York family—our devices, our castles—but were directed toward King Henry and Queen Marguerite. A chained swan, a spotted panther, an antelope, glittered under a sugary coating.

I noticed George's eyes widening with desire and he licked his lips while clutching his little knife in anticipation. He did not seem to have recognised the significance of these shapes at all. Although I too craved sweet and sickly things, as children often did, I felt a certain aversion to these new, unexpected subtleties, although I was unable to quite fathom why.

A hush descended over the hall.

Father stood—stiffly, I thought. The torchlight made a halo of his golden hair. His face was…*mine*, though older, careworn from his duties. My heart pounded against the cage of my ribs.

"While I was in London, as some of you may know…" he said in a voice a little slurred from what? Exhaustion? Despair? Reaching for his goblet, he quaffed a deep draught of wine as if laving a dry throat and continued, "Upon the Feast of the Annunciation his Grace, King Henry, decided on a celebration of new amity devised between the Houses of York and Lancaster. His Grace said it would forever, " *set apart such variances as be betwixt diverse lords.*" This Loveday took place at the church of St Paul's…" A grimace twisted his face as if the memory was abhorrent, "and all lords in attendance paraded through the church, holding the hands of our former foes to seal new friendships. The King himself, clad in his ermines and wearing his crown, walked before us. So, it is done…We must toast our new-found friends and pay special heed to our ever-loyal alliances to the Crown." He gestured to the trestle tables bearing their decorative but decidedly Lancastrian-flavoured delights.

Silence still hung over the hall; even George was beginning to look uneasy rather than ravenous. "Eat, eat!" ordered my Father, the Duke. His face looked grey, his eyes shining dully. "Show all how we value this new friendship!"

One of his supporters, a big burly knight in a thick red cloak and coiled chaperon, made the first move. He leant over one of the subtleties—the swan that was the symbol of the young Prince of Wales—and stabbed roughly into it with his knife. The red-striped jelly of the subtlety trembled and disintegrated. The swan was headless.

A sigh, a gasp went through the feasting hall.

I do not remember much about the end of the banquet, only that much wine was drunk, many men muttered in the corner, and both my parents were as still as statues, not speaking, barely eating. Edward and Edmund attended on Father, giving each other worried and perplexed glances as they refilled his goblet and tried to tempt him with rich dishes.

I tried to eat part of one of the subtleties—the rear leg of the King's panther—but the sickly sweetness almost gagged me and I spat it out onto a linen napkin. Beside me, George, recovering his appetite, downed all and sundry, his lips smeared by that rich rarity—sugar—and coloured with yellow saffron. However, it was too much, even for him; he was noisily sick into a nearby voider, which a server carried out to the midden.

At last, my Father the Duke rose, turned sharply on his heel and stalked out of the chamber with my mother at his side, signalling the end of the banquet. Household servants swept in, some clearing the crumbs of the meal into metal voiders to be handed to the town's poor, others peeling off the soiled linen table cloths and picking up discarded napkins. As the knights and lords and ladies departed, the candles in their branching candelabras were blown out; coils of smoke curled up to the rafters, forming nooses round the heads of the corbels high above.

I expected the nurses would hustle us children off to bed immediately, for the hours had grown late, but instead the Chamberlain came seeking us, grim-faced." My Lord George, my Lord Richard, Lady Margaret, you will come with me."

We walked down the hall toward our Father's private apartments, Margaret striding a few paces ahead, looking very grown-up in her coronet, George holding his sore belly and making pitiful whimpering noises.

"Margaret, what's going on?" I ran forth to catch her up. "We still don't know much. Isn't it *good* that Father and the King's party are friends once more?"

She turned and looked down at me from her great height— she was a huge girl, taller than any girl her age I had ever seen. "Dickon, don't be silly…" She saw my dismay, and suddenly her face softened and she patted my arm. "Forgive me, little brother. You're young, too young yet. You will come to understand in time."

We were taken to a small ante-chamber adjacent to the solar. Dark wood gleamed; tallow burned in silver cups set with red gems. A painting of Jesu stretched on the wall, agonised, blood runnelling down from the wounds made by the Crown of Thorns.

The Chamberlain bowed and then backed off to the door, slipping silently out into the hall. With no one to give me guidance as to my expected behaviour, I sat down on a nearby stool, dangling my feet with the pointed shoes Mother had recently purchased from the Cordwainers. George dropped onto a small Spanish rug; green as grass, it was as furry as a dog's back. I feared George might spew on it, as he had at dinner, and Mother would be angry indeed. She liked her luxuries, and they were all costly.

Voices sounded in the next-door room; the door hung open a slight crack. It was Father and the anger he'd suppressed earlier burst out in a flood. Weariness had vanished from his tone; now fire burned and flared. "Christ, Cecily—the humiliation of it all!"

There were murmured noises of sympathy from Mother.

"It was disastrous from the start, when the King retired to Chertsey and then Berkhamsted. He was supposed to have done so to allow deliberations between the parties to take place without signs of prejudice...but he allowed Somerset, Egremont, Clifford and Exeter to come before him with their grievances, nonetheless. My worst foes!"

"You know Henry is addled in mind," said Mother.

"He is, but not enough for parliament to permit me to remain Lord Protector of the Realm. As we both know, as it stands today, Queen Marguerite is the true ruler of England. I see her hand in all this madness...and, by God, the harridan will try to destroy me."

"Destroy you? She hates you, I cannot deny it, but you are..."

"Her worst enemy. The one she fears might unseat her son. The one who *should* unseat her brat—Somerset's bastard..."

The sound of Father's boot-heels clicked agitatedly on the floor as he paced. I glanced over at George. He'd stopped moaning about his sick belly and was listening intently to my parents' conversation too. Margaret was a dark statue near the door, poised as if ready for flight.

"Cecily, it has gone beyond mere loathing. Marguerite has the stomach of a man when it comes to war—far more so than her husband! Lancastrian loyalists attempted to ambush me and your brother Salisbury as we journeyed to the meeting in Westminster. When their ruse failed and they were beaten off, another treacherous band tried to attack young Dick Neville on the road. Fortunately, the bastards proved themselves both inept and stupid. But I have no doubt they will try their luck again if given the chance. Who knows—one wrong slip on my behalf, and Queen might get lucky."

"Do not say such things, husband." There was a strained sound in Mother's voice I'd never heard before, not even when Ursula died. It was as if a strong façade had broken; a hard shell cracked to reveal vulnerability. It was not comfortable to listen to. We had been reared hearing tales of nought but our parents' might and right; they had seemed invulnerable, a hero and heroine from times of old who would prevail against their enemies' ploys. Now…we heard fear. It infected us, plague-like; made us sweat, sitting with laboured breath in that tiny room beside the solar.

"A deal was reached in the end, was it not?" Mother again. Now I heard the sweep of her skirts, in tandem with the nervous clatter of Father's boots.

"Of sorts." He laughed a bitter laugh. The Archbishop of Canterbury came to visit my party at Blackfriars and then fared to visit my lord of Somerset at Whitefriars. The only way out for was to agree to the demanded bonds and pay reparations for the dead of St Albans. If the followers of Lancaster could not hurt me with their weapons, they would hurt my finances instead." He laughed bitterly again. "I must give payment to Somerset, Clifford and the rest. Set up chantry chapels where priests will pray for their slain kinsmen's souls—Christ knows, that lot need all the prayers they can get to free them from Hell's flames!"

"Richard…you have taken all the blame!" Mother's voice was strident; she now sounded vaguely incensed rather than afraid.

"I could see no other course; everyone in London was expecting a fray, even looking forward to one, but I wanted to prevent more bloodshed. It is not quite as bad as it sounds,

Cecily—the King still owes me money in arrears from my time in France and that shall take some of the bite from this decision. For all he is foolish, Henry is not a monster. What he is not is a King."

"Hush, Richard; there may be listeners. Servants with big ears passing nearby."

"Why should I care now? I have been close enough to having an accusation of treason flung at me already. However, I do not believe anyone in Ludlow would betray me—least of all the children who are, I trust, the only ones who are near enough to have heard my remarks."

The footsteps in the other chamber drew closer. George sprang up from the rug, clutching my shoulder for support, and we both stood in awe as our father entered the room. Margaret dropped into a deep curtsey that was unusually graceful for her—she was so tall and spare she was always bumping elbows and knees and getting a telling off for unladylike deportment.

"Lord Father, we greet you," she said with perfect politeness, her head bowed.

George and I fumbled with our bows. Father looked us over, a weary sadness in his eyes. They were blue, the hue of my own. "So…I imagine you've heard all I had to say to your Lady Mother, the Duchess."

"Oh no, my lord, we would never dare be earwigging…I mean eavesdropping…I mean listening in to conversations that don't concern us!" George lied, his face beneath his dusky-gold curls angelic and unbelievably sincere.

"Hmmm." Lips pursed, the Duke glanced down at him. "Unlike most young boys then, in my experience. How odd."

"Of course you are right, my lord Father." George changed his tune at once. "We *were* listening!"

A ghost of a smile crossed Father's features. It somehow made him look even more tired. "Well, with truth and honesty declared, I shall tell you and your Lady Mother the rest of my wretched story about the Loveday."

"Was the Wicked Queen there?" breathed George.

"Yes, she was indeed, dressed like a peacock and with a face twisted as if she'd sucked a Spanish lemon." Father ruffled George's hair. "Once we had come to an agreement with the Lancastrians, the King led all the court in procession to St Paul's. First came your Uncle Salisbury holding the hand of young Somerset, that vengeful puppy who is as vicious as his father ever was in life; then your cousin Dick holding the hand of Henry Holland—Exeter—the rogue who I should never have wed to your older sister, Anne." He sighed unhappily. "And to think, I believed their union would help unite our fractured families! He is a coarse and violent man, with more brawn than…than *this*…" He tapped the side of his head.

We stared, unused to seeing our noble father so perturbed, not knowing if we were meant to laugh at his jibe about the intellect of our brother-in-law, the Duke of Exeter.

"And what of you, Lord Father?" asked Margaret, curious and probing, unlike most other maids her age. She liked to learn more than sewing and dancing and prided herself on her knowledge.

"Me? I had the joy of walking hand-in-hand into St Paul's with Queen Marguerite."

Mother appeared behind our sire, her towered headdress a black blot against the light of the many torches bracketed around the walls of the ante-chamber. "Jesu, surely you did not, Richard!"

"I did. At times, King Henry is not such a fool. He knew where the enmity runs deepest. I swear the Queen would have skewered me if she'd had a weapon on hand; as it was, she merely stabbed me with blazing glances from her eyes."

"What will happen now, husband?" Mother's face floated closer, a pale moon, still beautiful despite her age. The Rose of Raby, fairest of the many children of Joan Beaufort, the daughter of John of Gaunt and his mistress Katherine Swynford.

"We pay our debts," the Duke shrugged, "and prepare for unrest. Despite swearing oaths on Henry's Loveday, our

Lancastrian 'friends', are still filled with the desire for revenge. The Queen too—after all, you know what men said about her and the elder Somerset. She will not let his death go unpunished."

Mother murmured in assent and inclined her head.

"I know it was your wish to travel home to Fotheringhay."

Mother nodded. "Yes, it is my wish, Richard. We have been long away. Edward and Edmund have not been as attentive of their studies since the younger boys arrived at Ludlow. They prefer to preen like peacocks to impress their brothers. I even heard from the priest of St Laurence's that some unseemly behaviour took place…"

I gasped audibly, nudging George with my elbow. A beating was forthcoming; I was certain of it.

Father seemed to only be half-listening to Mother's words. "Cecily, I cannot let you go."

"What?" Mother's plucked brows rose as did her voice.

"It is not safe. You would need to cross the whole middle of England with your entourage, passing not so far from Coventry, which seethes with the supporters of Lancaster."

"You think your enemies would strike so openly? Strike against a woman and children passing peaceably to their home."

"Maybe, maybe not, but strike they will…and you are not just any gentlewoman, nor are my children ordinary children but of the blood royal. I am no fool, wife. I will not have treacherous serpents strike at the very heart of my family. Even if you reached Fotheringhay unscathed, it is not a castle wrought for war. The walls are weak; if my enemies should come for you, the defences could easily be breached."

"So…we are to stay here at Ludlow?" Mother sounded shocked and a little dismayed.

My Father looked thoughtful. "No, I do not feel that is ideal either. I must prepare for possible future battles…"

George and I glanced at each other. So it might come to war!

Father continued to talk, "Edward and Edmund have no distractions from their studies from now onwards—and prepare for what will be their first military encounters. Yet I would like you and the rest of the children nearby—close enough that I can summon you to take shelter at Ludlow if necessary. And if nothing untoward happens, if hostilities cease, then I will see you safely on to Fotheringhay."

"I hope you do not suggest retiring to Wigmore!" Mother said testily, wrinkling her pert nose in disgust. "You know I dislike it. So old-fashioned, and I cannot help but think of how years ago Maud Mortimer had the head and..." she glanced out of the corner of her eye at us children "*other* parts of Simon de Montfort displayed above the banqueting table."

"Montfort was a traitor to the crown," said Father, perplexed.

"Yes, he was...but, Richard, severed heads *in* the Great Hall? So uncouth!"

Father smiled faintly at that. "You need not fear wife—I had not planned on Wigmore. Usk."

"Usk? I do not think you have taken me there before."

"It is just over the Welsh border, a quiet place, out of the way...but the castle, though small, has thick walls. Just the place for a few months sojourn. I have spent some months refortifying it and adding to the apartments. I have also endowed the nearby priory which contains the shrine of Saint Radegund; I am sure the prioress and her nuns would be delighted to meet the Duchess of York."

Cecily nodded. "You are my husband; if it is your wish that I take the children to Usk, then I can do nought but obey you."

"It would ease my mind. Remember, at Usk you are not so far from the Severn either; if the worst happened, a ship could be found to bear you away to safety."

"Let us not speak of such eventualities—and pray to God they do not happen."

Usk was some fourteen leagues from Ludlow. A little town, grey-stoned, ringed round by dark forests, I noticed Mother's visage darken in dismay when she set eyes upon it. However, she offered no complaint, and George, Margaret and I were soon ensconced in a small but cosy tower of Usk Castle, which stood guarding the crossing point of the river.

The castle was tiny compared to our homes at Fotheringhay and Ludlow but it had a close, calm feel; at night, instead of the constant murmurs of the household busy at all hours, I heard nothing but the rush of the wind in the trees, the yap of distant dogs in the town, the burbling of the nearby water.

The castle itself was once known as Brynbuga; we learnt that from our new tutor, who was half-Welsh and had dark eyes and a cheerful face berry-brown and coiled hair like a ram's. Once the ancient Romans of the 20th Legion had dwelt nearby in a fort known as Burrium; when the wind was high and the moon sailing in a sea of frothy cloud, I would often convince myself I heard the tread of ghostly, armoured feet in the woodlands and saw the moonlight shine on crested helms. George, who was often woken by my nightly restlessness, would tell me to be silent or he would crucify me as the Romans crucified Christ. He did not mean it, but still, his words stung; I would lie silent in the dark, a burly sheepskin pulled up to my cold nose, trying not to move and annoy him further.

There was a vast round tower set in the castle wall; the soldiery lived there and George and I spent much time visiting them, although Meg said we shouldn't, for they spoke uncouthly with much bad language, and some were Welshmen too. We ignored her warnings and lingered in that all-male world where we chattered incessantly of hounds and hawks, hunts and horses, oblivious to the bemused smirks of the hard-bitten warriors who protected us, day and night.

Sometimes, though, I grew tired of the smoky chambers where grizzled men with scarred faces chomped meat and polished halberds and swords, and went with Meg to feed the doves in the great dovecote in the bailey. Face upturned, soft feathers falling on my cheeks, I watched the birds hop from crevice to crevice, their soft voices echoing amongst the dung-speckled stones. At other times, all of the family would leave the castle and go to the priory, built centuries ago by Richard de Clare for a group of Benedictine nuns; on Mother's instructions, we would leave offerings at the shrine of St. Radegund. It was beautiful, with polished marble altar top and a vast painting of the saint wearing a white headdress that flowed over her shoulders and a robe decorated with Fleur de Lys. A crown gleamed upon her brow, and tame wolves and other beasts peered up at her through a golden oat-field.

"I wonder if one of Radegund's wolves would eat a nun," said George thoughtfully, eyeing the five elderly Benedictine nuns who inhabited the priory. They were all from noble houses but with their fierce, unsmiling faces beneath their wimples, they looked as dry and unappealing as withered autumn apples.

"Course not," I whispered to my brother. "Nuns are holy."

"Nuns are stringy too, I'd wager," George sniggered, pointing at Sister Agnes who had no teeth and looked as if a strong wind might blow her away. "Not much meat for wolves!"

"Stop it; both of you!" Meg had inserted herself between George and me, brows black and threatening. "Mother is nearby praying in the chapel of the Magdalen and will not stand for your foolish disrespect. George, I should send you to Sister Agnes to apologise."

"Apologise for what? She didn't hear me; she's half-deaf…and what I said was true!" He stuck his tongue out at Margaret and then, when she put her nose in the air and ignored him, began to pull on the edges of his mouth with his fingers, making himself as grotesque as the winged stone gargoyles perched along the priory church's roof.

I bit back a laugh as he danced like a court fool around a mortified Margaret but suddenly all mirth died away. The prioress Joan had entered through an arch near the vestry and strode up to

Mother, drawing her aside, out of the Magdalen's chapel with its rows of candles in rich, ruby glass cups. Moments later, Mother strode down the church nave and flung open the west door. As the door swung open, against the glare of daylight I could see gathered men and waiting horses beyond.

"George, Meg, something is happening!" I hissed, clutching at my sibling's sleeves, getting their attention.

Even as George ceased his japery, the Prioress bore down on us like a black raven, her sleeves billowing in the wind of her speed. "Children, you must leave at once. Your sire's servants await. God go with you."

We burst out into the subdued autumnal sunlight. Faint warmth flooded over us; the sky was mostly blue, the birds singing as they soared to and from the church spire. A scent of distant smoke hung in the air; the year was turning, the first hint of gold appearing in the leaves of trees on the distant hillsides.

It was my favourite time of the year, approaching my nameday. Soon I would be seven years old. Seven was a propitious number, I was told...

The servants in our retinue were sombre, their voices low and hushed. We children were thrust into a waiting chariot; our nurses clambered in after us, pale-faced, frightened, followed by an armoured guard who sat clumsily with an unsheathed sword across his knees. More soldiers in harness gathered around the carriage, affecting a tight formation.

Margaret cleared her throat; being the eldest by some years, she felt she had the most right to speak. "Where is my mother, the Duchess? I beg you tell us why we are being removed from the priory in this manner?"

"It is for your safety, my Lady," replied the man, lifting his visor. His face was shiny with sweat "You are being taken to Ludlow under armed escort. Her Grace the Duchess has taken horse and is already well upon the road."

"Our safety? What has happened?" Meg's fingers knotted in her skirt. I shook my head; blood pounded in my ears.

"A battle has taken place at Blore Heath, my Lady. My Lord the Earl of Salisbury was on his way to Ludlow with his forces when he was attacked."

"By whom?" Margaret swallowed; I heard George's breath slither through his teeth.

The soldier hesitated a moment. "Lord Audley and his army."

George and I glanced sharply at each other. Lancastrians, King's men. Our enemies.

"And?" Margaret tried to sound grown-up, but a tremor clung to her voice.

"My Lord of Salisbury was victorious. Audley was slain…"

Margaret's eyes were luminous green-gold in the shadows of the chariot. Although we knew Father had feared renewed conflict, we did not think it would come so soon. The Loveday had taken place in St Paul's so recently, where Father had held the hand of Marguerite the Queen…

"The Earl is on his way to Ludlow," the guard continued, "so too my lord of Warwick, who brings the Calais garrison with him."

"There will be fighting, then!" exclaimed George, almost excited.

"Maybe, my Lord George," said the guard. His armoured finger ran down the blade of his sword.

Meg kicked George with her delicate green shoe. "Be silent, George. It is not the time. We must pray…for peace."

"Girls!" George muttered mutinously, crossing his arms across the front of his velvet doublet.

I said nothing for fear of provoking him, but I thought Margaret was right. We did not need more bloodshed, and maybe God was the only one who could intercede and change men's hearts. As the chariot rolled on over the rutted Welsh roads, my stomach began to roil with fear. Next to me, Meg was toying with her set of coral rosary beads, a gift from Mother.

Click…click…click. The sound was at first irritating then strangely soothing.

God and the Blessed Virgin would surely protect us.

Ludlow seemed a different place when we arrived. Clattering over the stone bridge in our carriage to enter the town, we stared out the window in fearful consternation. Cannons were being rolled along the stonework into positions of readiness. Sunlight gleamed on armour, on the tips of bristling pikes and spears. The streets were filled with armed men wearing the Murrey and Blue of York. The Falcon and Fetterlock badge ~~was~~ gleamed everywhere.

At the Hospital of the Holy Trinity and St John the Baptist, facing out across the sluggish waters of the Teme, the poor men who were inmates were gathering up their meagre possessions and leaving the premises, hobbling on sticks and canes as they sought shelter further up in the town behind the second gateway. The townsfolk milled on the cobbles, throwing barricades across the front of their shops and houses. Women and children were crying; dogs barked in mad excitement before being dragged away by their owners. Barrels of drink and salted meats rolled by the carriage, pushed by puffing, sweating men. They were followed by wains laden with food—supplies going up the steep hill to the castle gates.

"Maybe there will be a siege!" George crouched on the cushioned seat, half-hanging from the window despite the trepidation of the nursemaids. "They'll try to starve us out or poison the well by throwing dead horses into it. The French Queen might bring up a great catapult and toss human heads over the walls…"

"George, *enough*!" Margaret pulled him back from the window by the seat of his hose. "There won't be any such fighting. Father will…*talk*. It will be fine. You will see."

She sounded doubtful and George smirked knowingly. "You're a girl…you don't know anything about such matters, nor should you. You should stick to your sewing, Meg. Although I've heard you're very bad at it!"

The chariot was now ascending the steep incline of Broad Street, the horses slowing as they laboured beneath their load. The crowds pressed against the carriage-side, despite out escort, striving to get to perceived safety behind the tower of Broadgate. The chariot swayed and I felt like I was slipping, falling, and I clutched George's arm, inadvertently pinching him, which made him squeal and strike at me with his fist. The whole world had grown ominous; topsy-turvy.

Reaching the castle after what seemed an eternity, the walls were black with archers, the main gates stoutly guarded. We were hustled in and marched straight into the nursery as if it was feared hostile forces would snatch us from right under our parents' noses. We were brought supper like inmates in a prison cell, I thought; outside the big oak door, the tramp of iron-shod feet sounded. Sentries.

George and I took to hanging from the high window as our nurses shrieked and clutched at the backs of our robes, fearful we'd go tumbling down to our deaths. We were ecstatic when we caught sight of Edmund and Edward in the courtyard, practising sword fighting with each other as they waited for news.

"Ned, Ned!" I yelled. No one could miss my eldest brother; he had a bright new suit of armour and shone like the sun; he was also the tallest man in the castle bailey. Helmetless, his hair lifting on the breeze, he grinned up at us and waved. Edmund made a rude gesture behind his back and pretended to prick his brother's posterior with the tip of his sword. Edward swung round and they fell together in playful sparring.

"I wish we could join them," said George plaintively, jumping on one our clothes chests and swinging his heels against it in order to make a loud noise that annoyed the nurses.

I wished for the same, but even more, I wanted things to be as they were. Safe. Certain.

But that was an impossibility now. Battle-lines had been drawn.

Before the next day was out, Father's forces and those of our Uncle of Salisbury were joined by those of Cousin Dick, the Earl of Warwick. Salisbury's Eagle banner flew alongside Father's Falcon, and now the Bear roared alongside too, clutching a craggy stave in its paws. George and I were brought forward by our tutors to meet these esteemed kinsmen—but only briefly, for they were about to engage in a council of war. Our brothers, regarded as full-grown men now, were set to join them in their talks, but we boys would not be permitted to do so.

Uncle Salisbury, Mother's brother, was a man of middling height with a strong-featured, pleasant face and a round, shining bowl of mixed brown and silver hair. Broad-shouldered and bluff, he bent and kissed Mother's hand then turned to us, hands on hips, thumbs looped into his glistening golden belt. "Be not afraid, children," he said. "We will prevail."

"I'm not afraid," said George. "I am *never* afraid…"

"He's never silent, either," interjected Edward, with a wry grin.

Cousin Dick intrigued me. Aged around thirty, he had dark, slightly-curling hair that blew roguishly across his brow—rather different to the neat cap worn by his father Salisbury. His face was bronzed and his eyes, a bright almost startling blue, were slightly lined from squinting into the sun on long rides and sea journeys. He wore scarlet and walked with a swagger in long leather boots; not only was he a sea-captain, but it was said he was a pirate too when the fancy took him and often apprehended ships in the channel.

He was glancing thoughtfully around the Great Hall, and his keen gaze happened to land on George and me. He stalked over; drawing near we could smell the scent of horse on him and salt from the sea—he'd ridden hard from the port to reach Ludlow.

"Greeting, my young cousins," he said, speaking to us with grave dignity, as though we were fully grown and not just unimportant small lads.

George was on Warwick in a flash, chattering about how he wanted to ride out with him and Father and Uncle Salisbury and smite down the enemy hordes. Warwick merely tousled his hair. "One day…" and he looked in my direction. "It is your name day soon, young Richard, I seem to recall."

I nodded; I had hardly thought of it since our mad carriage ride back to Ludlow. "It is on the morrow, my lord."

"Here…this is for you. Keep it well." He reached to his belt and pulled out a small dagger, probably for his own use at table. It was well-used, but it was a fine piece with a bone hilt carved into a growling bear. Little red jewels were set in the bear's eyes. "You and George will be the men of the House of York when your brothers and his Grace the Duke are away at war."

I took the knife with gratitude; George was glaring, red with jealousy, but what could he say? It was my birthday gift!

Then Father strode across the chamber, resplendent in green and gold and a silver chaperon, and clapped Warwick heartily on the shoulder. "It is time for us to confer, Dick…Ah, what is that in my son's hand? Has he learnt a new trade as a pickpocket?"

"No, my lord Uncle," laughed Warwick, "it is my gift to young Richard. It's his birthday soon, after all. Had you forgotten?"

"Yes…*no*," said Father emphatically. "But I have had more important things on my mind than a child's name day, needless to say." He nodded in my direction. "Put that knife away for now, Richard—I don't want you stabbing anyone. Give it to your tutors for safe-keeping."

Clutching the knife close to my tunic, I bowed. "Yes, Father." Father turned back to Salisbury and Warwick and both George and I were escorted back to our guarded nursery chamber. The fire roared in the hearth and it was cosy; beyond, we could hear the armed men gathered in the bailey singing rough soldier songs. We went to look from the window. The town and castle were lit by hundreds of flambeaux and watchfires. Clouds were flying over a round, pitted moon, and the woody smell from the campfires kindled by the levies camped down by the river was oddly cheering, despite the gravity of the situation.

I looked at my dagger, resting on the mantlepiece of the newly-put in fireplace, one of Father's renovations for our added comfort. I had convinced my tutor that I would only look at it this one night, then he could pack it away with my other items. Again, I felt pride at owning it…but I felt a little sad too. Cousin Dick had remembered my name day. Father had, in his commitment to his cause, forgotten me, the least of his sons.

I retreated to bed, tucked in beside George who was snoring lightly, his head resting on the bolster. Eventually I slept.

In the morning, I woke to see sunlight splashing on the floor. I rubbed my bleary eyes. One of the nurses was standing by the bed, cradling in her hands an object wrapped in fine cloth. "A gift from his Grace the Duke for my Lord Richard," she said. "For his nativity."

He had not forgotten after all! Reverently I took the gift; it was a jewelled leather sheath for the knife Cousin Dick had given me.

"Look, George!" I pushed at George's shoulder. He was still snoring and did not wake.

Outside, the forces of my Father and his allies marched from the castle and set out upon the road to Worcester.

Chapter Four

The army was back and gloom hung over the town of Ludlow like a shroud. Men spoke in hushed, fearful voices; the streets were empty with not even a stray dog running loose. On the fields beyond the River Teme, Father and his supporters set up a great defensive encampment with huge earthworks and barricades and artillery dragged into position.

His original intention had been to march to London and seek an audience with the King to present his grievances—he'd sworn his loyalty to the crown before the high altar of Worcester Cathedral so all men knew that he had no wish to harm the old monarch. But then news had come; King Henry was not waiting for his arrival and in no mood to treat with him. The Mad King's own army had been mobilised and it was twice the size of Father's. Even worse, Henry himself, who hated war and could barely lift a sword, was riding at the head of his men with banners raised. To fight him would be high treason with perhaps no chance of a pardon for anyone on our side of the conflict…

George and I were in our nursery Tower playing a game of Alquerques. We were bored and hungry; our allotted food portions had grown slender in anticipation of a possible siege.

"Do you think we'll die here?" moaned George suddenly, knocking the board away and sending pieces whirling across the floor. "Do you think they'll break in and cut off our heads and set them on the town gates? I *knew* Meg would be wrong. I knew we'd get stuck here!"

I was as nervous about the future as my brother but pretended strength; after all, I was now seven. Soon, God willing, I would get sent to a noble household to become a page. "Don't be silly, George. They say Henry is very forgiving."

"But Father has antagonised him on more than one occasion—although do not mistake me, he had full right to do so! But if the King thinks he has committed treason, I doubt he'll forgive him again. And if Mad Harry confers with the devil French-woman his wife, then we are all doomed. Doomed!"

"Queen Marguerite is up north," I said, sensibly.

"But for how long?" George's face was dark as a raincloud. "She's the one who'd truly like to see us all dead. We're threats to her son, her precious little bastard boy…"

At that moment, a warning bell sounded from the mighty-towered gatehouse in the outer bailey. Almost falling over each other in our haste, we rushed to the high-arched window. Below, through the dimness, we saw torches bloom to life and a party of riders gallop into the inner ward past the dry moat with its rows of newly-sharpened stakes. As they drew closer, my straining eyes discerned the shapes of Father and our Uncle and Cousin, amongst many others. They rode to the keep, dismounted, and went inside.

"It's Father!" I hissed. "Something's happened, it must have. He would not have left his men otherwise."

"I wish they'd let us out," said George. "It's not fair that we are left in the dark like babies, even though we might be in danger!" He kicked at the door, lip outthrust in a petulant pout.

Time crept on. Our nurses wandered in and out bringing food and toys and stoking the fire, but they would not or could not answer our queries. After a while, they tucked us into bed but although the candles in the iron candelabra burnt low, we could not sleep.

Shortly before dawn, the steward came to the nursery and in a sombre voice bade the nurses dress us. Instantly we were up, wild-haired and heavy-eyed. In silence, we followed the steward down into Father's solar. Mother was there, seated on a chair, with Margaret hovering about her, hair unbound like a hoyden. We bowed as was expected but Father brushed our gestures of respect aside. "Sit, children, I must speak to you."

We sat on stools already waiting for us. Father looked grey-faced and worn; he strode back and forth in nervous agitation. "I haven't much time; I must soon away," he said, "but we…we are undone. King Henry approaches in warlike mood and…and Andrew Trollope has defected and flown to the King's side. He was one of Warwick's captains and a knowledgeable soldier and he helped advise me. He knows my thought in this conflict; he knows how many men I command and what weapons and artillery I hold. All my plans were revealed to him."

Father took a deep, shuddering breath. "I have had to make hard decisions tonight. I thought of surrender…"

George and I glanced at each other. *Surrender!*

"…but even though pardons have been promised, I have my doubts as to whether they would ever truly be given. Not now. And no pardon was offered for Salisbury—the King wants blood retribution for the death of Lord Audley."

"We…we cannot let the King kill Uncle Richard!" cried Margaret, horrified.

"No, we cannot…will not." Father was firm.

"Is there to be a siege then, Father?" George spoke up, almost brightly. I am sure he was imagining he could stand atop the walls and hurl down stones and dung onto the heads of enemies below. "I told the others there probably would be."

"No, the castle has not enough provisions for a protracted siege. Such an action would only inflame our plight. What I must do is not an act of honour…but one of necessity" He took another ragged breath. "I must flee, leave England. Warwick, Salisbury and Edward will go to France, while I will fare through Wales and take ship to Ireland, where many men still support the House of York. Edmund shall accompany me on my journey."

"I was born in Ireland!" exclaimed George. "I would come with you, Lord Father."

Father bit his lip. "And here must the truth be spoken, the reason I have summoned you at this early hour and despite your young ages. Your dear Lady Mother already knows what must befall. When I go abroad into exile…you must all stay behind here at the castle."

A terrible silence fell over the solar. A log cracked on the fire, making us all jump. Mother's visage was stone as she stared into her lap.

George was the first to speak. "Lord Father…sir…sir…" he stammered.

"I am sorry, George," said Father quietly. "It is farewell…for now. We will meet again when it is…safe. God protect you, my children, my lady-wife."

So saying, without an embrace for any of us, he sharply turned on his heel and left the chamber.

After what seemed an eternity, Mother rose from her seat, dignified though pale. "You must be brave, as befits the children of York. Make your sire proud by your courage. The first thing we all must do is attend chapel and pray. Pray that we may be delivered safely from our enemies."

On October 13, all the soldiery left in the fields near Ludford Bridge surrendered to King Henry. He let them live. Father and our brothers were long gone, along with Warwick and Salisbury.

The King did not approach the castle but he allowed his men to enter the town in great groups without captains to hold them in check. George and I were in the Hall when we heard the banging on drums coming steadily closer from the direction of the River Teme. The sound washed up and over the castle like peels of thunder. At the same time, clouds of smoke began billowing into the clear, cold October sky; huge black plumes that flared out across heaven and drifted in the wind. The scent of burning wood, hot and acrid, drifted to our nostril.

One of Mother's ladies began to weep. "Jesu, they are firing the town! They will kill us all!"

"Mary, be silent," said Mother with fierceness. "Go to your quarters or see to your prayers—your wailing is of no help to anyone."

Sobbing, Mary fled and Mother gathered George, Margaret and me together. "Come, children, I shall assess what is happening in the streets beyond."

Leaving the hall, we climbed the uneven, worn steps to the castle wall-walk. The garrison was on patrol, armoured feet and halberds clashing; archers with bent bows massed on the heights of the great red Towers. The smell of burning was even more fierce here; ash rained through the air, making my eyes and nose run. Meg started to cough and covered her mouth with her hand.

"Your Grace…" One of the soldiers barred Mother's way. "It is not safe up here…"

"Nowhere is safe," she snapped. "I will pass."

We walked along the wall; Mother's headdress belled and flapped as if it were a living thing as clouds of smoke and ashes eddied around her upright figure. George and I might have found the scene amusing if we had not been terrified. The wind was rising, blowing more smoke in our direction—and bringing the sound of screaming to our ears.

Standing on tiptoes, I reluctantly peered through the crenellations atop the wall. The town below, the familiar, friendly town with its angled timber houses, had become a scene from Hell, reminiscent of the Doom Paintings on the chancel arches in many churches. Red flames licked greedily at rooftops, consuming beams and tiles, jumping from one house to another. In the streets, people surged this way and that—and were met by armoured men in the colours of the King and his supporters. The invaders looked scarcely human, faces smeared with soot, mouths open in bestial roars of victory as they stormed between the flaming houses, striking out at fleeing townsfolk. A huge barrel of ale, stolen from some inn, was set down on the cobbles and broken open; Lancastrian soldiers slurped at its contents like pigs at a trough. Drunk, one man lurched forward and stabbed a fat merchant in a white chaperon, who was using a staff to beat the raiders from his smouldering shop door; the man screamed in agony and fell, and dead or alive, the Lancastrian horde thrust him into the flames with much laughter. At the same time, other soldiers had gathered a bunch of girls and women together; they chased them from side to side of the street, as if they were herding kine. I recognised the one who had blown a kiss at Edward when we went to St Lawrence's; she was not so confident now, her hair tangled, her gown torn off her shoulder. A man caught her round the middle, dragging her towards one of the many alleys that snaked through the town. Others raced after him, I saw them rip the rest of her garments as she screamed...

"Richard!" Mother pulled me away from the horrific scene in the street; her fingernails were like daggers impaling my small shoulder. "I forbid you to look."

"We should help them..." I said weakly, choking on smoke. From below the yells and shrieks and unholy laughter grew louder. Bells were clanging in church towers, adding to the din.

"There is no help we can give. But there may be some slight hope. I have seen the banner of the Duke of Buckingham, my brother-in-law, your uncle-by-marriage. We will fare out of the castle to meet him...and to offer our most humble surrender to the King's forces. For all that he is on the opposite side of this conflict, he will keep us from harm, for the sake of my sister Anne."

"Mother...we dare not leave the castle!" said Margaret, horrified. "Those ruffians..."

"Would not dare touch a daughter of York," said Mother.

In haste, we descended from the walls and Mother made her intended actions known to the constable. Mouth open like a hooked fish, he gaped at her, waving his arms in distress as he tried to dissuade her from her course.

"Open the gate," she ordered. "Remove your Lord's banner from the towers. Inform the captain of the garrison that I shall go forth to offer surrender to the Lancastrian forces. You need not fear; it is an unwritten law that if a castle should surrender without siege, its inhabitants should be spared."

Ashen-faced, the man bowed and hurried away. "Come," said Mother. She was like a warrior-queen from an old legend in her huge, wind-damaged headdress. She took my hand and George's; it was not a comforting hand-holding as one's nurse might do after a fall; it was an iron grip, cold and hard. A grip that said, "*Do not fail me.*" Meg walked behind, wretched with fright but struggling to emulate the seemingly unbroken hauteur of our mother the Duchess.

We stood for a while in the outer bailey, waiting. Smoke rolled over us in acrid clouds. We heard thrown objects strike the great wooden gates that faced outwards toward the town— perhaps casks that the looters had emptied out in their drunken frenzy.

The constable and steward came rushing towards us, their long robes flowing, the hems streaked with mud; the chaplain was trailing behind them, his cassock billowing, and the captain of the garrison in ash-smeared breastplate and sallet. They all tried to persuade Mother against her chosen course of action.

Rain began to fall, chill, drizzly; now the sky was black with clouds as well as smoke from the burning. The gold and green on Mother's fine brocade grew dark; her headdress drooped further. "I will not be gainsaid," she insisted. "Opening the gates and surrendering is the only way."

She turned from the men to face the gates, her shoulders back, her chin proudly raised. Beads of water trailed down her smooth white brow, high and shaved as was the fashion. The captain glanced at the constable, who made a small weak motion of assent with his head. The priest prayed, his voice a nervous mumble.

The castle gates began to creak open, the portcullis rising with a noisy groan as men heaved on the chains that levered it up and down.

Together, we walked out into the ransacked town, the shadow of the walls black upon us. Behind us the priest was now on his knees, arms raised to heaven, crying out words from the Psalms, "Be gracious to me, O God, be gracious to me, for my soul takes refuge in You; and in the shadow of Your wings I will take refuge until destruction passes by." The captain had his hand on his sword hilt, watching our progress with frustration; we knew he would die for anyone of us but his true duty was to the castle and its inhabitants. Every step we took bore us further from the safety of his sword-arm.

Around us, the market square was a scene of carnage and destruction. Animals lay slaughtered; stalls were crushed and overturned. Crushed fruit mingled with blood, broken crockery, piss and ale. An old man lay spread-eagled on the cobbles, his head staved in. A woman with a bloodied face howled at his side, her shrieking animalistic, inhuman with grief.

Mother led us through the wreckage and up the age-worn steps of the Butter Cross. The stone blocks were slimy with gore and drink. We stood near the top, under the drizzling sky, as Mother cast her gaze about the ruination, looking for a worthy from the Lancastrian side to whom she could call the surrender.

Like rats,. drunken Lancastrian foot soldiers and archers began to emerge from the alleyways and the taprooms they had broken into. They approached the Butter Cross, grinning and nudging each other.

"Look at the fine lady up there!" one hooted. "God's teeth, is that the Duchess of York herself? You come out for a bit of fun, my Lady?"

She refused to answer, to even look at the leering creature. The man loped up, grinning, stinking of wine and beer, sweat and lust. He was a head taller than Mother but she was standing on a step above him and stared him down eye to eye, almost daring him to lay hands on her. His filthy, bloodied paw reached out, trying to grope; she did not move an inch. We children cowered, clinging to her hands.

"Think of what you do," she said to the miscreant in a flat, toneless voice, "and what the outcome will be if you touch me or mine…"

He made a growling, almost disappointed noise in his throat and suddenly reached out and ripped a jewel from her dress. That seemed to make him happy. "Look what I have, lads!" he screeched, holding the gem up flashing green fire into the smoky air.

At that moment, he was struck by the charging body of a great white horse. He was flung onto the cobbles, the breath knocked out of him.

"Arrest this man!" An armoured warrior sat astride the white destrier, the golden plume on his helm flying out in the wind. His mount, as heavily armoured as he, was caparisoned with cloths bearing silver knots. Immediately soldiers wearing badges shaped into similar knots rushed forward and laid hold of the man who had robbed Mother, ripping the jewel from his hand and dragging him away into a corner of the square. There they gathered, circling him like wolves; I heard a gurgling shriek. They had slit his throat.

The rider leaned forward, mailed hand outstretched to take the gem from the blood-smeared captain who walked back across the square. Then he turned his steed's metal-bound head and spurred it up the steps of the Butter Cross.

"My Lord Humphrey," said Mother. She tried to keep her voice steady but a tremor of relief was audible.

The rider was the Duke of Buckingham, Humphrey Stafford, our uncle-by-marriage. His wife Anne was Mother's sister, our aunt. He raised his visor; we saw a broad, rather florid face marked across the cheek by a long, pale scar. He had taken that wound at St Albans, protecting King Henry. Protecting him from Father and Warwick's men…

"Lady Cecily, what, by God's Teeth are you doing out here?" he snarled, furious. "You could have been killed…or worse. And your children! By Christ's Nails, why did you bring them into the middle of this looting!"

"I came to find you or some other great lord in the service of his Grace King Henry…Came to tell you that the castle will surrender on any terms the King wishes. I know you are a good man, Humphrey, even if we do not see eye to eye on many things. I beg you, let no harm come to the residents of the castle…and beg his Grace call off these ruffians before a thriving town of *his* subjects is destroyed utterly."

"I will accept your surrender and have the news conveyed to the King at once," said Duke Humphrey. "I cannot promise anything about the sack of the town; I do not approve but it has gone too far to stop, I deem, without having permission to hang looters. I also cannot promise the safety of your goods within the castle…"

"I care nothing for my goods," said Mother.

"Then I will see the household is escorted to safety."

"I thank you, my Lord Buckingham." She bowed her head, looking suddenly wan and weary. Ash smeared her cheeks; her veil was black with it.

"And so you should, Duchess Cecily; as you should humble your pride." He tossed her the green jewel his men had wrest back from the thief before killing him. "Here is your tawdry gewgaw. Now, come, walk alongside my horse—but forget not, my Lady, you are not only under my protection, you are also my prisoner."

Mother's lips went the colour of chalk but she nodded. "I understand, my Lord Duke."

Buckingham turned and let his gaze fall upon us children, ash-strained and bedraggled on the muddy and bloody Butter Cross.

"Jesu, what a bunch of ragged urchins!" he said, but there was a hint of sympathy in his voice. He beckoned to Margaret. "Come forward, child; I will carry you on my horse."

Rain was sluicing down now, cold and unpleasant, gathering in my collar. Some of the fires around the town were dying away in the deluge but the smell of burnt woods—and flesh, whether beast or man's, was unbearable.

Mother handed a sodden Meg up to the Duke; she sat awkwardly behind him on the high-lipped saddle, clinging to him for dear life, her hair hanging in wet tendrils. The Duke spurred his horse on a few steps and we all followed; the ground was churned up mud, its stickiness sucking at our ankles. Mother's gown, trailing behind her, was ruined. We slipped and slid, half-falling on unnameable, horrible things we dared not gaze upon.

The Duke glanced over, then wheeled his horse towards us. "The smallest one, I can take him too. It will take too long for him to walk back to the keep; his legs are short and he is struggling already. I am not a monster; I have a grandson only a little younger than he."

Silently, Mother lifted me—an odd sensation, for a great lady such as she never manhandled her children—and I sprawled over the pommel of the Duke of Buckingham's saddle. His destrier snorted and stamped, unnerved by my added weight. Buckingham calmed the beast with a gentle command. "I will not let you fall," he said to me, as I perched almost in his lap, muddy, shivering and wet.

"Thank you, Lord Humphrey," said my Mother, the Duchess.

The Duke guided his steed forward with the pressure of his knees. "You, madam, shall walk, however, along with the bigger boy. I would not have you forget through small kindnesses that I may offer—you are still my prisoner."

Chapter Five

Tonbridge Castle's walls rose stonily around us—our new home and our prison. It was a soft enough imprisonment, however, with plenty of food and drink and warm clothes to wear. Mother had it the worst; her sister Anne sternly took her in hand with many a rebuke for her pride. She was allowed to wear only the dullest of robes and headdresses as if she were a penitent, and she was made to attend upon her sister like a servant, walking at her heels while Anne swished along in fine brocades. Mother was always a pious woman, but she spent more time on her knees in that castle chapel, praying that her sins be absolved, than she ever had at Usk or Ludlow.

We children had tutors; they were eager to rap our knuckles or birch us for insolence, but I cannot say they were evil men, just doing what the Duke and Duchess paid them to do. They still treated us as the offspring of a Duke, making no mention of our imprisonment, although much attention was paid to daily praising the old King, as if we didn't know he was truly about as effective a ruler as a sheep. Still, he had won the day at Ludford bridge, and we had lost—at least for now.

Uncle Buckingham was not so bad and seemed to have less resentment against our family than he might have done, considering the ugly wound he had taken at St Albans. When he had time, he would show us his fine horses and let us play with some of the hounds. Sometimes he would even tell us stories of his exploits—how he became Earl of Stafford aged but one year when his sire was killed in battle, and how he was knighted by King Henry V.

Aunt Anne liked us less than her husband, even though we were of close blood. She wore a stony face in our presence and constantly found fault. "Your dress is rumpled, Margaret!'

61

'Moderate your voice and stop scowling, George!' 'Richard, speak up when I speak to you; you are not an infant anymore."

Margaret whispered that Anne's constant ill mood was not only on account of Uncle Buckingham's ragged scar, which had ruined his looks (George and I quite *liked* the scar, thinking it gave him a roguish, almost piratical air) but because their son, Humphrey, Earl of Stafford, had taken wounds at St Albans and never recovered—he had died a year or so later, bedridden, leaving behind a small son named Henry for the King. Uncle Buckingham called the boy 'Harry' when he spoke of him.

We soon got to meet young Harry, who was several years my junior. George and I watched him come rolling into the inner bailey in a gilded carriage as if he were a prince of the realm with banners flying and horns bellowing. We were confined to the side-lines near the clustered servants—a deliberate ploy, we decided, by miserable Aunt Anne to make us look and feel unimportant.

Out into the bailey stepped our Cousin Harry, plump in a velvet doublet as red as blood, a feathered cap sitting at a jaunty angle on his gold-brown curls. His wide, well-fed face beamed as members of his grandparents' household rushed over to pay their respects to him.

George and I were not invited over but were left standing in the gloomy shadows of the keep as Harry was whisked away to his apartments, a veritable army of servants and nurses trailing in his wake. He even had his own Fool, prancing along beside his master with the bells on his hat and shoe-tips jingling, and seven musicians playing on pipes and flutes who followed him into the castle.

"I don't think much of him," sneered George. "He's a little prig. He did not even glance at us, Richard."

"He may not have seen us in all that great crowd of servants. I am sure he will be introduced properly to us soon," I said, trying not to damn my small cousin from the very start. I did not want to judge. And if we could befriend Harry…well, we needed friends.

"Aunt Anne and Uncle Humphrey mollycoddle him. You can tell whenever they speak of him. Harry this, Harry that…Harry the moon-shines-from-his-buttocks! He's a fat, spoilt little piglet, that's what he is!" George laughed nastily.

I did not tell George that Harry's appearance reminded me a little of George himself—for I did not feel like having my arm twisted or my foot stomped on by my mercurial brother. George had lost interest by now anyway; the crowd was dispersing and he saw the cook coming out of the kitchen with some mince pies cooling on a tray. She placed them on a bench near the door, above the reach of any passing dogs.

But not of passing children. George was always partial to a few pies. He took one, then two, and gobbled them down. Then he grinned at me, in that devious way George had. "Don't look so shocked, Richard. Take one while you can. Otherwise they'll all end up on the table before fat Cousin Harry."

That evening, there was a feast held to mark the arrival of the Duke of Buckingham's small heir. Even Meg thought such a celebration was excessive and rolled her eyes at the thought. "He is what—five, maybe? He'll be carried off to bed asleep before the night has even begun!"

All three of us were dressed and washed, put in our best clothes (though nothing that might outshine the special Stafford child) and paraded into the hall. We were seated at a bench well below the salt; Meg shook her head and said it was shameful for us to be there, even if we were prisoners. Mother was seated across from us, hands folded in her lap, white-robed as if she were a nun. Her expression was shuttered.

On the dais at the top of the Hall, the Duke and Duchess of Buckingham sat in splendour beneath a canopy adorned with Stafford Knots and running antelopes. Little Harry Stafford was beside them on his own little gilded chair, kicking it with his heels as he waited impatiently for the first courses to arrive. He was wearing a circlet on his curls and a long, silverish robe with Bohun swans picked out on it in crystal.

"Next they'll make us kiss his hand; you watch!" George whispered in my ear. "You'll have to go first, Richard!"

Needless to say, nothing as terrible as that happened, although young Harry got the choice cuts of meat, the foil-coated pies fashioned into crowns, the huge sugary subtlety shaped like a castle. He devoured almost all of it himself then tossed some to his pet dog, a little yapping brown-and-white spaniel that ran excitedly around his chair.

Later in the evening, we were finally invited up to officially meet our cousin. By that time, his eyelids were drooping and he looked cranky. After our names had been given, he stared at us appraisingly. "I'm a descendant of Edward III," he said proudly.

"So are we," I said, gesturing to George, Meg and myself.

That did not go down well. Harry's face went red and he stormed out of the Hall, his dog bouncing and yapping around his ankles. I noticed Aunt Anne giving us a hard stare from beneath her canopy.

As we were shunted off to the confines of the nursery, George crowed, "Did you see that old witch our Aunt glaring? I dare say you're due for a birching, Dickon, because you insulted her precious Harry!"

I was afraid then and cursed myself inwardly for my honest tongue. I spent the night tossing and turning, anticipating the birching I was likely to receive. Fortunately, it never came and Uncle Buckingham winked knowingly at me when we passed in the chapel.

Over the next little while, George and I gradually came to know Harry. At first, we suspected Aunt Anne kept him away from us since we were seen as bad influences on his tender little Lancastrian soul, but in the end, it was his own inquisitiveness that drew us together. We soon were playing ball and other childish games under the watchful eye of the servants and nurses.

He was younger and whined when he scraped a knee or lost in a game of Hoodman's blind or Nine Men's Morris, but we learned to ignore that. He was spoilt and over-proud but we ignored that too. Being his friend meant we were allowed more time in the stables and kennels even when the Duke was not in residence.

Slowly we began to forget that our freedom was curtailed; that we could not travel to our Father's holdings, nor see our other relations; that we could not contact our brothers who were in exile. We dwelt in a strange, safe little world behind the walls of Tonbridge Castle, doing childish things and thinking not of the troubles beyond the outer gates.

We did not even long for our freedom when, surrounded by Buckingham's guards, Mother rode out of the castle without us, to fare to Coventry where the King was holding parliament. She was to plead for clemency for Father and for all her children.

Men called the Parliament that year the 'Parliament of Devils', for Father, Edmund and Edward were all attainted; our family now had nothing, no lands, no castles. We were nobodies.

But Mother spoke the King fair and he gave her an income of £1000 marks that we might not starve. 'The infants have not offended their King!" Mad Harry had told her as he set his seal upon the order.

At least we would not face complete penury, but sometimes we saw Harry Stafford smirking at us, his face flushed with too much knowledge for a child his age. He liked to creep around and listen in on the adults' private talk. "Your Father is attainted," he would mutter spitefully. "So you should all bow to me now!"

But the Wheel of Dame Fortuna was turning, and in the next year, when July's sweltering heat caused shimmering ripples in the air and the River Medway turned slow and sour, we saw the castle full of armed men and a messenger dustied from long riding amongst them.

"What is going on, George?" I breathed to my brother.

"How would I know?" he shrugged. "Shall we try to find out?"

We began to run out toward the clustered soldiers, but suddenly one of our tutors, Master Kitchell the rather-black-hearted Latin teacher, raced from the apartments and grabbed us both by the scruffs of our necks. I was nearly pulled off my feet by the strength of his lunge; my throat hurt where my collar had cut into it.

"No, this is no place for you!" Kitchell thundered, his bushy brows waggling over piggy, blood-shot eyes, and the way he said 'you' implied this ban was solely upon the children of York and not the other residents of the castle.

Without further ado, George and I were herded into the nursery; the door was shut firmly behind us. We could hear footsteps echoing in the hall and voices muttering furiously. Outside in the castle bailey, the clash of armour and the neighing of horses grew louder.

I pressed myself to the door, praying none of the nurses would barge in to see what we were about and leave me with a bruised ear. I could make out words, jumbled and indistinct, but I got the gist of what was being said:

"Lord Faulconberg, John Dynham and John Wenlock attacked Sandwich under the cover of darkness. Mundford is dead, executed at Rybank Tower! The Earl of Warwick had already stolen half the ships but now the port is lost—"

I jumped back from the door as if the wooden panels had burst into flame. Great hope leapt in my heart. Edward was with Warwick. If our Cousin Warwick was sailing the seas near England with a mind to land, then Edward would also be coming home, glorious Edward—and following him, God grant it, my Father and Edmund! The placid acceptance of the past months died away in my soul. Now I wanted nothing more than to leave Tonbridge, to leave this soft but sure captivity.

George was poking at my back with bony fingers. "What is it, Dickon? What have you heard? Tell me!"

"Hush! There may be more!" I pressed my ear against the door again, a cold sweat breaking on my forehead.

Again, the buzz of excited voices, some more distinct than others. "Warwick...landed with two-thousand men. The young Edward of March is riding with him under his sire's banner of the Fetterlock. They are gathering many supporters and heading with all haste towards London..."

My breath hissed through my teeth. *Edward*! *He was here!*

"The King and Queen are at Coventry," a man's voice grated. "They've an army with them. They'll stop Warwick and March if they march north." A harsh laugh followed.

"The army's not so large, Rodge; not so large at all, and you said yourself that Warwick is gaining supporters wherever he goes. He's well-loved, is the Earl. You know what men sang even before he arrived back in England...

'*Send home, most gracious Jesu most benign,*
that noble knight and flower of manhood
Richard Earl of Warwick, shield of our defence,
Jesu! restore him to the honour he had before!'"

"Shut your mouth! He's a fucking traitor; he deserves his head on a spike, not adulation. His fame will be short-lived, I have no doubt—his Grace the Duke is riding out as soon as possible to meet the King and then to deal with these fractious miscreants, I pray for once and for all."

George was shaking my arm. "Tell me, tell me! Your face is as white as a ghost's, Richard!"

Overcome with emotion, I almost fainted into my brother's arms. "George," I cried, clasping his hands, "Edward and Uncle Dick are back in England! Soon we're going to be free! There's going to be a great battle and then we can leave this place and never come back!"

With Warwick and Edward marching to London and beyond to take on the King's army, our family's position as prisoners at

Tonbridge became more apparent. No longer were we permitted to roam about the bailey and the corridors; we were confined to our respective rooms. Luckily, George and I were housed together, so I had some companionship; we only saw Meg and Mother at Mass. There was no more game-playing with young Harry Stafford, and we were not even permitted to watch the Duke march out to the battle at the head of his contingent of knights, archers and foot soldiers. Our main nurse, a termagant called Tillie, told us this was for our own protection since the onlookers might turn on us, as we were the sons of a traitor.

Over the next week or so, George and I amused ourselves playing with marbles and staging pretend battles with toy soldiers of lead. Our tutors seemed flustered and uneasy and old beetle-browed Kitchell whipped us for stuttering in Latin and blotting our papers with clumsy hand. We were dragged to the chapel even when we need not, to pray for the safety of the Duke of Buckingham as he took to the field. At every turn, I could feel hostile and accusing eyes upon us and my ears burned—what kind of a son was I if it was not my Father's cause I prayed for? And Edward, tall laughing Ned, fighting his first real battle?

Outside our chamber, the rain splashed down, adding to our darkened mood. The heat of previous weeks had broken and England was struck by thunderstorms and tumultuous downpours. Through the narrow, ancient window-slit of our room, George and I gazed at morning skies the hue of bruises, with clouds rearing on the horizons like siege-towers. Birds wheeled in rising winds; rain began to hammer on the pointed tower-roof of the nursery.

"Richard, if they do not let us out of here soon…I…I will jump!" George suddenly ran to the window and grasped the shutters, hauling himself up.

Panicked I grabbed the back of his leaf-green hose, almost ripping them from his body. He yelled out at the possible indignity of exposed buttocks and fell back on top of me, making us both collapse onto the floorboards. "You great lump!" he yelled, pummelling me. "I was only jesting!"

"You shouldn't act the fool! You might really have fallen!" I whacked him back and we rolled on the floor like angry village boys, not the sons of a royal Duke...even though an attainted Duke, stripped of lands and wealth.

When we had ceased hitting each other, our childish passions burnt out, we stared one to the other—and then George began to laugh. I was red-faced and panting but gradually I began to laugh too. "Jesu, Dickon," said my brother, "I swear I will go mad if we have to stay in this place much longer!"

"As mad as the mad old King!" I cried, still laughing.

"Yes!" cried George. He whipped a coverlet off the bed and wrapped it about his shoulders mimicking a King's long mantle. "I am Mad King Henry...and I think I am a dog!" He fell to his hands and knees and began to bark and caper around.

I shrieked with mirth and began to join him at his new-found sport of insulting our less than competent sovereign. "You're not Mad Harry, I am!" I cried. I jumped on the bed, waved my arms in the air and rolled my eyes. "I howl at the full moon! I am a lunatic!"

At that very moment, there *was* a howl from deep within the twisting corridors of a Tonbridge Castle. It was exactly what one would expect to hear from the throat of a madman. Only it was a woman's voice. Immediately we fell still and silent. "What was that?" I whispered.

George shook his head. We crept to the window, stared out through the drizzle. A courier must have reached the castle from afar, unbeknownst to us; the stable-hands were leading a lathered brown horse to a trough. Suddenly a serving girl appeared, trudging through the muddy bailey. She appeared to be weaving from side to side as if drunk—or sick. Slowly, she collapsed in the mud and lay face down.

George gave a sharp gasp. "Pestilence! It must be the Plague."

We glanced at each other in terror. A hundred years ago the Black Death had ravaged England, killing thousands, from the lowliest peasant to the highest noble. Towns were left empty, villages abandoned; the dead were hurled into pits together, rich man beside poor. Everyone feared the pestilence would return one day bringing blackened skin and bursting boils…

A strident knock sounded on the door. George and I both jumped back in fright. "Lord George, Lord Richard." It was our frightful nurse, Tillie. "I bring tidings."

She staggered into the room, eyes streaming and red. She looked ill, dazed. We stared, alarmed, scanning the puffy, pouchy face. That wasn't a bubo growing on her chin, was it? No, it was just a wen.

George sprang towards her, then stopped as if he feared contamination. "Tell us truly! Is there sickness at Tonbridge?"

"No sickness," she said, her voice strangled with suppressed sobs, "but you must come at once. Your mother the Duchess has asked for you. She waits in the Duchess Anne's solar."

We glanced at each other. This could be the most dreadful news—or it could be what we had dreamed of hearing these past days. With thudding hearts, we made ourselves presentable then proceeded to the solar.

Inside, Mother seated upon a stool. Her garments were dark, plain, mourning clothes—yet a necklace of white roses circled her throat, outshining any darkness. Although her face bore its customary serene expression, revealing nothing, I noted a flush of colour on her cheeks, a hint of a tilt to her mouth that I had not seen for a long time. Margaret was with her, kneeling at her feet.

"George, Richard, a battle has been fought at Northampton." She paused. "The Earl of Warwick and Edward are victorious, aided by the defection of Grey of Ruthin."

"Hurrah!" George punched the air.

Mother turned on him furiously. "George, be silent. Keep yourself in check. Your Uncle, the Duke of Buckingham was slain defending King Henry's tent. This household is in mourning and my sister made a widow, no matter what the outcome of this battle means for us. We had been treated well at Tonbridge; show gratitude to those who have fed and dressed you."

George hung his head but I could see the dancing, happy light in his eyes. He clearly hoped soon he would regain the status stripped from us by Father's attainder.

"What will happen now, Lady Mother?" asked Meg, fidgeting in a simple brown kirtle; she was not properly dressed for the day, so swiftly had the momentous news come to Tonbridge.

"Edward will send for us, of course," said Mother, "and we will leave this place for London. After that, your Lord Father and Edmund will return from Ireland."

"And?" Meg's brow lifted.

"He will speak with the King and Parliament will be held. I have no doubt the foolish and improper attainders will be lifted." She smiled suddenly, unexpectedly—a surprise, since she was not overly given to smiling, thinking it undignified. "The House of York is in the position now to ask for what should rightfully belong to your loving sire. We hold the cards. With Humphrey dead—God assoil him—and the Tower in Salisbury's hands, the tables have turned at last."

Before a fortnight had passed, the family was ready to leave Tonbridge. We had taken few of our possessions; Mother said they were to be given to the poor—they were now from a time she had no wish to remember.

Little Harry Stafford was waiting, to our surprise, having railed at his nurses until they bought him into the courtyard to say farewell. I was not sure how to speak to him, since he had been close to his Grandfather, having lost his father already. I merely bowed my head and tried to look solemn. George, however, was racing around, filled with energy at the thought of our upcoming freedom.

Before I knew what was happening George and Harry were trading insults. "My grandfather died because of your family," Harry said with bitterness. He was desperately trying not to cry. "He was your kinsman too. He protected you at Ludlow. Don't you care?"

George was fully playing the ass now, uncaring as to the damage he could cause. "Care? My Father always taught me to tell the truth…" (A lie—George could lie like no one else!) "and the answer is…no."

It was meant to hurt and clearly it did, a stupid, needless jibe. Harry launched himself at George, his small body barreling into him and knocking his legs out from under him. George was caught off-balance and fell heavily onto the cobbles. As his posterior hit the ground, he began to yell and shout as if he was dying. But Harry, young though he was had not finished with him. As George attempted to stagger up, Harry rushed him again, slamming his head full into his face. Blood spurted from George's perfect Plantagenet nose!

Meg, standing beside the chariot and about to alight, cried out in alarm and clutched at George, whose bloody hands were curling into angry fists. "No, stop it; this is shameful!" she thundered but he tore himself from her grasp and grabbed the collar of his opponent's doublet—his opponent who was now the Duke of Buckingham. The smaller child hung in mid-air, legs kicking angrily, trying to poke George's shins with the long toes of his imported poulaines.

I had to do something before things went too far. I ran at George as a knight gallops at the quintain in the tiltyard and swatted at his hands. "Enough!" I cried, attempting to sound authoritative. To my relief, he dropped the new Duke who gave a roar and crawled in his direction with fury in his young eyes.

"Stop, *stop*, you are both disgraces to your families, especially you, George!" Margaret rushed over, grabbing George's arm once again and shaking him as a terrier shakes a rat.

"You started this unseemly row! Apologise to our cousin. At *once*…or…or I'll thrash you in front of all."

"I—I will not!" George yelled, his hand pressed to his nose. Blood still spouted, spattering his doublet. "Look what the Stafford brat has done to me?"

"You got what you deserved," I said solemnly. "You should not have said what you did."

"You are as bad as Harry, Richard!" cried George. "Why do you defend him? That Lancastrian! You're a traitor and I hate you!" Pushing me aside, he sprang into the waiting chariot and pulled the thick red velvet drapery across the window so that he would not have to look at the rest of us.

I turned to face Harry and attempted to make amends for George's hideous affront. "I am so sorry for George's behaviour…and…and for the loss of your grandfather."

Harry's round face was red as flame. "No, you're not. You're not sorry at all. You are all traitors; it is in the nature of the Yorks to be treacherous! I hope you all die horribly. Go away!"

The vehemence of his ill-wishing shocked me, but at that moment, Mother and Aunt Anne entered the courtyard, walking slowly toward the chariot. Our Aunt had aged in the days since her husband had died at Northampton; wearing stark-black, she looked a gaunt skeleton next to her sister. It was more like ten years between them instead of one. She had been married to Duke Humphrey for many years and her grief was clear to behold. She did not even have Uncle Buckingham's body to bury at Pleshey, which was their original choice for joint interment; already, in the aftermath of the battle, local monks had chested him and buried him in the House of the Franciscans in Northampton. I could not help but feel a sense of pity towards her, even though she had not been especially kind to us. As a child, though, I could say no words without giving offence.

I merely bowed to her before clambering into the chariot beside the sulking, bloody-nosed George and Meg, who was sitting crushed against the side, afraid of getting George's blood on her gown.

Mother gave her sister a brief, cool embrace, spoke a few words next to her ear, and then joined us in the carriage, moving regally as a queen. I noted her under-gown was purple, the colour of royalty.

As the chariot rolled out into the Kent countryside, our armed escort galloping alongside, I felt almost deliriously happy.

A new day was dawning. The House of York was ascendant, and all the world in that moment seemed fair and bright.

Like all worldly things, my joy would prove fleeting...

Chapter Six

Arriving in London, our chariot was escorted through the crowded, smelly, exciting streets to the house of Sir John Fastolf in Southwark. We would reside there while our parents' castle of Baynard was prepared for us, its recent Lancastrian tenants having departed, by force or by choice we neither knew nor cared. Fastolf had been one of Father's supporters, serving him in France when Joan of Arc was riding about dressed as a man and inciting the French to war. The lords burnt her at the stake in the end. Fastolf himself was dead these past months, however, and his home in Southwark was placed at our disposal, no doubt because the ties he had forged with Father long ago.

As the carriage trundled into Southwark, rocking over the muddied cobbles, I stared out, eager to see the great city of London for the first time. I could smell it already, even within the confines of our carriage—scents of a rank river mixed with dung, smoke entwined with the sickly smell of butchered meat from the flesh-markets.

My eyes grew huge. Buildings were crammed everywhere, stretching down impossibly long streets. Narrow tenements stretched toward heaven, wedged between the shops of wealthier men, their walls hung with painted buckram and their doors ajar to entice visitors inside. Bagpipes wheezed and a hurdy-gurdy churned out a lively jig. Bear-baiters gathered around a pit, hooting as they poked a mangy bear with a pole; cockfights took place outside inns with names like 'The Tabard' and 'The White Hart.' Gutters steamed, full of muck, and children no older than I played in the slime, stark naked. Cripples hobbled by on sticks; the ill and afflicted sat cross-legged on the roadside, holding up their begging bowls for alms. I crossed myself and threw a few pennies into their midst at Mother's insistence—"It is truly a curse not to be whole and perfect of body, " she said.

George, who had snivelled through most of the journey then taken to kicking me in the shins whenever I drifted off to sleep, suddenly seemed interested in what was going on. He leaned over me, trying to get a good view of the streets beyond our chariot. "I wonder if we'll see Bankside? That's where the bagnios and stews are! Ned told me all about them back in Ludlow!"

"George!" Mother's voice was the crack of a whip as she sat upright. "Draw the curtain at once, I bid you. It is not seemly you gape out the window like a common oaf."

George fell back on the seat, chastened and sulking once more, his arms folded defensively over his chest.

"What's a stew?" I whispered in his ear.

He gave me a hateful glare. "Not telling you…baby Dickon."

I decided to ignore him for the short remainder of our journey. Soon we were driving towards a large moated manor house faced by a great drawbridge. Beyond it flowed the River Thames, a sluggish grey snake, and on the opposite bank, the louring bastions of the Tower of London, glowing pale as the feeble sun broke through the ragged grey clouds that stretched overhead.

Then the view of the Tower was abruptly cut off. The chariot was rocking over the drawbridge, its wheels making a terrible din on the boards, and then we were in the courtyard, gazing up at tall crenellated walls and a sea of vast mullioned windows.

Mother alighted the carriage, helped by a host of servants who appeared as if from nowhere, wearing Father's colours of Murrey and Blue. They bowed to her as if she were a Queen. We followed next and were whisked away to the nursery area to be bathed and fed and clothed in new garments.

Excited, we raced about our spacious new chambers like mad things, bouncing on the beds lined with fustian, playing with toys, hazelwood swords and a marble chess set, that were waiting—gifts from Ned, we were told. However, when night fell and the tapers set about the room began to gutter and the busy castle grew quiet, I felt much more subdued, even uneasy. I gazed out the glass prisms of the window, sparkling dully in the candlelight, at the blue dimness enfolding London, hiding thief and murderer, peasant and noble. We were free and Edward and Warwick were victorious at Northampton but Father was still in Ireland, and uncertainty cloaked the date of his arrival. What if his hated foes banded against him before he even got near to us? Somerset hated him with a passion that could only be assuaged by blood.

I continued to stare into the night until the sky grew black, lit only by hard stars like a thousand watchful eyes, while the candles around the chamber melted down into pools of red wax and George, oblivious to my worries, began to snore.

"Edward!" Waving frantically, I leaned out of the tower window. Down below, in the courtyard of Fastolf's Place, I spotted my newly arrived brother, tall and magnificent on his great white horse. He grinned up and me and waved back and I felt so much pride, I thought I would burst. Then I was away from the window casing and running down the castle corridors, the wind of my speed making the great wall-to-floor tapestries flap. Bursting from the door, I skidded across the rain-slicked cobbles, almost crashing into Ned, who had dismounted his steed and thrown the reins to one of the stablehands.

"Whoah, little brother!" he said, catching me under the arms and throwing me up into the air as if I were as light as a feather. "You ran at me so fast I was afraid you might knock me down, and how undignified would I look before the household if I sprawled on my arse in the mud."

He was smiling, though feigning anger; I knew he jested, for the idea of me sending him sprawling was ridiculous—I was a slip of a boy, thin and small, while Ned was broad as a castle wall. I'd need a battering ram to bring him down.

"It is good to see you, Dickon," Ned said, setting me down on my feet. He looked older, more mature somehow—no longer the eager youth at Ludlow but a man who had his first taste of warfare. And it suited him. He was dressed in rich blacks and red, with a velvet bonnet and a brooch that bore the York Falcon in white, shining gems.

"And you, Ned. George, Meg and I have missed you so much! What was battle like? Did you kill many men? Why have you not come before now? It seems a hundred years since you went away!"

He laughed at my boyish eagerness. "There will be other times for talk about deeds of arms, Richard. I must speak to our Lady Mother on matters of import and then I must leave Fastolf's Place again. Everything has changed—since Northampton. I must meet Cousin Dick and Uncle Salisbury at the Tower later today; it is now my duty to sit in on the councils of lords in all high matters of state. That is why you have seen nothing of me since my return to England."

My disappointment in finding out his visit would be brief showed in my downcast eyes and slouched shoulders. Ned punched me gently on the arm with a huge fist. "Do not fret, Dickon. I promise I will return when I have more time. Look…I will let you in on a secret. You mustn't tell anyone, not Meg, not George—especially George, for he would blab it to all and sundry. It is about the message I carry to Mother."

I glanced up, wondering what secret he might be about to impart.

"Do you promise not to tell a soul?" Edward teased. "I would find myself in a predicament if it became common knowledge that I told my infant brother my news before the great Duchess Cecily."

I nodded. "I swear…by St Anthony and St George," I breathed.

He leaned over, the dangling ends of his burnished brown hair brushing my upturned cheeks. "Little Richard...our Father the Duke has returned."

A month later, Mother was ready to go forth to meet Father at the meeting place he specified at Cheshire. Surrounded by a bodyguard in the livery of York, she processed out of Fastolf's Place seated upon an ornate chair draped in blue velvet that was drawn by four coursers. All down the streets people gathered to stare—and they cheered at the spectacle and hurled flowers in her path.

I cheered with them, shouting as loud as I could to compete with George and the clarions that blew from the head of the entourage. Mother did not glance back and her courses and high seat were soon lost in the press of bodies and tangle of houses.

It was, I remembered, my eighth birthday. In the excitement of all that had recently befallen, it had slipped my mind. "Oh, I am eight today!" I suddenly piped.

"Well, then, here is a nativity gift from me!" tittered George. He gave me a hard pinch on the arm. It hurt for hours after, and my tutting nurse laved it with lavender water. George said I was lucky he did not give me eight pinches, one for every year.

The York children had to remain behind while our parents were reunited, but that was no great hardship, although we were eager to see Father and Edmund after their exile in Ireland. As most noble children, we were used to being separated from our family for extended periods. Ned had extricated himself from other duties to attend to his younger siblings, and almost daily we met him in the gardens of the great house, which were filled with apple, cherry and pear trees, and beds full of sweet myrtle, thyme, sage and winter savoury. Caught in Autumn's snare, the trees were turning, leaves gold and fluttering before the winter wind stripped them away and left stark skeletons behind. Gold, gold like a king's crown, all around us—and it seemed to me those brief days were also golden, with Edward as our companion, playing hazard and knucklebones, watching George and I thrust at each other with our wooden swords while shouting out encouragement and giving us pointers on how to parry, how to strike a fierce buffet to down your foe.

Toward the end of this spell, our belongings were packed and our household moved from Fastolf's Place into Baynard's Castle in anticipation of the return of the Duke and Duchess of York from their travels. The castle was, in reality, a huge manor house, built by the unfortunate Humphrey of Gloucester on the site of an earlier castle. It stood in the vicinity of House of the Blackfriars and the great church of St Paul's, one of the busiest parts of the city, where preachers cried from Paul's Cross and the Paul's Walkers passed on the daily gossip.

The Thames flowed directly alongside Baynard's Castle, its turgid and relentless waters lapping the castle's lowest walls. Many wharves and jetties thrust out into the deep waters, and the cries of sailors and gulls hung sharp on the air. The mansion itself had four vast wings that enclosed a central courtyard, while two polygon-shaped towers of dim red stone overlooked the activity on the river. Men said some of its foundations were built by the ancient Romans.

Arriving by barge, George and I were quick to explore the great house; everything had been polished and painted; the dais in the great hall was decked in swathes of cloth of gold and the walls were hung with the richest Burgundian tapestries. Unicorns, harvesters, ladies and lords at play reached from floor to ceiling in a riot of colours.

"We are truly princes now," said George, arms folded contentedly, as he watched the house servants bringing in basket-loads of candles, the washer-women hauling linens in and out from the laundry, and the constant stream of wine kegs, barrels of salted meat, dried fish, jarred spices and other delicacies for the cellars and kitchens. Then he turned to me, speaking in a quiet, sly voice, "Do you think Father will go for the crown? The Mad King was soundly trounced at Northampton. They've stuck him back on the throne but we all know…he doesn't truly rule. His grasp on England is slipping…"

Shocked, I nudged him with my elbow. From birth, we had heard the tales of our heritage, and how many considered our claim to the throne superior to that of the King. But even so, Henry was crowned and anointed, and unless he decided to abdicate, only one thing would put Father on the throne. It was the thing not even children dared speak, for it was High Treason. Imagining the Death of the King.

"George, that will never happen and you mustn't ever say it again!" I whispered. "The bad counsellors will be afraid now that Edward and Cousin Dick have beaten them; the King will listen more to Father's advice…"

"You're such a dim-witted mutton-head. The Beauforts and Cliffords will never harken to a word Father says. The Lancastrians have been beaten on the field before; it changed nothing. Northampton may even make them more determined to cast Father down."

He was right and I knew it but dared say nothing. A lump hung in my throat. I wished we were back at Fotheringhay, where, in my earliest memories, all had seemed calm and protected from the storms that blew elsewhere.

But I had no time to brood. On October 10th, George, Margaret and I, dressed in our best, were hustled out of Baynard's and escorted to a vantage point near Westminster, ready to watch the arrival of our parents into London. After spending hours fidgeting and being told off by our tutors and nurses, we finally heard a fanfare of trumpets in the town beyond and drew ourselves up into positions of respectful dignity. George was wearing blue, his favourite colour; I wore dark red; both of us had small black bonnets and neat leather shoes buckled in gold. Meg was dressed in a yellow gown of silk; the ends took off like sails when the wind blew.

The procession drew near, accompanied by drummers and pipers. We could see Mother's velvet-furled chair drawn by the gorgeously caparisoned coursers, and her veils, jewel-bespangled, spinning out from the peak of her headdress to twine around her narrow shoulders. But before her rode Father on a destrier, wearing white and blue raiment emblazoned by Fetterlocks; standard bearers cantered alongside him, and when I saw them, I gasped, for the banners, streaming out against the rain-washed sky did not bear his personal symbols. The bore the Arms of England. The royal arms of the King.

"I told you!" George hissed in my ear. I said nothing but bit my lip and tried to keep dignified.

The procession had reached us, the trumpets blasting out their fanfare, making our ears ring with their incessant shouts. Close at hand, I noticed something else besides the displayed Arms of England that alarmed me. One of Father's loyal servants was walking before him, and in his gloved hands he carried an unsheathed sword, point upwards towards the sky.

It was how a King processed with the Sword of State carried before him.

A mutter went through the crowds massed on the street. They were as confused as we were by what they were witnessing. The cheering faded a little.

Father went into the Palace. Mother alighted and followed him, surrounded by her ladies. We had thought she might join us or that we might be required to wait patiently on the streets till our Father re-emerged, however long that might take. It was, after all, our filial duty to honour and support our sire the Duke.

Instead, there was a flurry amongst our attendants. A man I'd spotted in Father's cavalcade was talking urgently to them, his face serious. All of a sudden, all three of us were gathered up, thrust into a carriage that suddenly rattled around the corner, and whisked back to the louring riverside battlements Baynard's

Castle. Armed guards galloped at our side, and once we were inside the fortress, the huge iron-bound gates were slammed shut and barred.

"I don't understand," said Margaret miserably as we gathered before the fireplace in the nursey, warming our hands before the freshly-stoked blaze. "I was sure we would meet with Mother and Father…"

"I can guess what's gone on," said George, smug. "If you're too slack-witted to guess, I'm not telling."

Meg glared at him. "Sometimes, you are a horror, George. Where do you get it from?"

"I know what he means," I butted in, not wanting to see them fight. Things were uncomfortable enough. "I'll tell you if you want…I-I think Father is going to try to ta…"

One of the nurses noticed us conversing and strode over, sternly clearing his throat. "You have had your outing for the day, Masters George and Richard. Idleness is not seemly, nor respectful to the good Duke and Duchess who even now seek the best for all. Pick up your books, I bid you; soon your tutor, Master Elder, will come round to hear your Latin. As for you, Lady Margaret, your governess shall be coming soon to check upon your needlework. So it is best you retire to the solar to await her."

Gloomily we dispersed, Meg hustling away with a grim visage, us boys mournful at the thought of more hated Latin— especially when our minds were on other things. No one came to us, however, much to our surprise. Peering out the window, we noticed crowds massed in the streets beyond the castle barbican. My stomach began to churn queasily; memories of the sack of Ludlow, the screams, the fire, the blood on the steps of the Butter Cross ran riot in my mind.

"What do you think they are there for, George?" I asked my brother. "D'you think they're hostile?"

George leaned on his elbows on the window-ledge. "Probably just waiting to cut off our heads," he said, attempting to sound nonchalant and failing; his face was the colour of bleached linen.

"Look, George, look!" I suddenly pointed to the grey, sluggish river. A barge was sailing swiftly toward the nearest wharf to the Castle gatehouse; Father's banner streamed above it in the wind. It docked and my parents stepped onto the quay and hastened toward the gates, which had open with great clangour. "Father is back. Mother is with him." Relief flooded me in a hot cascade.

"But something's happened." Intrigued, George was hoisting himself half-out the window in his usual careless way. "The way he walks...he is *furious*, Dickon! "

I yanked George back from the sill and peered out the window myself but it was too late—Father and Mother had vanished into the shadows of the gatehouse. The huge doors banged shut again.

"We must find out," said George, eyes glittering.

"How?"

"The nurses cannot hold our hands going to use the privy. Besides, we haven't seen the old witches for hours. They are in the hall, gossiping. For something has happened. Something important."

"George, you shouldn't call them that!" I rather liked a few of the nurses—when they did not chide about tangles in my hair or dirt smears on my face. They were preferable to the stern tutors with their birches and their sour, sallow faces.

"It's true, they *are* witches." George tossed his curls arrogantly. "But I care nothing for such a gaggle of ugly old geese. I want to know why Father is so wrathful."

"How will we find out? He won't tell us! We're too young!"

George's expression resembled that of a malevolent imp. "What if we just happen to overhear. Up in the gallery. There won't be any minstrels lurking about there tonight."

I was worried about the nurses catching us but my desire for knowledge overrode my concern. "Let us go then..."

Tentatively we opened our chamber door, peered out. The corridor was empty, the torches and cressets unlit. No sign of nurses or servants—perfect. Side by side, George and I ran through the gloom, swift and silent—we had changed our buckled shoes for soft leather ones. We felt like footpads, running through a midnight street; it was quite exciting and touched by danger-we knew we'd be thrashed if caught.

Soon we reached a winding, narrow staircase leading up—it went to the Minstrels' Gallery that jutted out across the back of the Great Hall. Climbing, we entered the confines of the gallery—no one else was there, thankfully; it would ruin all our plans if the servants decided *they* also wanted to eavesdrop from there! A small dais was set up for the musicians; someone had left a crumhorn on a stool. Behind this stand was a huge faded tapestry showing David and Goliath; Goliath bore an oddly complacent expression as David smashed his forehead with his shot.

Below us, in the body of the Hall, we could hear a tumult of anxious voices, raised in a confused roar...and then a fanfare of clarions to announce the entrance of Father.

Abruptly the gaggle of voices died away. The silence was eerie...and strained. "Come on!" George beckoned me with his hand. He tiptoed toward the jetty of the gallery and peeped over the edge. Grabbing the stool, I joined him and peered down into the hall.

The massive chamber was filled with servants and other members of the household, but they had all grown so silent it was almost as if dead men walked. The hush was both eerie and ominous.

Father was standing on the Lord's dais, his shoulders tense, his movements filled with agitation. He glanced up once, and terrified he might see us, we dived for the floor. "Out, all of you!" he cried, gesturing to the gathered crowd.

"Not a good idea to look over after all," George panted. "We might just be visible from where he's standing...but look, we can still find out what's going on."

George crawled a few feet on hands and knees, then pressed his ear to a spot in the jetty wall. A mousehole gaped in the oak panelling; we wanted to believe it would go down, down into the bowels of the castle.

Mousehole or no, we need not have worried about hearing. Suddenly our Lord Father began to speak—well, almost shout. "They did not support me! Behind Henry's back they talk of his weakness—those who do not have their noses in the trough—but when the time for change comes, courage slips away like morning mist. No man should have denied the crown upon my head!"

George and I cast each other quick glances then, unable to help ourselves, we risked peering over the jetty wall again. Down below the Hall was now empty save for Father, Edward, Edmund and Cousin Warwick. Even the pages and squires had been dismissed.

"My Lord Father..." Clearing his voice, Edward spoke up. "Today's actions were not wise—it was too soon. You should not have placed your hand upon the throne as if in ownership."

Father whirled around and grasped Edward by the front of his jerkin. He was almost dwarfed by Ned, but his fierceness was undeniable and Edward stumbled forward an inch or two before finding his footing again. "It was my *right*. How dare you defy me, boy. How dare you question!"

"I do not!" Edward pulled from his grasp and went down on one knee. "Well I know the crown is your right by blood and more. But we must be subtle, we must not cause fear in those who waver. I pray you do not think I speak out of disrespect or that I am but a hapless youth who knows little. I have been blooded on the field of battle, and my sword will always be ready to defend you."

The Duke stared at his huge son for a moment then wearily clapped him on the shoulder. "I know, Ned. You did me proud at Northampton. Yet I cannot forget how the lords in parliament stared at me today; how they asked me if I should like to speak with the King, who was 'resting'—lying in a stupor, more like, with drool upon his lips."

"You have the Queen sore afraid, though, Father," said Edmund. "She has fled for Wales with the young Prince."

Father nodded. "She is the serpent in the bosom of our land; men hate her and yet fear to cross her. She is the enemy, not old Henry, who would gladly, I deem, spend his last years in a monastery!"

Warwick stepped over to Father. "We are not undone yet, Richard. This is only a setback. If you cannot openly claim your birthright, we must submit your claim to parliament. My brother George, Bishop of Exeter, has expressed willingness to aid with your claim. He will present to parliament a roll of your ancestry, showing to all men your noble Plantagenet descent through Lionel of Clarence and Edmund of Langley. When it is laid before the Three Estates for examination, surely they cannot deny what is before their very eyes."

"Then let him come to London, Warwick. Let him come soon."

George pressed up again me, in the dust and gloom. His voice was an excited rasp. "Dickon, it's happening. The church will provide proof. Parliament will have to listen. Our Father shall be King after all!"

George Neville arrived at Baynard's Castle within days. A cheerful, learned man, he was as unlike his brother Warwick as the moon differs from the sun. They shared similar colouring and resembled each other in the cast of nose and chin, but George's face was fuller and less weather-beaten—his pursuits were mostly indoors, in his beloved scriptoriums and libraries. His hair was cut short, as was considered fitting for a churchman, and he walked with a little stoop that he had obtained from long hours leaning over great, hide-bound tomes and religious texts. He had a pair of magnifying spectacles—two pieces of glass embedded in horn— which he had imported from Italy to aid his strained eyes during his studies, but he was vain, like most of the Nevilles, and would not wear them in public, keeping them concealed in the long sleeves of his robe.

After settling in and dining with Father, Mother and Cousin Dick, he came to see George and me in the nursery. He was particularly interested in my studies, and I guessed he was contemplating what kind of a churchman I might make—it was a good position for younger sons with few lands. But I had no inclination to became a priest, even though I worshipped the Lord-God as all good children should, and I turned shy with his probing questions. I dared not tell him I wanted to fight in battles beside Edward and that as much as I loved books, I did not wish to spend my life cloistered away with them.

"You have excellent handwriting, Richard," he said, inspecting some of my schoolwork. The tutors lurking in the back beamed, pleased with themselves. "I am sure there is some kind of career you…"

"I am very interested in horses!" I said brightly. "I am small but can ride well already. I want to be a knight."

Cousin George was no fool; he sighed and smiled wanly. "Ah, all the same, you young lads. Well, if you ever change your mind and decide upon a career in the church, I will speak for…"

"My thanks, my Lord Bishop!" I interrupted. "I most certainly will remember your kindness."

"If talk of a future as a cleric brings no interest, perhaps I can interest you in something else," said the Bishop. "Indeed, your Father asked me to show you—and young George—the scroll I crafted to show the Duke's, and your, royal ancestry."

Both George and I clamoured to see. The Bishop gestured us to follow him and we scampered down the halls alongside him, nearly tripping on the hem of his robes in our youthful eagerness.

The Bishop took us into Father's private closet, where he did his administrative duties. A large desk heaped with parchments stood beneath a tall thin window that admitted a shaft of yellowish light. There were half-burnt candles everywhere, white and waxy.

Atop the heap of correspondence, maps, and seals lay a new parchment scroll, very large and long, its velum pale and new.

"It was a bit of a rushed job," admitted Bishop George, almost as if to himself, "but it needs urgent presentation to parliament, so we must make do." Deftly he lit two thin tapers, giving us extra light, then smoothed out the parchment on the desk.

Before us stretched a genealogical roll—our ancestors laid out before us, depicted inside ornamental roundels. At the top was, naturally, Adam, naked and bearded; below him was wise Noah, complete with Ark, alongside his son Japhet, who was the forefather of all English Kings. Further down were the old Kings of Britain such as Brutus and Arthur, and then the Saxon Kings with odd names such as Egbert, Ethelred and Alfred.

Bishop George swept his hand over the roll, as if none of these figures was important. His finger came to rest on the roundels near the end of the scroll. "Here," he said, "you see the Lord Duke's rightful claim to the crown. There is your noble forebear, King Edward III—here is his third son, Lionel of Clarence. Lionel was a great tall man just like your brother Edward—maybe even taller! Alas, he died young, in Italy, not long after his second marriage to the beautiful Violante Visconti."

George and I made noises of disbelief; we'd met *no one* taller than our brother. Our Bishop cousin continued on, ignoring our mutters. "Lord Lionel begat a daughter Philippa in his first marriage to Elizabeth de Burgh, Countess of Ulster. Philippa married Edmund Mortimer, third Earl of March. Their granddaughter was Anne Mortimer, your sire's mother who died, alas, just after his birth. Now, look you here…" His long finger, slightly stained with inks, swept across the parchment to yet another roundel. "There is Edmund of Langley, first Duke of York, a younger son of great Edward. He married Isabella, daughter of King Peter of Spain, who some call the Cruel and others the Just. They had three children, a son Edward, who had no heirs, a daughter Constance, and another son, Richard of Conisbrough.

This Richard married Anne Mortimer so that their offspring had two lines of descent from King Edward."

"Conisbrough was our grandfather," said George, more solemn than was his usual wont. "They executed him for plotting against Henry V. He's buried in Southampton."

George Neville nodded. "An unpleasant business, most unfortunate for all. It should never have come to pass, imprisonment would have been punishment enough but, but…it must have been God's will…Just as," he said brightly, "it will be God's will if your father the Duke ascends the throne. Look what I have written here—how Henry IV acted unlawfully in usurping the crown of King Richard, and therefore the right, title and estate of the crowns of England and France and the lands and lordship of Ireland belonged by right, law and custom to Richard Duke of York."

I was hardly listening. When George had mentioned our grandfather's execution in Southampton, a cold sensation had gripped my heart and I could have sworn the candles flickered and sank low for an instant. It was as if a dark presence had entered the chamber, an ominous spectre like the scythe-wielding figure of Death painted on the walls of many churches. I almost expected to see a rag-furled skeleton grinning beside George Neville's ear, crooking a bony finger. But there was no one there…and outside the little window, the sun must have emerged from behind a cloud, for suddenly the room was filled with light and flying dust motes.

"Father is the rightful King!" said George with joy. "Parliament must see that it's all true. It is set out here clearly. All those last three Henrys on England's throne—the first a usurper…" he puffed himself up with pride at his use of such adult words, "and then the offspring of a usurper, and then a raving loon!"

I said nothing and George jostled me angrily and said I was a bore, always solemn and overthinking things. But I truly could not join in his gleefulness. Marguerite the Queen was out there still, and even if old Henry abdicated and shuffled away to a monastery, she would be hiding in the wilds, angry, vengeful—waiting like a monstrous she-wolf, a great spider in a web.

Waiting to strike…

For two weeks parliament debated Father's claim. Two weeks we saw Father stalk about the Great Hall like a caged beast, wondering what would be decided in the end. Fearful we would cause offence with our innocent childish curiosity, Edward and Edmund took us out of his way, down to the riverside below the postern gate where we could fish in the river from a small, private jetty.

"Don't fall in, George." Edward put the toe of his boot against George's posterior, threatening to tip him into the murky waters. "I won't fish you out."

George let out a squeal; he was relishing his possible new position as a true prince of the realm and had endeavoured to dress the part, wearing burnished-gold velvet and smart red hose.

Much jollity filled our hearts that day, but as George and I pulled out small, shining fish from the waters and clambered in the shallows where all sorts of amazing finds turned up—shards of pots, ancient coins, a rusty blade, a lead arm that Edmund said might have come from an old Roman statue—I overheard my older brothers talking to each other.

"I still have no idea why he set his hand upon the throne." Edward was shaking his head. "It did not help his cause. Indeed, I deem it caused harm. He should have gone before Parliament from the first and not acted…rashly."

"I think long years of waiting overwhelmed his good sense," said Edmund. "In Ireland, he would stand on the top of Trim Castle, looking in the direction of the sea, desperate to return home. It built inside him, like a wave, and once that wave broke the dam, its surge could not be stopped. His ploy might have worked if he had come to England at the head of a mighty army, but then his crown would have been bought in blood. He does not wish for that. Enough blood has been spilt."

"Yes…" I glanced over my shoulder; Edward was stroking his chin thoughtfully. "Maybe you are right, but sometimes, Ed, war is the only way. Some things may only be bought with the sword. Not through truth. Not through good deeds. Not even through blood right; not when your enemies oppose you, no matter what."

"When Father set his hand upon the empty throne and the lords pretended they knew not his intention and asked if he had come seeking an audience with Henry …"

"My heart sank to the bottom of my boots," murmured Ned. "I felt shame! And it grew worse. When Father did not receive the accolades he expected, he stormed to the royal apartments in a rage and locked himself within. It was not his finest moment; Uncle Dick and I had to coax him out!" He stamped nervously from foot to foot; the boards of the flimsy jetty creaked beneath his great weight. "Edmund, I hope you do not think me disloyal to our sire's cause, but Jesu, what if, in the end, the palace guards had dragged him out…or worse. A swift strike by some Clifford or Beaufort lackey and we might have ended up fatherless, with everyone's hopes and dreams destroyed."

"Of course I do not think you are disloyal, Ned," said Edmund. He flicked a pebble into the river; it cast wide rings as it vanished into the murky deep. "You speak only truth. Well, what's done is done. We must now wait on Parliament's decision."

"But if they say 'no'? What do you think Father will do? He will not, cannot, let it lie. If his claim is rejected, that would be the moment his enemies would rise to crush him…us. And this time, I fear there would be no mercy but accusations of high treason, pushed by the Queen."

Edmund shrugged; worry-lines crossed his brow. The cold October light was in his hair, catching fair strands and turning them faded gold. "And if they say 'yes', do you think our troubles will be over then?"

Edward folded his arms across his padded doublet and stared out across the Thames with its bobbing boats. "No...but I have a strong sword arm, and so, I trust, do you."

The news we were waiting for came with a whimper rather than a thunderclap. It was not bad news but it was not exactly what Father wanted to hear, either. No one in Parliament wanted Henry deposed—his ineptness was not regarded as tyranny; unless he decided to abdicate, he could not be forced to give up the throne. Instead, it was agreed that Father would become Henry's heir, and Ned his heir after him. This meant young Edward of Westminster, the Prince of Wales, was formally disinherited. The old rumours about his possible illegitimacy rose up again and whirled around London and beyond.

"What about the Queen? Won't she fight?" I asked once, while the household celebrated our new status as royal heirs with a feast. All the tumblers were tumbling, the Fools turning cartwheels, a bear dancing, the jellies on the table wobbling...and I felt a nervous sensation twisting the pit of my belly, a feeling that all this happiness was transient, passing. Always my mind ran away from joy to the sorrows I'd known—from Ursula's death to the terror of the sack of Ludlow.

George, seated at my side wearing a brightly-hued feathered cap that made him look like a small peacock, glowered at me, sugary jelly glistening on his lips. "Oh, Richard, can you not be happy for a change? The Queen's only a woman, albeit an evil one; now that he's got her on the run, Father can easily defeat her."

I knew better to argue with George; it was like arguing with the castle wall. I merely shrugged and stabbed at my portion of the subtlety. A pink castle wall crumbled beneath my knife.

"All will be well," my brother continued, imperious. "Did you not pay attention when we were told that Father's claim was accepted? While the lords debated the case in parliament, a crown that was hung suspended high above the chamber suddenly fell to the floor with a great clangour! Men believe it is an omen—an omen that the Mad King's reign is almost ended and our Father will soon sit on the throne."

Omens. I had seen them too. A dead crow in the gardens, its legs gnarled and pointing at the sky. A lone magpie, the sun glinting off the white feathers in its outstretched wings. A clumsy elbow that spilt expensive salt on the table near my Father's seat.

But I dared not speak of these signs, especially not to dismissive George. I could only wait and in the darkness of my bedchamber pray that nothing untoward would happen to my family.

Queen Marguerite was on the move. Escaping from Wales, where she had abided at Harlech Castle in the care of Jasper Tudor, she took ship to Scotland with her son, the boy who had been prince, the disinherited boy who was a little younger than me. Mary of Gueldres, the dowager Queen of King James II, took them in and offer her support.

Around the same time, the Earl of Northumberland raised an army and began to pillage the north, particularly the lands of the Nevilles. Hearing of these actions, Marguerite wrote to her own loyal men, Henry Duke of Somerset and Thomas Earl of Devon, and bade them ride to Hull with their levies. In haste they went, along with the experienced solder Alexander Hody and the treacherous Andrew Trollope, who had deserted Father at Ludford Bridge.

Father was furious—and surprised. He had not expected Marguerite to move so swiftly, not in winter. "I fear I shall not be able to spend Christmas here," he told us, after gathering the family in the solar, where a huge blaze burned in the new fireplaces to stave off the growing chill of December. "The Queen moves against me. Already she has written to her supporters in London in the name of her son, calling me a forsworn traitor, a mortal enemy with an untrue claim to the crown. I cannot allow Marguerite to continue fomenting unrest, nor can I permit the pillaging of lands belonging to my allies. I will ride north as soon as I may. With luck, I may capture the She-Wolf herself and put an end to her meddling."

Mother said nothing, her face like white marble. She knew her duty. For her to take her place as Queen, the old Queen must be dealt with.

Father placed his hand on Ned's arm. "My captains and I have decided on a course of action. Edward will ride to Wales to deal with Jasper Tudor who has amassed a great force there. Edmund will come with me to the north, to learn the arts of war."

"Edmund…" Mother suddenly glanced up, breaking her stillness. "He is only seventeen."

"So was Edward at Northampton," said Father. "There is no reason why he should not have his first taste of battle. He may not have Ned's height, but the arms master says he has done well in his training."

I glanced at my brother Edmund, green-robed, bursting with the excitement of going on campaign for the first time. He noticed my look and turned, smiling, "I shall write to you, Dickon."

"Do you promise?" I said feebly.

"I promise."

We had little more to say, for with that, he was off with Father to learn the duties of a prince. Mother, with no word to any of us, went to the chapel to offer up prayers to God for the safety of her husband and sons.

Edward stepped forward, steadying me with a hand strong as iron. "We will prevail, Dickon. We might all be back long before Twelfth Night and join in the Christmas revels!"

"Back for you to kiss wenches under the mistletoe, Ned," laughed Edmund.

"Indeed," grinned my eldest brother, and he ruffled my hair in reassurance.

Snow fell shortly after Father's departure from Baynard's Castle. The world around us became one of cold white flakes. Part of the Thames froze; with jealous eyes, George, Meg and I watched local children skating on skates made of the shoulder blades of animals. We begged our nurses for permission to join them 'just one time' but were chided by the head nurse, Amabel. "You may not indulge in such a dangerous pastime. You are the offspring of the greatest lord in the land. Every year foolhardy children fall through the ice—they often do not find their bodies till spring, when they are caught up in the weirs!"

Days moved slowly toward the Christmas Feast; we children looked toward it with eagerness, for it would brighten the dull days without Edmund and Edward at home. It was also Advent, a time of fasting. As infants, we were exempt from the worst of it, but the grownups ate but one meal a day consisting of plain fish and tasteless winter vegetables, and perhaps the occasional egg. Meat, milk, cheese, wine and ale were all forbidden. This meant the grownups were fouler tempered than usual and inclined to chastise us for any perceived wrong-doing.

In the Great Hall, servants were gradually preparing for the upcoming festivities. Boughs of greenery were brought in; holly and ivy swathed mantlepieces and hung from the great beams with their eroded carvings of kings and angels. The Advent Wreath was set upon the dais, its candles burning brightly. There were three purple ones, symbolising penance, and one rose-hued one that had only been lit a few days before—the Gaudete Sunday Candle of Joy. The final candle, the white one at the heart of the wreath, would not be lit, of course, until Christmas Day.

"I wish our brothers were here with us for Christmas," I said quietly, not to anyone in particular.

George overheard. "So do I, but think of it, Dickon—more food for us!"

"If only we knew what was happening," I said. "Edmund said he'd write. He hasn't."

"We *know* what's happening," said George. "Nothing at all. Father and Edmund are safe in Sandal Castle and Ned is camped out on the borders, making sure Jasper Tudor's forces do not cross into England."

"And remember..." we both jumped in alarm, almost guiltily as Mother's chaplain strode across the Hall towards us, "Violence is forbidden in this holy season; it is the time for reflection and peace. Thus it was ordered long ago, at the Council of Toulouges. Bishop Drogo decreed that the peace must be kept from the start of Advent to the octave of Epiphany."

I wondered if our enemies knew of this ancient decree, or would honour it if they did, then told myself I was being foolish. For all that the Lancastrians were enemies, they were still God's children and as pious and God-fearing as we were. However, I knew they also thought God was guiding them and protecting them in their endeavours—even as we did.

Nonetheless, as George and I retired to our chamber and we lay together beneath the coverlet seeking the warmth, with the gentle rush of the snow against the window shutters, I only dreamt of happy things, of the Christmas celebrations to come.

We were woken by an eerie howling, a screech that rose to shudder the tiles of the turret above; both George and I sat bolt upright in our bed, clutching each other. The fire had burnt to embers; a thin rim of ice ran round the edge of the window.

The nurse tending us for the night shifted on her pallet and sat up, her visage a fat white moon in the gloom. Scrabbling to her feet, she lit some candles and tossed some more wood into the brazier, muttering apologies for letting it burn out.

"What was that noise, nurse?" I asked, shaking with the cold—and a horrible sense of expectation. "You must have heard it too."

"It was just the wind, I am sure of it, Lord Richard," she murmured. "It's blowing a gale out tonight. The snow's a foot deep."

"Just the wind..." George, looking sleepy-eyed again, pulled the coverlet up around his face.

Teeth chattering, I scrambled out of bed and scuffled toward the window.

"What do you think you are doing, Lord Richard?" the nurse cried, dropping the poker with which she'd been stabbing the sluggish fire. "You'll catch your death. Come away."

"I...I thought I heard something else! Horses! And that howl...it wasn't the wind! It was the gate being hauled open!"

Before the nurse could reach me, I had unlatched the painted wooden shutters covering the window. The gale snatched them from my small hands, blowing them inward with a terrific bang. Snow gusted in, putting out the fledgeling flames in the brazier. George roared as freezing flakes blew over him. The nurse's hand reached for the collar of my woollen nightshirt.

I managed to evade her. The wind was wild, whipping like a living thing around the bedchamber. Tapestries flapped madly; the candles died again in our ferocious gust. A candelabra blew over with a metallic clang.

I leaned out into the storm, whiteness accumulating on my eyelashes and frosting my bed-knotted hair. Below, far below, torches swayed; figures moved in the gloom.

All too clearly, I was reminded of our sojourn at Tonbridge, when the messenger had arrived to say that the Duke of Buckingham was slain. The terrible scream of despair from Aunt Anne, animal-like...

"Come away!" The nurse's arms were around my waist like thick, binding ropes; I was dragged back, half-falling, as the wind came in with another great gust. The last three candles died in that frigid blast and the room was plunged into freezing darkness. Somewhere deep in the castle, a bell began to toll, hard, metallic, funereal. George began to yell and pulled himself from the bed. He stumbled, crashed into a wall, then a table, tipping over a basin of wash water. Cold water splashed over the mats on the floorboards and ran in icy rivulets around my toes.

And then came the knock on the door, fierce, urgent. "Open...*open*."

Gasping, the nurse fumbled in the dark, lifted the wooden latch. Outside stood the chamberlain, eyes practically starting from his skull, his hair thrust up in greying tufts.

"W-What is it?" the woman stammered. "Oh, I am afraid..."

"I have come for the children," he said, gesturing to me and George. "It is on the command of the Duchess Cecily."

"Oh, dear Christ, what had happened?" The nursemaid sank down like a great deflated blancmange in her white apron.

The chamberlain beckoned us forward. "Be brave, my lords," he said, and there was a crack in his voice as if he held back tears. Instantly I knew that some evil had befallen but I refused to let myself think upon it. As I walked behind him, my mind became confused, filled with a nameless dread; I staggered through the halls as if I'd imbibed ale, while the cressets and flambeaux blurred in my strained eyesight.

George and I were admitted to our Mother's solar. She stood beside the dying fire; to our surprise her hair was down and uncovered. This was a shock—we never saw her hair. Her tresses fell to her hips and were a deep dark chestnut-brown. Little streaks of silver caught in the flickering firelight. Her face was taut, a skull, suddenly aged.

I was reminded of...Aunt Anne.

"My sons," she said, and her voice was hoarse, "I must send you from me this night. You will go from Baynard's to the house of the widow Alice Martyn."

"But why?" George blurted, still sleep-addled, not grasping the gravity of the situation. "What have we done wrong to be punished so?"

Mother's lips tautened; suddenly she grasped the carved mantle of the fireplace as if she feared her knees might give way.

"George, Richard, young though you are, tonight you must put your childish ways from you and show the bravery of men. You are scions of the House of York, of the old royal blood, and you must never forget that…"

I knew now what her next words would be. Reaching out in silence, I clasped George's hand in my own. His fingers were clammy.

Mother breathed in deeply. "A messenger from the north has ridden hard, so hard he killed his horses beneath him. He brings news from Sandal. Queen Marguerite's forces…they broke the Christmas truce; they lured your Father from the safety of the castle." She swayed again; one of her ladies, hovering in the shadows, made to support her but she elbowed the woman away. "Children your Father has fallen—he has been slain by the Lancastrians. And your brother Edmund…" Now her lip began to tremble; we watched in horrified fascination for we had never seen such emotion revealed, not even when Ursula died. "Edmund almost escaped. Almost. But black Clifford caught him on the bridge at Wakefield, I am told. He stabbed him through the heart to avenge his dead father, right at the door of the chapel of the Virgin Mary. His tutor begged that Clifford spare Edmund for his youth…but Clifford the Butcher wanted blood."

Beside me, George began to make small, desperate noises. I was struck dumb…and numb. Waves of cold then hot swished through my body and I felt my head spin. Father…and Edmund. I would never see my brother again, never hear him laugh as he joked about with Ned. Never look at that face that was an older version of my own. Edmund who, I'd learned, loved music and danced well…

"The Queen's army is set to march on London," Mother continued. "I do not trust, after what Clifford has done to my poor son, that they will leave any male scions of the House of York alive. Therefore, you must abide with Mistress Alice until I decide what is the best course to take next. Now, wipe your tears and remember who you are. Go, get dressed in your warmest travelling clothes—but be swift. By the time you are ready, a carriage will be waiting in the courtyard."

"What about you?" I asked miserably. "And Margaret?" I did not want to lose the last of my family.

"Your sister and I shall stay behind, Richard. Pray God, being but weak women, we may be protected from axe or sword or swift dagger in the night."

But not imprisonment, I thought, a sick feeling rising in my belly. I thought I might spew upon the floor.

George was tugging at my arm. "Richard, don't just stand there like you're moon-mazed! You heard Mother. We must get dressed and go before they come to stab us too!"

Alice Martyn's house was not far from the Steelyard where the Easterlings, the men of the Hanse, lived in their own walled community where no women were allowed and where every bedchamber held a suit of armour. Her abode was not a great house, but it was not a hovel either, squeezed in between the lumbering, stone-vaulted mansions of the vintners. It had a tall, over-arching timber-frame and amber glass in the windows. Inside, was a wainscoted hall and a kitchen and buttery. Furnishings were quite sparse compared to what we were used to and a musty smell permeated the air as if the rush-mats had not been changed for far too long. Indeed, the rooms looked a little tired and shabby, the Arras faded and repaired, the draperies full of dust. We saw only a handful of servants, all aged and gnarled, peeping at us through the doorways.

"I do not like this." George wrinkled his nose as our attendants deposited us in the cramped solar of the house, ready to meet Dame Alice. "Why did we have to come here?"

"You know why. I am sure it is a good place to hide. No one would expect a Duke's sons to dwell here."

"That is for certain," George sneered.

"Mistress Martyn is a widow, Mother said. She may not have much money, but we must not complain, George, not if it is safe…"

We stood to attention as we heard the soft patter of shoes on the floorboards. A woman entered the room, tall, slender, neither old nor young, wearing a modest headdress and a simple gown. We did not need to bow since we were of superior rank, but from a sense of politeness instilled in us by our upbringing, we both did so.

"My Lords," she said. "I am Dame Alice Martyn. Your house is at my disposal until other arrangements can be made."

"Do you have a garden where we might shoot at butts or play other sports?" said George, sounding embarrassingly rude.

"Only a small one, Lord George. And I am afraid you cannot play outside. It is important you stay hidden."

George stomped his foot, making a loud bang that echoed through the room. "Jesu!" he swore. "Our sire and brother have been murdered and now we have to live like paupers too!" Suddenly he seemed to have realised what he had said. The awful enormity of all that had taken place washed over him and his face reddened and crumpled. "Father is dead…" he began to weep, pressing his sleeve to his eyes.

Joining in his misery, I began to weep too, great wrenching sobs that tore at my chest and made it hard to breathe. I clung to my sobbing brother, and the lady of the house, the widow Alice Martyn, knelt and gathered us into her arms and held us until the tears stopped and we lay in her embrace like limp rags, not the sons of a fallen Duke, merely two young boys who had lost their father.

From that moment on, Alice was our friend, and George never spoke ill of her house or her hospitality again.

We never found out exactly who Alice was or how she became an acquaintance of Mother, but we assumed they must have been at court together in the Queen's service at one time. Asking for details was out of the question, nor did it matter. She was nurse, governess and tutor all in one, keeping us amused with games of chess or Nine Men's Morris and reading to us about brave Sir Gawain and the Green Knight as the cold days of winter stretched on towards spring.

One day, however, we found her staring out of the large mullioned window towards the street. Her hands were knotted together. "My young Lords," she said softly, "I must speak with you."

"Are we to go back to Baynard's now?" I asked.

A shadow passed over her face; she shook her head. "No. I am afraid not. Children, I have heard from her Grace the Duchess, your esteemed Mother. She no longer considers my home as safe enough."

"But no one ever comes here!" cried George.

"No, but unrest is growing again. Children, another battle has been fought—at Mortimer's Cross. They say three suns shone in the sky, a token of the Holy Trinity. Your brother Edward led the army against the Lancastrian host and was victorious. Jasper Tudor's father Owen—he who dared bed Queen Catherine of Valois—was taken and beheaded in Hereford."

"Edward!" I squealed in excitement. "He…he won? He avenged Father and Edmund?"

Alice's lips drew up. "Yes, he did. There is now no man in England who would be a better King than Edward of March. He has proved himself on the field of battle yet again. He has not forgotten you, his brothers, either—he told his troops the Three Suns shining above the battlefield also represented the remaining three Sons of York."

"Why must we leave then?" George asked. "Does this victory not mean, Ned will…will take the crown?"

Alice stared down at her hands. "He will take it if God is good. After the battle, it seemed that he would be swiftly acclaimed…but Queen Marguerite has not surrendered; she is determined to march on London and assert her rights."

"The old harridan!" shrilled George. "She should have given up when she was beaten. After all, our…our side has possession of the old Mad King since Northampton, hasn't it?" His eyes glittered, dark and fevered. "Ned could…could threaten to kill him!"

Alice's face was solemn. "Hush, George and listen. Your brother won the day at Mortimer's Cross, but alas, only a short time after, the Earl of Warwick was routed at an engagement at St Albans. Worse, he had old King Henry with him, a prisoner in his tent, and when the Earl's ranks broke, the King was taken back under the control of his wife."

I gasped in alarm, my joy at hearing about Edward's success against our enemies turning to cold fear. "Cousin Dick, is he…"

"Lord Warwick escaped," Alice said reassuringly, "and I am told he has flown to meet Edward and plan their next move to defeat the Queen. However, should Marguerite enter London before Lord Edward or Warwick can stop her and finds his two young brothers, both in line for the throne…" Her words trailed away, the meaning all too clear.

"She'd have us killed, "whispered George.

"Maybe. At the very least imprisoned. She would certainly use your lives to attempt to negotiate with Edward. So, you must go and with all speed, for the Queen's army marches as if the devil was behind them, and perhaps he is—in the form of your mighty brother bearing his sword of vengeance. Your Mother sends word that a simple unmarked carriage will arrive for you after dusk."

"Tonight!" squeaked George.

"Yes, tonight."

"And where are we being sent now? To a strong castle far across England?"

Alice gave us a pitying look. "No, children, you are going further than that. You are to take ship and leave the country—you are going to take refuge in Flanders."

Chapter Seven

Sea wind whipped my hair into snarls; on my lips, the taste of salt lingered, bitter, stinging. It was dark and George and I were being hurried by cloaked men onto a small cog pulling on its mooring ropes against the wall of a vast harbour. One lanthorn lamp cast dreary rings of yellowish light over wet, slippery cobblestones rimed with tangled seaweed cast up by storms. A sleety rain was falling, pale in the wan glow from the lamp.

It was the first time I had seen the sea, a midnight expanse that rippled and shifted like a living creature. Away, beyond the harbour wall, it boomed as it struck harsh fists against the land. My child's mind imagined all sorts of creatures submerged in that ebon tide—sea-serpents and many-armed beasts, sirens singing deadly songs, a Whale as big as that which swallowed Jonah.

"Do not dally, my Lord Richard." I glanced up into the seamed visage of our guardian, John Skelton. "We must be aboard and on our way to Burgundy—there's a storm coming and the captain must try to outrun it."

George and I scurried over the plank leading onto the deck of the cog. An old man with a white beard flecked by sea-spume and a tunic of boiled leather straining over a wide belly made a curt bow in our direction—I guessed he must be the master of the ship. Then we were hurried down into the hold with Master Skelton on our heels.

The hold was close and rank, smelling of the ever-present salt and of cargo and supplies—sheepskins, wool and hanks of desiccated meat and fish stored in barrels.

George and I sat down on grubby pallets between two great casks of ale. "Jesu," George murmured, "if that lot moves when the ship rolls, we'll be crushed to death."

"You'll just have to pray to the Virgin that the storm misses us then, Lord George," said Skelton, dryly, hunkering down next to the pallets. "Best not to think of such possibilities. Why don't you…sing?"

"Sing!" George frowned. "Why should we sing?"

"It will pass the time," said Master Skelton, glancing upward. The hold had now been sealed; footsteps thundered and men shouted above. The ship rocked slightly and water began to slap against the prow. "Ah, we're off, can you not feel it? Let us hope we have passed unseen in the night like a ghost."

I sat still as a stone as the ship ploughed into the dark and frothing sea. The slamming of the waves against sturdy wood rattled my nerves and before long, I was on the floor, George beside me, both of us groaning and holding our bellies. John Skelton pushed a nearby pisspot towards us. "Try not to get sick everywhere, my Lords," he said. "The journey will be unpleasant enough without being soaked by puke."

We continued to heave up what little we'd eaten on the journey to the port, and John Skelton began to sing on his own, since we certainly were in no fit condition to do so. He had a fine, strong voice that rose above the creaking of the ship, but the words, as I lay with my belly griping in agony, reminded me, with a fresh burst of pain, about what I'd lost and what I might lose in the days ahead:

Winter wakens all my care,
Now the green leaves wax bare.
Often I sigh and sorrowful mourn
When it comes into my thought
How this world's joy comes to nought.

Now it is and now it is not
As if it has never been
As many men say, so it is—
All goes away save God's Will:
All men die, though we like it ill.

All that grain that grows so green
Now lies fallow in the wooded dene
Jesu help that it be seen
And shield us all from Hell!
For I know not whither I shall fare
Nor how long there I dwell.

After a few hours, the worst happened—the threatened storm hit. Wind screeched through the riggings high above and the ship rocked violently, timbers groaning like souls in torment. Several kegs broke loose, making a great thunder, but fortunately the sailors had packed the hold better than we had feared. Most objects were tied down with rope and weighted with stones—so George's fear of being crushed would not come true.

Other fears came instead, fears of the black seas opening up and swallowing the cog and all its crew. Fears of freezing water pouring into the hold, rising to cover us, to drown us, as the fishes drifted in to nibble at our cooling white flesh...

And then...the storm abated with one final boom of winter thunder, loud as the blast of a cannon. The ship slowly righted itself, no longer listing in the swell, waves no longer smashing with all fury against the prow.

Whey-faced, brow awash with sweat, John Skelton glanced upwards at the closed hatch. "I do not know where on the sea we might be, my Lords, but I think God has calmed the storm for us."

"Took Him long enough," said George irreverently as he rolled over and spewed one final time.

Master Skelton sputtered.

I was not listening to either my brother or our guardian. Clambering to my feet, unsteady in my puke-stained shirt and hose, I listened carefully to sounds outside the hull.

"Master Skelton, George!" I cried after a few seconds. "I can hear seagulls crying. Lots of them!"

John Skelton sprang to his feet, swaying slightly. "So can I. That many birds together must mean we are drawing close to the port. Soon you'll be in the care of his Grace, Duke Phillip of Burgundy."

The harbourside was dismal. Rain sluiced down, making tiny rivers over the cobbles; severed fish heads, sliced off by fishermen the day before, eddied by, their eyes glutinous and staring at the sky. A man wearing a long, hooded cloak against the weather strode over to Master Skelton and spoke quickly in French. Skelton nodded and George and I were herded through the deluge to a waiting carriage.

"Not another ride!" George groaned.

We climbed in and Master Skelton clambered in after, as did the man who greeted us, who were presumed was Duke Phillip of Burgundy's emissary. As the chariot began rolling away from the port, bouncing through ruts and puddles, the man removed his hood, revealing an arrogant, bored face with hooded eyes and a large hooked nose. "I am the steward of Bishop David of Utrecht," he said in heavily accented English. "We shall fare to his Castle as swiftly as we may. You may call me Monsieur Hugo Jouffrey."

"We are going to a Bishop?" George yelped, sitting bolt upright. "What? This cannot be right. We were supposed to be guests of Duke Phillip."

Jouffrey stared down his long nose at George. "His Grace the Bishop is one of the Duke's…how you say it, *natural* sons. You are too young to know much, but Duke Phillip does not want to involve himself too closely with English squabbles. To show favour to one side over the other may not be politic…"

"A coward then!" George cried, half-rising. "Is he going to see us thrown in a dungeon too?"

"The children have not eaten and have spent hours consumed by sickness," said John Skelton, thrusting George back into his seat. "That is why they are fractious and speak out of turn. Master Jouffrey, is there any sustenance for them?"

"The enfants will have to wait till we reach Utrecht," said the man with a sniff. "Time is pressing. My duties are many…and you are late arriving."

John Skelton frowned; I could sense his anger. "We could not help the bloody roughness of the sea slowing our passage! Look, the bairns are worn out and they need to get new clothes on before they are presented to the Bishop."

Awful Hugo sniffed again as if a bad smell lingered in the carriage—he was probably right, since we had sweated and vomited all through our sea-crossing—but still. "The Bishop is currently in Bruges with his father, attending to urgent matters of state. The children of the late York…"

"The brothers of the next king of England…!" growled Skelton. A muscle jumped in his jaw.

"The children of York," Hugo repeated as if Master Skelton had not spoken, "shall wait in Utrecht, where they are safely out of the way. They do not warrant the time of either Duke Phillip of Bishop David, not until we know for sure how…" he gazed down his long, beaked nose at us, eyes like little mean beads, "how this unseemly war for the throne plays out in England."

"This is outrageous," said Master Skelton. "Not having them at court is one thing but…"

"It is what it is," interrupted Monsieur Jouffrey. "The Good Duke must take care of his interests first. It is only out of his extreme kindness and generosity that he has agreed to have these *enfants* here. Now let us not argue. We will reach the town of Utrecht before long. You are more fortunate than many in these troubled times; at least you will have a roof above your heads."

The sky was lightening, the clouds streaking out like dark banners against the faded blue firmament when we reached Utrecht. The entire town was surrounded by a ring of dark water and we had to cross a bridge to reach the crenellated gatehouse. The sky and the clouds were reflected in the waves of the nearby river, which Master Skelton said, in a hushed voice, must be the mighty Rhine.

Inside the town walls, standing proudly on older Roman works, were close-pressed merchant's houses, far more colourful than those we were used to in England. Church bells rang out from towers and belfries—so many it made our heads hurt. George put his hands over his ears.

Hugo Jouffrey smirked. "Utrecht is known for religion. It has been a seat of Prince Bishops since St Willibrord came to convert the Frisian heathen centuries ago. You will soon see the Cathedral of St Martin's, the heart of the town, and the great Dom that overlooks all. There is an Abbey dedicated to Saint Paul, and a House of the Teutonic Knights, as well as collegiate churches and those serving the various parishes."

The carriage was slowing down; ahead, the street was blocked by men in florid hats rolling barrels and great wheels of cheese over the cobbles. Watching them, my belly gave a hungry grumble. I tried to put my discomfort aside and looked out of the window for the landmarks Monsieur Hugo had mentioned.

Out of a haze of steam rising where the burgeoning sun smote the townhouse roofs stood the great Cathedral. I had seen a few cathedrals but this one had a particularly large tower with an airy lantern-shaped dome through which birds soared and wheeled.

"That is the Dom." Hugo flapped a languid hand. "The tallest church tower in the land. Thirteen bells it has to summon the faithful. The Bishop has a private chapel on the first floor, and the elite of the city guards are billeted in rooms below."

Our carriage crossed the cathedral close; beggars were outside the huge doors of the Dom, hands extended, yelling and yammering in tongues George and I did not understand. Court French was one thing; all good young English gentlemen learnt it, but this hodgepodge of dialects and local tongues confounded us. Monsieur Jouffrey cast a few pennies from the carriage window, watching as the poor scrambled to grab them, kicking and snapping at each other like beasts. "Curs," he said haughtily, yanking the velvet curtain over the window, "but the Church say we must help such scum, no? Never mind...we shall be at his Grace the Bishop's house shortly."

True to his word, the carriage entered a narrow street and stopped before a great white house with a stout wall and a pair of thick wooden gates, which were closed.

Jouffrey looked perturbed, stuck his head out of the carriage and bawled something in French that we could not catch. The gates remained closed. Monsieur Jouffrey shouted again, his voice high and strident. Still nothing. Flushed, he flung open the door and stalked like a lanky spider to the gate and pounded on the small inset doorway. Seconds later, the door creaked open and he stepped inside, shouting and gesticulating.

"Maybe they won't have us," I gulped. "Maybe they want us as prisoners instead. They don't seem very glad we're here."

"Do not be afraid, Lord Richard," said Master Skelton, but I noticed his hand was near to the dagger at his belt.

A few minutes later, Hugo returned, expression full of peeved annoyance. "There is trouble in the town. Talk of a mob rising. His Grace the Bishop tends to be...at odd with many of those in his parish. It is deemed too dangerous to have you stay here."

"So, what is to be done? The children cannot go back to England—and they need food and rest. Soon!"

"Bishop David sent a courier with instructions while we were on our way here. He has a more remote property not so far away which may be suitable. Castle Duurstede is undergoing renovations and so the household is small and comforts lacking but it has strong walls."

So we continued onwards, back out of Utrecht and into the countryside. Dusk was starting to fall again, turning the flat surrounding landscape blue when we finally reached our destination.

The castle of Duurstede was set amidst a haze of dark trees. An earthwork protected it and a deep moat into which rainwater splashed from the nearby trees, causing great, widening rings. A drawbridge crossed the moat, leading to an entrance beside a stern, square tower of old-fashioned style. Several round towers, under heavy builder's scaffolding and only partway built were dotted around the curtain wall. Another great tower, as big as the one at the gateway was also partly raised—it was in modern Burgundian style with pointed conical turrets bristling like teeth.

We passed below the arch of the gate and entered a courtyard filled with stone blocks, new-cut wooden beams and other builders' detritus. The horses were reined in; the carriage juddered to a halt. Jouffrey exited first, officious, impatient, and the rest clambered out and stretched, breathing in the fresh air of early evening, while a meagre handful of sullen servants came to carry our meagre goods into the castle.

Monsieur Jouffrey conversed with an old, bent man I guessed might be the steward and then led us into a rather shabby and ancient-looking looking hall block led at the rear of the house bailey. Part of it had been pulled down, but one half was still intact. Inside, we could have cried. The corridors were dim; only one or two torches were kindled to light the way. Our bedchamber, situated at the rear of building, overhanging the moat, had one rickety bed with no hangings and a single faded coverlet; the floor was brushed clean but had no rushes or rugs for warmth. No one had lit the fire; the room was freezing and a few patches of damp dappled the walls. A small table had a water pitcher on it and a cloth but when I approached, I saw it was empty. A large spider crawled in the bottom.

John Skelton made a disgusted noise in his throat. "Monsieur, where are the staff?"

"Mostly with his Grace in Bruges," said Hugo Jouffrey. "Due to his Grace's building works, this palace has been mostly vacated. There is an old bailiff, his wife, a cook, a pantler, a few other menials and a small contingent of soldiers to keep the place fast in the Bishop's absence. Oh, and a laundress will come once a week to assist with your laundry. If you need to, you can hang your clothes above the privies to kill any lice that might thrive in them."

"That will not be necessary," murmured Master Skelton. His fists clenched and unclenched at his sides. "We keep ourselves as clean as we may."

Hugo glanced disdainfully at us, in our sweat and vomit stained garb from our arduous trip on the seas. "Really. I will have to inform you that there are no bathing facilities here at present, although water and cloths can be supplied."

John Skelton bridled but said nought—what could he say? We were refugees, cast adrift on the seas of fate.

"I bid you adieu, then," said Hugo Jouffrey, and he stepped from the chamber without any proper acknowledgement of George and me as Duke's sons, and hurried down the hall as if he could not wait to be away from us.

"Well, this is a sorry predicament," murmured Master Skelton. He sat on the edge of the bed. "I am sorry, boys. But at least you are safe."

I tugged on his sleeve. "Is the Duke of Burgundy angry at us? D...d'you think he is in with the Lancastrians?" I shivered.

"It's all politics, Richard," said Skelton. "Warring between France and Burgundy. The French heir is at loggerheads with his father, King Charles, and is also enjoying Philip the Good's 'largesse.'"

"I'll bet he has it better than we do," moaned George. He rubbed his arms. "I'm freezing!"

"No doubt. But you must see that harbouring the heirs of York is even more displeasing to King Charles than giving succour to the errant Louis, since the French naturally support England only when a rabid Frenchwoman rules through a sick old man. Duke Philip, I suspect, is fearful that Charles may think he has gone too far in harbouring both recalcitrant son and Yorkist princes. He is afraid of invasion—of being annexed by France. Always a fear for Burgundy."

He turned from us and unlocked our travelling chests. "Here, put on your nightshirts and throw those stained rags you're wearing on the floor. I will find the laundress…and also someone to get the fire started and some meat and fish for your dinner." He smiled grimly, his face taut and weary beneath a haze of dark stubble. "It looks like I may have to run this place myself while we are here."

"My brother when he is acclaimed king will reward you," I said.

Master Skelton ruffled my hair. "I am sure he will, young Richard, but it matters not—I was always a lover of your Father's cause. God rest his soul. Now, let me be about my business; I shall return ere long."

John Skelton left the bedchamber, shutting the heavy wooden door with a soft thud.

George flung off his ruined clothes and dragged on both nightshirt and a great woolly night-robe, which he drew up around his cheeks. With only his dusky gold curls poking out, he looked like a rotund sheep—a rotund sheep with miserable, angry eyes.

"I hate this place," he said to no one in particular.

Over the days that followed, to keep us amused Master Skelton took us into the local village of Wijk bij Durstede, with its spireless church, great mills and the slow-moving expanse of Kromme Rhijn, the Crooked Rhine. Later still, he paid for a chariot to bear us to the town of Utrecht to keep us amused; after all, the townsfolk may have had grievances with the Bishop but they had none with us. We walked along vast canals lined with wharves, where the locals built walkways that led to cellars hiding below the rows of fancy dwellings that towered above. We prayed in the grand cathedral of St Martin—St Martin was the patron of soldiers—and we lit candles for Edward and implored the Almighty to give him a final, decisive victory over the Lancastrians so that we might return home. For even more good luck, we lit more candles in the ancient churches of St Salvator (of whom we'd never heard) and Holy Cross. In the ruins of a Roman building near the Cathedral we sat on broken stone and ate sweet sticky pies and bread and cheese purchased by Master Skelton.

Back at Bishop David's palace we still heard nothing from our either Bishop or the Duke of Burgundy. However, the staff the Bishop had left behind were, after their initial reticence, far kinder than unpleasant Monsieur Jouffrey and soon the place did not seem quite so dreary. The laundress would sing to us as she worked; the far cook with the face like an apple would bake us special pies and tarts and give us huge slabs of bread heaped in melting butter. The guards let us practice archery in the bailey, and some kind soul found us some rugs and a second quilt.

And then, at long last, a messenger arrived; he wore a device I had not seen before—a large pewter badge with a sun-burst. He also wore the White Rose of York. With him were a gaggle of emissaries from Philip the Good.

George and I were taken into the solar of Duurstede Castle to hear their tidings. We were leery and afraid after having received so much bad news. But Duke Phillip's men all smiled, haughty in their high fashion, their tall hats and richly-coloured chaperons; they bowed and fawned on us, treating us as if we were the highest of princes. A chariot was coming to bear us hence; we would be carried to Duke Philip's grand palace at Bruges forthwith; Philip was most eager to meet the sons of York; a sumptuous banquet would take place in our honour.

I turned my questioning gaze to the messenger wearing the York Rose. "My Lords," he said, "all is well in England. Your Lady Mother, her Grace the Dowager Duchess, send her greetings."

"And our brother, Edward?" I asked, nervous, biting at my lower lip.

"Felicitations are also sent from his Grace the King. Long live his Highness, Edward, fourth of that name."

That night George and I huddled in our room discussing what we had learned that day. Mother's fears had not come to pass; Queen Marguerite had never entered London. Her army had reached the gates, a shining host demanding entry; the citizens denied them entrance and threw cauldrons of waste down upon their heads. The Lancastrians were forced to slink away like scolded dogs.

Edward had marched out to confront his adversary at a place in the north called Towton Field—and there my brother crushed them utterly. Late snow had blown across the battlefield, straight into the faces of the Lancastrians, hampering their vision and causing their arrows to miss their targets. Our forces had snatched up their fallen missile and shouted mockery at the enemy line as they put the collected arrows to their own use. At one point, Lancastrian horsemen hidden in a wood attacked the left flank and the Yorkist line began to break, but Ned himself had taken control and pushed the enemy back. The battle lasted most of the day. In the end, the Lancastrians fled the field—and were cut down as they ran, their dead bodies clogging the stream that ran across the field and turning its water red with blood. The Lancastrian Lord Dacre died there, shot by a York archer hidden in an elder tree; faithless Anthony Trollope fell too, and a few days later, the Earl of Northumberland succumbed to grievous wounds.

"I wish I had been there," breathed George, eyes shining in the candlelight. We were too excited by the momentous news from England to sleep.

"We're too young to fight."

"Yes, but we could have travelled with the baggage...or acted as squires."

"They killed the boys in with the baggage when Harry Five fought Agincourt."

"Richard!" George rolled his eyes in irritation. "Do you have to counter everything I say? It wouldn't have happened—the ones who slaughtered the boys at Agincourt were Frenchies. Englishmen wouldn't behave like that, not even Lancastrians."

I wasn't going to argue with my insistent brother. "It would have been good to watch Ned win," I said. I hoped we could agree on that point. "The messenger said at one part of the battle he was nearly killed, though. I would not have liked to see that." I shuddered at the thought of Edward slain, his head taken to join those of Father and Edmund on Micklegate in York. "Sir David Ap Mathew, his standard-bearer, managed to step in front of him and deflected the blow of a mace when Ned stumbled on rough ground."

"A Welshman saved Ned; imagine that!" said George, marvelling.

I sat up, the coverlet slipping away. "And Cousin Dick! Did you hear that part, George? When they were attacked at Ferrybridge, he slew his own horse and shouted to the men, 'Let him fly away who will, for this day I will tarry with him who will tarry with me!' And his soldiers all stayed and fought and were victorious."

"One day we'll fight too." George stretched out, the candlelight glinting on his long golden eyelashes. He stifled a yawn.

"Will we? There will be peace now. Peace."

George rolled onto his side, curls a tumble. His looked smug, knowing. "Don't count on it, Dickon."

Several days later, George, Master Skelton and I travelled in one of Duke Phillip's personal carriages to Sluis and then on to Bruges. Great celebrations took place upon our arrival; we were no longer unwanted guests but royal princes, brothers of a victorious young King. On the narrow streets of the city, crowds filled the streets and squares to stare and wonder.

Duke Phillip's palace in Bruges was far larger and more opulent than the Bishop's Castle at Dursteede. A large retaining wall enclosed several courtyards and the white-washed ducal apartments. A tall thin tower overlooked all, its machicolations and black and white crenels like rows of uneven teeth. The palace complex stood near the busy market square with its flowers, stalls, covered Water-hall where produce from arriving boats was sold, and the mighty tower of the Mint which cast a long shadow over the activity below.

Upon alighting from our carriage, Duke Phillip's chamberlain, a jocular, burly man in a fur-trimmed red robe, gave George, Master Skelton and me a grand tour of the palace before escorting us to our apartments. The Burgundian Court was one of the most flamboyant and wealthy in Europe and it was overwhelming to see the gold work and heraldic designs in every chamber, and the courtiers dressed in vibrant and exotic garments that glittered with multi-coloured gems. Their hats were extraordinary, towering high above their heads till they looked giants, and their shoes were even longer and more tip-tilted that those worn in England, the ends glittering with gold.

The palace had two chapels and an oratory. The main chapel, for general use by the household, was dedicated to St Christopher. Inside painted statues stood in niches below a canopied wooden roof painted with stars, while cressets burnt brightly, illuminating a tapestry of St Christopher bearing the Christ Child on his shoulders.

"We should say a prayer of thanks," I nudged George as I stared up at the saint's benign, bearded face. "St Christopher is the patron of travellers; he, along with gentle Jesu saw us safely to Burgundy, after all. And when we leave, he must aid us over the sea again."

George, for once being agreeable, nodded and together, with approval from Master Skelton, we placed offerings on the altar and lit candles to give special thanks for our safe delivery to Bruges after our not-so-merry adventures. Then the Chamberlain, waddling in his opulent crimson robe, took us onward into the palace compound to show us the *espicerie*, the Spice Room, with its pungent fragrances, where he allowed George and me to thrust sticks of barley sugar into a pot of cinnamon before herding us onwards through the tapestried corridors.

"Do you like jewels, my little Lords?" said the Chamberlain. "I am sure you will be impressed by these! They glimmer hot as the sun, cool as the moon! I am sure your guardian Monsieur Skelton would like to see too—to view such marvels is a rare honour!"

He led us down a stair to a vault heavily guarded by men in highly polished *whyte* armour. A door was opened and we were given a brief glimpse into what the Chamberlain called the *chamber de joyaux,* which held the Duke and Duchess' jewels, coin and plate. Coronets, collars and armlets glimmered into the light of candelabrum, attesting to the Duke's great wealth.

"That was deliberate boasting!" George whispered in my ear as the door shut again and the Chamberlain beckoned us on. "That man is trying to impress upon us how wealthy and important Duke Phillip is, even if we are the King of England's brothers!"

Master Skelton overhead and gave us both a stern look. "You are doubtless right, my young lords...but it would do well if you day nought. Remember you are the Duke's guest."

Passing out of the hall-block into hazy sunshine, we followed the wide, waddling red back of the Chamberlain through the palace gardens, where pear, apple and cherry trees surrounded roseries and herbal beds, to behold a large ornate bathhouse built on the orders of the Duke's wife, Isabella of Portugal. We were informed by our guide that we could use it upon request if we so wished. We had never seen a whole building dedicated solely to bathing before and we even more astounded to hear there was a room where the Duke would sit, with a fire raging near his feet, to sweat the dirt from his skin before diving into a cool tub.

Finally, as our own feet began to grow rather sore from walking, the Chamberlain escorted us to the guest quarters which were situated at the back of the Duke's own apartments. Everything was richly coloured, the walls hung with a huge Arras showing hunting scenes. Satins and silks were in abundance, cloaking the bed in sea-blue splendour. Fires burned in iron braziers and Portuguese rugs were scattered on the floorboards, increasing the warmth of the room. Dried fruit and plates of sweetmeats stood on a table alongside rose-water in a bronze ewer draped with blanched linen napkins for our faces and hands.

It was completely unlike our cold reception in Utrecht! Master Skelton spoke some quick words to the Chamberlain and then turned to us, kneeling before us on the plush rugs. "My Princes," he said, "blessed sons of that great lord, Richard Duke of York, now is the time I must leave you and make my own way to England. You will be safe now, and you will be treated as princes of the blood should be treated. Enjoy Duke Phillip's hospitality while you can; King Edward will send for you soon."

John Skelton had become more a friend than guardian or tutor; tears in our eyes, we hugged him farewell and then waved as he passed down the halls. Life, it seemed to me, was full of too many farewells…

We did not have time to mope, however, for within the hour the Duke's own squires and pages came to attend us, dressing us in the best clothing from our small clothes' chest. Upon finishing, we were told to expect the Duke of Burgundy to greet us himself.

George became officious, asserting his new-found importance as Ned's brother—and heir presumptive. "Remember to stand up straight, Richard…and to let *me* speak first. Because I'm older than you, and even more important—until Ned marries, I am heir to the throne of England!"

"I am second after you!" I retorted.

"Yes, but still second! I have no intention of dying before you, Dickon!" he laughed.

Footsteps sounded in the hallway. A squire in a salmon-pink doublet with immensely puffed sleeves entered the chamber, and in a loud clear voice announced the Duke and Duchess.

Duke Phillip was a man of middling height. He wore black velvet from head to toe and an extraordinary chaperon with a dangling, jewelled tail. Around his neck gleamed a collar embossed with the firesteels of the Order of the Golden Fleece. His nose was thin, sharp and aristocratic, his complexion pale. His hands were long and tactile, adorned with a single signet ring. "Welcome, my young Lords, George and Richard of the House of York," he said. "You are most welcome to my palace of Bruges. Do you like what you see?"

"Oh yes, sir!" George was eager to impress our host. "I shall carry word of your house's beauty and your lordship's generosity to my brother the King of England."

"Which one are you?" The Duchess of Burgundy moved forward, peering into our faces. "I know one is named George and the other Richard. You are both, what? Around nine years?"

A spasm of annoyance crossed my brother's features at being thought younger than his true age, and I prayed he would not act foolishly. "I am George of York, your Grace, and I am fully eleven years old."

I fixed my gaze on Duchess Isabella Her sire was John I of Portugal and her mother Philippa of Lancaster, which made us distant relatives—although her Lancastrian roots made me wary. We were surprised to see her at Bruges, for Master Skelton had told us that her marriage to Phillip was unhappy and that she dwelt at a rival court in a castle called La Motte-au Boi. But perhaps, tied to Phillip by their sons if nothing more, curiosity had brought her to see the children of the new ruler of England, the King who had replaced old Henry.

Isabella was a tall woman with a plain horsey face. We'd heard she had not married till she was ancient—around thirty—and that the court women laughed at her because she dressed as plainly as a nun. She was not dressed plainly now, however—her butterfly headdress matched Mother's in its enormity, and her gown was wrought of blue cloth of gold and cinched by a silver girdle. She grinned at George; her teeth were rather large. "My apologies, my Lord George. At least I make apologies, no?" She had a strange accent, tinged with the lilt of Portuguese. She gave her husband a glance. "Has his Grace apologised for sending you and Lord Richard to David's castle in the back of beyond? No? Ah, sometimes he forgets about children; he has so many himself—over fifty last tally! Do not take his carelessness as an affront, young princes—I also dwell far from his Grace and he frequently forgets all about me."

"Wife, the young lords should not hear such tales!" The Duke's large ears went red with embarrassment. "It was my decision from the start to keep their whereabouts hidden, hence a journey to Utrecht instead of Bruges. It was for their safety, as I am sure you realise." He gestured to George and me, the rings winking like eyes on his fingers. "My humble palace is at your disposal. Would you like to see my collection of *mappamondes* and other such bibelots? They might amuse such intelligent and curious young men."

George and I agreed at once, although we did not understand what a *mappemonde* was; Lancastrian Isabella, with her towering hat and tales of her marital dissatisfaction, made us feel a little uncomfortable and we were eager to avoid her probing gaze. Dutifully, we followed the Duke out of the chamber after bowing respectfully to the Duchess and then scurried down the hallway at our host's heels.

"Ladies," he murmured, casting us both a look once we were well out of Isabella's hearing. "You will not understand the difficulties at present, my dear little lords—but I am sure you will know the woes of which I speak someday in the future!"

Duke Phillip guided us up a flight of stone steps to where a wooden gallery bisected the building, connecting his quarters to that of his wife. In this long gallery hung dozens of maps of various parts of the world, hung up along the walls like tapestries.

"*Mappamondes*…Mappamundi!" I laughed. I had heard of similar maps of the known world but had never before seen one.

"Look closer," said Duke Phillip, "but do not touch—some of the maps are very fragile. See—look here—Jerusalem, centre of the Christian world!"

We followed his pointing finger. Sure enough, Jerusalem was painted on the stretched canvas, a circular wall with battlemented towers at the heart of the map. *"Thus says the Lord God: This is Jerusalem; I have set her in the centre of the nations,"* quoted the Duke.

George and I began to hunt on the map for other notable cities. We soon found Rome and Paris but were disappointed that London was omitted—clearly, we English were still thought to be barbarians at the edge of the world. So, we shifted from towns to strange peoples of the world—Blemmyes with eyes in their chests, Monoculi hopping on a single giant foot, dog-headed Cynocephali and Troglodytes lurking in deep caverns. After that, there were animals—camels and elephants with riders on their backs and a unicorn with a horn as long as its own body.

Once we had taken a good look, the Duke called us to him and we proceeded a little further along the gallery. Other maps swirled by—I saw the Hanging Gardens of Babylon, and Adam and Eve naked and unashamed in the garden. There was a labyrinth with a half-man, half-bull raging at its heart, and the tall Pillars of Hercules at World's End.

"Now," said Duke Phillip, "something a bit different. My collection of *orloges*."

George and I glanced at each other, confused once more.

"Clocks and other oddments," said the Duke.

George and I crowded in to see. At home, we mostly still used hourglasses or the sound of ringing bells to mark the hours, although a few of the religious houses had mechanical clocks. Before us, were rows of astrolabes, a bronze cock that crowed noon and midnight with the use of a bellows, a sundial set in crystal, and, Philip's obvious pride—a gilded brass clock shaped like a cathedral with spires rising several feet into the air. On its face was a roundel with hands that went around by means of springs, ticking off the hours.

Magic.

George and I bent over and stared and the Duke joined us in watching the hands of Time, as entranced as any child.

Then, suddenly, he stood back and clapped his hands. "Enough of viewing my little keepsakes. A banquet will be held in your honour, my little Lords. You will find amazement at what you will see, and I have no doubt you will then go to Edward, your kingly brother, to tell him how fine Burgundy is, and how perhaps, now, a new alliance can be forged."

The feast was as grand as we expected. George and I sat next to the Duke and Duchess under a vast silver canopy bearing his Firesteel emblem. Many dishes were served—a salted haunch of stag, sturgeon stewed in vinegar, spiced chicken slathered with egg yolks, wild boar roundels, pigeon pie, capons stuffed with minced veal. The main courses were followed by wafers and cream, pomegranate seeds and gilded sugar plums dipped in honey. George looked as if he were in heaven, his lips and fingers smeared with sticky sauce.

I was more interested in the entertainments the Duke had provided. Along with the usual fire-eaters, stilt-walkers and minstrels, every table was graced by an automaton—a moving figure made of metal. Phillip had perfected the art years ago at the infamous Feast of the Pheasant, where a metal elephant, ridden by a man in woman's garb who was meant to represent Mother Church, paraded about the Great Hall. There was nothing quite as grand as an elephant tonight, but a jewel-spangled peacock tinnily spread its plumage, while a jet-black swan opened and shut its beak and a coiled serpent covered in green metal scales writhed over a bowl of golden apples.

As I watched, entranced, a man approached the dais and was beckoned forward by Duke Phillip. He was heavy-set, dark-haired, with a pleasant inquisitive face. "Here is one of your countrymen, my lords George, Richard," said Duke Phillip. "William Caxton, whose trade is printing books. One day, I wager, his books will be sold all over the known world."

"You are English, then!" I said as Caxton bowed to George and me.

"I am indeed, but my trade is here in Burgundy for now, my Lord. However, I pray you will commend me to his Grace, King Edward. I also bear a gift for his Grace...if it is no inconvenience, I would ask you to take it to him when you return to England."

He laid a book into my hands; large and heavy, wrapped in golden tissue. "I certainly will give this to Ned...I mean, the King," I replied.

George looked peevishly at me, annoyed that Caxton was not conversing with him, the next in line to the throne, but when he saw the gift was 'only' a book, he began to lose interest and instead turned his attention to the court Fool, who was tickling the back of his head with a pig's bladder.

"So how did you come to be here in Bruges?" I asked. I wanted to thumb through the hefty tome he'd handed me but I feared that would be impolite, as it was not mine.

He smiled, the edges of his eyes crinkling. "I was an apprentice of Robert Large, the Mayor of London, who was also Master of the Mercer's Company. When he died, God rest his soul, he left to me a sum of twenty pounds. I decided to make my way in the world and ended up in Bruges, purchasing a printing press. I did not cut my ties with England, however; I am a Governor of the Company of Merchant Adventurers and will return one day. I foresee a great trade in printing books in English...Some day in the future, my Lord, I believe every man will know how to read and will have at least one book, should he so wish, within his household."

"Extraordinary, Master Caxton!" I gasped. "Every man?"

"Yes! Even those who do not possess great wealth but who are eager to learn...or to be entertained. Think of it, my Lord— Aesop's fables, the Canterbury Tales, the stories of King Arthur and his knights—all those and more! Books on manners, on warfare, on religious matters…" He shook his head. "Forgive me; I get carried away, but I feel in my heart of heart, that what I do is so important…"

"Maybe, when I am older, I can have one of your books," I said. "I like books, although my brother George does not." I glanced at George, who was still being teased by the Fool and paying no attention to me.

"Perhaps so, my Lord. You will return to London soon?"

I nodded. "The King wants us there for his Coronation."

"I imagine the occasion will be beyond compare," said William Caxton. "May King Edward bring peace and plenty to all, after these last unhappy years."

To my surprise and embarrassment, I felt my eyes fill with tears. I clutched Caxton's book in my thin hands. Yes, the time of sadness, the time of mourning was over.

Soon I would be going home, the brother to a new young King.

I wanted very much to see Ned. And Meg, for all her bossiness. And even Mother, despite her austere propriety.

I thought of her fragrance, the imported scent Mother wore, and my eyes became even blurrier.

Caxton murmured inaudibly, bowed again, and hurried away into the chaos of the Hall, where acrobats in silken streamers were tumbling and a bear with a spiked collar danced to the music of his master's flute.

Soon, soon I would take ship with George. Soon I would see the White Cliffs of Dover rise through the mist and rain. Soon I would be back in England, a prince of the realm.

Chapter Eight

The King entered the hall of the Palace of Plezaunce, where we had taken up residence. Tall and oak-broad, he flamed in red and gold, the leopards and lilies broidered on his sleeve, his golden collars burning with his new symbol, the Sunne in Splendour.

George and I stood still, side by side, scarcely breathing, as he approached us. Our brother, yet more besides. The avenger of our slain father and brother. God's Chosen.

Awkwardly, we both bowed; George's sharp elbow accidentally jabbed my side, making both of us wobble a little in mid-bow. George cast me a nasty, warning look but Edward, far from chiding our clumsiness, knelt on the tiles before us until we were all of one height, and he gathered us into his huge embrace, his head down to ours, his scent of sandalwood, horse-sweat and wine overwhelming us.

"My brothers, my dearest brothers," he said as courtiers and fine ladies with headdresses tall as steeples stared in amazement. "You have returned, safe and unharmed. God be praised."

"God be praised," we heard others murmuring.

He kissed us both upon the brow, first George, then me. Then he stood up, his huge hands heavy upon our shoulders. "The Three Sons of York stand here in the Plezaunce, united. May it ever be so!"

The courtiers in the chamber clapped in joy. Sunlight spilt through the high windows, lighting the room, catching on the rayed Suns on Edward's collar, making green and gold flecks dance within his eyes.

At that moment, I had never been happier; the storm had blown over and night had come to morning for the House of York.

It was time for Edward's Coronation. If half the lords in England still supported the Lancastrian cause, the people certainly did not. The folk of London cheered and celebrated, having put from their minds the foolish old King, his determined Queen and the boy who was no longer a prince. The former monarchs and their son were in hiding in Scotland; they might as well have been at the ends of the earth.

Ned journeyed from the palace of Sheen to the city, where the scarlet-clad Mayor and Aldermen appeared to grant him admission in the prescribed manner. Four hundred local men on horseback, wearing verdant robes, joined the party, forming a special entourage for Ned as he processed to the Tower of London.

George and I had our own special part to play. Along with twenty-six others, we were to be created Knights of the Bath. The ceremony took place after sundown when the Tower was a haunted place, half-lit by torches, the shadows flitting. Guided by servants bearing candles, George and I were escorted to the upper chambers of the Tower and there separated. Our experiences would be individual; the mystical rites performed for each of us.

My heart thudded against my ribs as one of Edward's men, Lord Stanley, stepped forward to beckon me to my initiation. Of middling height, Stanley looked slightly sinister, with hooded eyes and a pointed beard that he was fond of stroking. I had heard men whisper that he was 'shifty Stanley' who played both sides when it came to loyalty, but I was too young to know much of his past. Whatever Stanley's history in the battles for England's crown, he was wearing a Yorkist collar now, hung with golden suns and enamelled white roses.

"Come, my Lord," he said. "It is time for your induction into the esteemed Order."

I followed him into a secluded chamber, vaulted and candle-lit, where a bathing tub stood waiting beneath a silk canopy. Mensura candles ringed it, nearly as tall as me, and the light of flambeaux bracketed to the walls shimmered on the water in the tub.

With surprisingly gentle fingers, Lord Stanley divested me of my short velvet robe and other garments and laid them neatly on a side table. Embarrassed to be naked in front of this great lord, especially since I was small and thin, I stood shivering, but he showed no expression either good or ill. His eyes were dark hollows, swallowing light.

Carefully so as not to slip, I climbed up the little wooden stair attached to the side of the bathtub and immersed myself in the water up to my neck. I struggled to bite back a gasp. The water was shockingly cold, a bath of ritual purification rather than of actual cleansing, good for the soul rather than for comfort. I floated below the surface, arms and legs greenish-white beneath the surface, trying to keep my teeth from chattering. My hair spread out around me, darkening on the swell.

I forced myself to ignore the discomfort; if I acquitted myself well, soon, I would be able to call myself 'knight.'

At the rim of the bathtub, Lord Stanley began to instruct me on all the duties expected of a knight. I must honour and protect women, I must aid the poor, I must show courage in battle, I must kneel before God Almighty in true repentance. Stanley's voice droned on and on, a low, gravelly monotone. He sounded bored; he must have performed this rite many times before with young initiates.

When he was done and I had solemnly sworn that I understood my new responsibilities, he reached out a knotted, ring-decked hand and assisted me from the bath. Wetness streamed around my cold-blued toes and I was even more afraid of falling, which would not only prove painful but mortifying in the circumstances.

But Stanley's hand on my elbow was surprisingly firm and I reached the floor of the bath-chamber safely, although puddling water in my wake.

"Come, Lord Richard," said Thomas Stanley, bowing his head. "You may lay abed a while and ponder your future and the will of Almighty God."

He led me to a small narrow bed set up in the corner of the chamber. I lay down on sheets of new, clean, pure white linen, shivering now after my trek across the chilly room. I pulled up the solitary coverlet, trying to get warm while praying fervently to God as I had been advised to do. The dampness from my skin and hair soaked into the sheets, making me even more uncomfortable. I attempted to forget my discomfort and turn my attention to God. I sought to recall every sin, every misdeed I'd ever committed, and prayed for absolution.

At length, Lord Stanley cleared his throat. "Rise, my Lord Richard. It is time."

Shivering, arms goose-pimpled, I climbed from the bed. Stanley shuffled over, carrying a long white robe which he drew over my head. "White," he intoned, "symbolising your newfound purity as a knight." The corner of his thin, dry lip quirked up—sarcastically, I thought.

As he finished dressing me, a bevvy of musicians entered the chamber and began to play on sackbut, flute and tabor. They circled around me, their deft motions making the candleflames flicker and shadows dance.

Lord Stanley put out his hand. "The chapel awaits, where you will begin the vigil."

Together we left the chamber and fared to Saint John's chapel, where the Knights of the Bath traditionally spent the night. The chapel was as old as the Tower itself with great thick painted pillars void of any carving, beautiful in their plainness. Three later panes of stained glass filled the narrow, round-arched windows, and figures of St John the Evangelist and Edward the Confessor gazed down from niches in the wall.

Kneeling before the altar, I hung my head in reverence. Beside me, Stanley genuflected then melted away like the smoke from the censers. The sound of the musicians' melodies faded into the warren that was the Tower. I was alone—with God.

But not for long. Soon the other new knights joined me—along with George, his damp curls wild, his white robe belling around him like a cloud. He dropped to his knees next to me, gave me a swift look from the corner of his eye. "We're knights now!" he murmured. "Or close enough—Ned still needs to dub us. Who would have thought it two months ago?"

"Hush!" an older youth admonished from behind us.

George's expression was disgruntled. "How dare he—I'm the King's heir."

"He's one of our fellows now," I hastily whispered back. "We can't fight, not now! We must follow the rules."

"Rules, rules," mocked George. "Typical Richard." However, he turned his attention to the great golden Rood soaring above us and put on his most pious face.

The night dragged on, seemingly endless. Our intentions were good but our knees less stalwart as we knelt on the chill tiles. Around us, we heard the other young boys and men shuffling about, equally uncomfortable as time went by. Taking my eyes from the Rood every now and then, I glanced aside at the slit of the window, high above. It was a shaft of darkness, framing one solitary star.

I held back a groan.

Around me, there was another shuffle of robes, muffled sighs, an openly murmured prayer to God for sustenance. and, from somewhere at the back, a muffled fart. Next to me, I felt George quiver, verging on laughter. I knew the whole chapel would erupt in a mixture of mirth and outrage if he could not control himself. So I pinched him and then pinched my own arm to remind myself that I was not to laugh either.

At last, the chapel began to lighten, the night passing to day. Red dawn light flooded through the eastern window, making bloody patches on the tiles. The priest entered and began Mass; we all observed with humility and full hearts. After Mass, with our confessions newly made (I worried a little for I forgot to mention pinching George in the middle of the vigil) Lord Stanley, accompanied by Ned's friend, Will Hastings, drifted into the chapel and gestured us into the hallway. "It is time to receive the accolade and your spurs from his Grace the King."

We were led to the Hall. Edward sat on a seat of estate, wrapped in ermine and red velvet, white roses with ruby hearts dripping from his long sleeves. He did not smile in his usual easy way but looked stern, a statue bathed in majesty, a king of red blood and white roses, a king as great as the fabled Arthur, hero of Britain of old.

One by one, a Herald called the new knights forward.

At last, my own name was called. I was the youngest and smallest of all the party. Trembling in both anticipation and nervousness, I knelt before the King...but I would not let my trepidation show, not in that high company.

"Do you swear, Richard of the House of York, to be a true knight and speak only the truth before man and God?"

"I do," I breathed.

"Will you be true to your sworn lord, protect women and the weak, and revere our Holy Mother Church?"

"I will." Beads of sweat crept down the back of my neck although the room was cool.

"Will you have courage in the face of death and show charity to the poor?"

"I will, so help me God."

Edward stood and beckoned to a waiting squire. The lad brought forth a belt and spurs; Edward girded the belt tightly about my waist while the squire attached the spurs to my heels.

A sword was then brought forth by a second squire; Edward clasped it in his right hand, the hand that wielded death at Towton, the hand that won vengeance and a crown.

He raised the blade; light flashed on the edge, blazing into my eyes, and for a moment I fancied I saw my dead father's face and Edmund's within that searing light. Then the flat of the blade clouted my thin shoulders, first the right and then the left.

Edward's voice rumbled through the hall, the most wondrous sound to my young ears. "Arise, Sir Richard of York. Be thou a knight."

We left the chamber in a blare of clarions, departed the Tower for Westminster, clad in gown and hoods and with white silk draped across our shoulders. Edward processed after us and we entered the ancient sanctity of Westminster Abbey, where Ned was anointed and crowned by our kinsman, Thomas Bourchier, the Archbishop of Canterbury.

As the Te Deums were sung at the finale of the Coronation Mass, I glanced over and caught sight of my Mother, gorgeously arrayed in cloth of gold as if she was a Queen herself. She was weeping, tears running like rain down her cheeks. She made no move to wipe those tears away. I had never seen her weep before. Tears of loss, tears of joy.

In the aftermath of Edward crowning, at the elaborate Coronation banquet, I saw Mother led to a throne at Edward's right-hand side. A few eyebrows were raised by some amid the celebrants—but not within sight of Mother. I heard she had assumed a new title 'Queen by Right,' although she would never wear a crown.

The banquet may not have had the automatons of the Duke of Burgundy, but it was still magnificent. A giant silver salt cellar shaped like a ship stood near the King's table; it was so large the servers had rolled it in on wheels. A cake as tall as a man had been brought in at the same time, borne on a bier by four stout fellows— when it was set down before Ned, the topmost layer erupted, revealing a Fool concealed within, who leapt up releasing a clutch of canaries that soared amongst the banner-draped rafters of Westminster Hall. The crowd roared with delight.

The food was bliss after our recent privations. A roast shoel, a young pig, lay stretched before my hungry eyes. There were imported partridges and stuffed capons and imported oranges that filled the mouth with a bitterness that was both delightful and hard to bear. There was sturgeon, salmon, herons and cygnets cooked in ginger, cinnamon or cloves. A *Crustafe Lumbarde* was set before the King, a tart filled with dates, parsley, cream and eggs, and sweetened by honey, which ran in liquid gold rivulets over its crust. Laughing, Ned thrust a huge slab into his mouth, while the crumbs fell down his royal robes.

"Eat! Eat! All of you!" he cried, pushing the rest away of the tart for the servants to deliver to his friends and kin.

His carver, whose position was one of great honour, was busy serving him, great, long, polished knives flashing in his hands as he carved the new King slabs of venison, boar, duck, swan. The Chief Butler, Lord Wenlock, was at his side, serving wine and other refreshments. In truth, he was also played the role of High Steward on behalf of George, who was deemed too young as yet.

Later in the evening, subtleties were brought out from the kitchens, each one more fantastical than the last. Mostly were on religious themes—angels and saints, but the Falcon of York appeared with outstretched wings, and a huge sugared White Rose glimmered on the High Table.

The height of the banquet, though, must have been the arrival of a member of the Dymoke family to be the King's Champion and deliver a challenge to the onlookers in the hall. It was a tradition since the days of King William Bastard, and I had never heard of the challenge being taken up, but that did not stop the fact it *could* have been, especially I knew there were still Lancastrian supporters lurking, even if some nominally had begun kneeling to the House of York.

First, the Garter King of Arms stepped through the doors of the banqueting hall, followed by a fully-armoured Knight, a clutch bright peacock feathers waving on his helmet as he rode a white stallion into the chamber.

"Does any man here challenge the right of the King?" the Garter King of Arms cried in a great voice, and the Knight, Sir Thomas Dymoke, flung his gauntlet to the ground with a grand flourish.

No one responded to his bold challenge. Edward sat in his chair like a glittering statue.

The gauntlet restored to Sir Thomas, the herald now strode to the centre of the hall, standing betwixt the trestle tables where the great and grand of England sat with their trenchers and goblets before them. Again, the challenge was uttered and the gauntlet flung with a clash upon the tiles floor. George and I both jumped at the noise and forced back nervous giggling. On his throne, Edward was smiling.

Lastly, the Garter King of Arms came before the dais with its banners of the Sun in Splendour hanging above the throne. For the final time, Sir Thomas Dymoke uttered the challenge and the gauntlet crashed down before Edward's feet.

Still, no one dared challenge the right of the new King and the room broke into cheers and celebration as the gauntlet was returned to Thomas Dymoke and he slowly and carefully backed his prancing steed out of the banqueting hall without bumping into a solitary page or server. Then the minstrel returned to playing, more food was brought out, and lords and ladies danced.

Near midnight, the King called an end of the feasting. None of the assembled nobles could leave until then, not even us children. As he left the chamber, he called for his esquires to bring George and me to him. We walked briskly down the hallway, trying to pretend we were not excruciatingly tired as Edward walked beside us, the holy chrism glinting in his hair, now more than a mere man—the Lord's Anointed.

"Sleep well, little brothers," he said, "for I fear you must be up early again tomorrow. George, it is my decision to formally invest you with a Dukedom on the morrow—you shall be the Duke of Clarence, like our ancestor Lionel, from whom we derive our prime claim to the throne. This, I am sure you understand, raises you to the highest rank of the peerage, and designates you as my heir until I am wed and have heirs of my body."

"Thank you, your Grace!" cried George. He grabbed Ned's hand and kissed it. He was already well aware of his position, as he delighted in telling everyone, but receiving this title was an affirmation.

Ned glanced over at me, his lips curving upwards. "I have not forgotten you, either, my littlest brother, but you are very young yet. I must have time to think about what is best for you."

"You won't make me a bishop or anything, will you, Edward…Highness," I stumbled. "Although a noble office, I do not want to be a priest."

"He wants to fight at your side, even though he is but small," interjected George.

Edward grinned. "No, I have no inclination to give you a Bishopric or such, Richard. Your heart would not be in it. You will just have to be patient while I deal with my new government and the running of this war-torn realm. And…" Unexpectedly, he draped a companionable arm around my shoulders, sweeping me into the shadows of a wall embrasure. "Let's give George his chance to shine in the sun, shall we? You know how 'being important' pleases him. I dare say I shall marry soon enough and produce an heir…" A strange hot little gleam came into Ned's eyes and he looked suddenly distant as if thinking of something or someone far away.

Abruptly he shook his head as if clearing it. "Off with you now, brother," he said. "Look forward to your future reward."

George and I continued to live at the Palace of Plezaunce at Greenwich. Lord Stanley saw to our needs, along with our kinsman, Thomas Bourchier, the Archbishop of Canterbury. George had his own household, though, and was being schooled as the heir presumptive. Suddenly he was much less interested in a young brother and more in strutting about in his finery and impressing the courtiers. He even began to harken to his tutors and learn what he should; George was nowhere near as foolish as he sometimes acted.

When I was not engrossed in my own studies, I would wander the palace or go down to the wharves that jutted out into the Thames. Far from the centre of London there quieter and cleaner, as was this arm of the river itself. The Palace itself was crenellated and embattled, surrounded by a sturdy wall. Duke Humphrey of Gloucester had built it around twenty years ago on the site of an older manor house owned by the Abbot of Ghent. Humphrey, the brother of Henry V, was a learned but unfortunate man; his wife Eleanor was accused of witchcraft and imprisoned for life and Humphrey had died not so long after—many said through unnatural means.

I liked to explore the grounds; the garden was bounded by a huge dark hedge and contained an arbour—both places good to hide in if I should wish to avoid George or my tutors. At other times I would ask permission to go into the adjacent deer park and fare up to the brick and timber tower on the nearby hill—Duke Humphrey had built it to spot any enemy ships sailing down the Thames. Puffing, I would mount the spiral staircase and run to the top, staring out over the verdant park, the palace and the ribbon of the Thames, and pretend I was watching for pirates—Easterlings or Frenchmen who had come to raid the city's wealth...I saw nary a one, though, to my childish dismay.

In November Edward finally created me a Duke like George. I would be Gloucester, like poor old Humphrey who had built the Pleazance. Later, I was made Admiral of England (although others performed my duties in my extreme youth), given Gloucester Castle, Kingston Lacy manor, and made constable of Corfe, a mighty fortress far in the West. Ned also presented me with lands and castles confiscated from the Tudor family, who were strong supporters of Mad Harry and his Queen. From their misfortunes, I obtained the lordship of Pembroke in Wales. Later still, I received the lands of Henry Beaufort, Duke of Somerset, although Edward took these lands back when he, mysteriously, became reconciled with Henry and even befriended him—they hawked and hunted together, even shared a bed in friendship. I never liked or trusted

Beaufort, though, nor he me, probably because of the lands, although that was no doing of mine, but he was soon out of the way—he turned his coat and rose against Ned, and ended up on the headsman's block after the Battle of Hexham.

So it happened with many who spoke fair then turned foul both in Ned's life and mine…

Chapter Nine

I had nearly reached my eleventh nameday when Cousin Dick, Lord Warwick came to my quarters in the Pleazance, seeking me and me alone, not George, not the King. I'd seen him often enough since Edward was crowned but it was the first time he had paid me much heed. In silence, he looked me up and down as if judging my worth, my strength. Even though I was a prince and he truly had no right to scrutinise me so, I reddened under his stare. I admired Warwick and hoped he did not find me lacking.

"Do you like it here?" he asked in a lazy tone. He had a dark, rumbling voice, tinged with a northern accent acquired from long stays at his fortress of Middleham in Yorkshire. He walked to the window and leaned on the sill, gazing out over the river where boats were passing by, heading toward London.

"Yes…yes, it is nice…" I stuttered, uncertain as to why he should ask such a question.

"Soft," he said unexpectedly, and he suddenly slammed the window shutter, plunging the room into gloom.

Not understanding my cousin's temperamental display, I jumped in alarm.

"Soft?"

"Yes, that's what you'll become, staying here. It's a palace for women and children. A place to grow fat and idle, listening to minstrels and playing games on the lawn."

"I *am* a child," I said boldly, feeling somewhat annoyed by his attitude. Ned had wanted me here, and Ned was surely right.

"Yes, Dickon, you are, but a damned big one now. Almost twelve, by God. I know you are tutored well, but reading and writing are not all you need to learn. Has the King employed a swordmaster for you to learn skills in arms?"

"George has one. They have let me…."

"Let me what?" His eyes were hot in his tanned, wind-burnt, pirate face. "Have you leant to fight or not?"

"I…I…they let me borrow George's wooden practice blade. Lord Stanley and Lord Hastings traded a few blows!"

"Hastings! Stanley! The only thing Will can teach you is wenching, boy, and I dread to think what Stanley would teach; the man swings about in the wind like a sail, not an ounce of loyalty in his body. You need proper training as a page and then a squire. It is the customary thing for noble boys. In that aspect, Edward has been remiss in your upbringing and your mother his accomplice, I fear."

"I like it here." Defiant again, I crossed my arms defensively over my thin chest.

"I am sure you do, lying about in idleness. It certainly seems to suit George—he has grown fat as a suckling pig since last I laid eyes on him. It is disgusting to behold!"

Cousin Dick sounded so outraged about George's slothful habits that I burst into giggles, which I tried to smother on the sleeve of my doublet.

My laughter seemed to leech the thorniness from Warwick. A wry, crooked smile moved his mouth. "Richard, I am going to ask Edward to release you into my care. I am going to take you North to my castle at Middleham. Once you are there, I will see you are taught all the arts a prince of the realm should know—which does not mean lounging about and daydreaming! You will be a page and live with other pages from good households. You will serve me and my friends at table and learn manners and decorum. You will be beaten if rude, insolent or fractious, no matter than you are a Duke. In return, you will be taught horsemanship and the warrior's arts; England may be at peace now but who knows, Mad Henry and his bitch still live."

I said nothing. I was happy here, true enough, but I had always dreamed of knighthood. Yet Middleham was far away—it was nearly in the land of the bloodthirsty Scots!—and going there in Cousin Dick's service meant I'd have to leave Mother, Ned,

Margaret and George. We had faced so much together, had the heart of our family ripped out by the deaths of Edmund and Father—it pained me to leave and made me fearful. What if I never saw any of them again? Death was cruel and life uncertain.

Warwick was scrutinising my face again, perhaps guessing the reasons for my reluctance. "I loved your father, you know—God assoil him. He would have wanted this, Richard. He would have wanted his namesake son to have a fitting education in the proper manner."

I thought of my sire, his tired, earnest face growing more distant in my memory each day, no matter how hard I tried to remember it. A hard little lump filled my throat. "Cousin Dick…if the King agrees to it, then yes, surely I will go with you to Middleham."

Ned agreed and before the month was out, I was travelling north in the company of my cousin, the great Earl of Warwick. Edward had tried to make provisions for me to travel in a chariot for at least part of the way but I refused—"To travel so would only befit a maiden…your…your Grace! I am tougher than I appear"

Edward had looked at me, stroking his chin thoughtfully though his hazel-brown eyes twinkled with ill-concealed mirth. "Hm, you may be right. You are a little young I'd wager to ride so far mounted, but then again, there will be stops along the way and Dick will accompany you and see that you arrive at Middleham in one piece. You are a fairly good rider anyway, are you not?"

"Y-yes, Ned...I mean, Sire. I am very good for my age."

"So be it, then. You ride to Yorkshire."

I was given a rather placid grey mare, known for sure-footedness and lack of ill-temper—a slightly embarrassing horse to ride for a young boy who dreamt of conquering enemies while mounted on high-strung white stallions, but one unlikely to kill me by flinging me off into a brook or dyke.

Cousin Warwick rode at my side, tall and rangy under the banner of the Bear and Ragged staff; he whistled occasionally, distractedly, to himself—I could see he was deep in thought, and not likely to enjoy chatter with a small boy. I amused myself by peering this way and that at the unfamiliar countryside—the rolling green fields, the little roads that wound over them, the thickly forested areas with their leaf-canopies of light and shadow, the slow rivers reflecting the patterns of the ever-changing skies. Everywhere we journeyed we passed pilgrims and journeymen on the roads, dressed in sun-faded hoods; there were nuns and monks with dusty toes and a passing troupe of players who did an impromptu skit in front of the 'mighty Lord of Warwick.' Cousin Dick gave them a tight grin and tossed them a few coins for their efforts.

Eventually we reached my cousin's colossal castle of Warwick, standing in the heart of Warwick-town at a bend of the River Avon. I was used to fine castles such as Fotheringhay and Ludlow and Baynard's but Warwick, high upon its eroding sandstone cliff, took my breath away. Its towers were massive, great broad columns rising starkly against the sky, their stonework glowing pale in the muted sunlight. Two towers were far larger than any of the others, their conical slate roofs topped with pennants that fluttered in the wind.

Dick saw my awe-filled expression and nodded in the direction of the castle walls. "You like what you see, young Dickon?"

"Very much, sir. Your home is impressive indeed."

"See that great Tower near the entrance?" Warwick gestured with a hand encased in red leather. "That one is called Guy's Tower. The one further along, tallest of all, is Caesar's Tower."

"I know who Caesar was, Cousin Warwick—a great Roman emperor. But who is this Guy? He must have been a very famous hero or commander to have a Tower named after him!"

"Guy of Warwick," said Cousin Dick, "was a noble hero of long ago, the son of Seguard of Wallingford. He sought to marry the Lady Felice, daughter of Roalt, Earl of Warwick—although she was far above him in status. To win her hand, he did as all good heroes should—he battled giants and fell beasts, including the Dun Cow."

"A...a *cow*?" A bull would make a formidable opponent or a wild boar, but a cow?

"Oh yes, young Richard, this Dun Cow was a most fearsome, foul-tempered monster who haunted Dunchurch, not far from here. It was a giant beast, thrice the size of a modern cow, with horns like honed spears; one of its ribs was saved for posterity after Guy slew it, and can be still seen today."

I was dubious and Cousin Dick laughed to see my expression. "So, we have a little sceptic here. To be honest, I agree—I do not truly believe there was any cow or any giants either. My daughters Isabel and little Anne enjoy the tale, though. Maybe you can go with them to the chantry chapel of Mary Magdalen at Guy's Cliffe, where you can see a great statue of brave Sir Guy."

"Maybe, sir," I mumbled. Although I would not mind learning more about this knight, Guy, the idea of being accompanied by two shrill little girls, no doubt chattering about all the silly parts of the legend and not the good things like the swords and fighting, did not hold much appeal.

We had no more time to discuss such an excursion, however, because our cavalcade was now passing through the huge gate with its jagged-toothed portcullis and a row of murder-holes, and I was entranced by the fineness of its construction and its war-like aspect. Then, as we passed from the dim passageway into the light of the inner bailey, I became aware of crowds rushing towards us, cheering for the Earl of Warwick. Up they came to him, unafraid; an old washerwoman even grabbed his hand and kissed it with bristly, withered lips. I gasped at her foolhardy courage and wondered if he or his guards would thrust her away, but Dick smiled down at her as if in gratitude, and all the women huddled in the crowd glanced at each other, dewy-eyed. It was then I realised how much Cousin Dick was loved by the common man, even as Ned was, perhaps even more so. I had often heard he was just and generous to those who dwelt in his household and on his lands, and regularly gave alms to the poor and the sick. In that instant, I made up my mind to do the same when I had come into my own as Duke. God had raised my family to high estate but I remembered well how easily it had been stripped away for a while…

Our horses were taken by the grooms and I was escorted away to a bedchamber high in one of the Towers. I had hardly time to change my garments and bonnet and wipe the dust of the road from my brow before a stout steward was ushering me into the Great Hall. Warwick was already there, resplendent in black, looking as if he had only been on a morning ride, not travelling on the road from London for some days. He reclined on a seat on the dais, at ease, his long, black-clad legs outstretched, his poulaine shoes pointing into the air. Beside him was his Countess, Anne, her face a pale, creamy oval beneath a henin furred with a pelt of red velvet, and on either side stood his two daughters, Isabel and Anne. Isabel was of similar age to me and was gazing curiously in my direction. She had dark hair that curled a little and I supposed she was pretty—not that I was a great judge of such things at eleven summers. The other sister Anne was younger, hardly more than a baby really; she had slick, straight hair that was dark blonde mixed with a strong hint of red. She seemed shy and would not look at me at all.

I made my best bow as graciously as I could and introduced myself to the girls. "Greetings, Lady Anne, Lady Isabel, it is my pleasure to meet you upon this happy day. I am your cousin, Richard."

"There," Warwick was saying to the Countess, "my young kinsman, the Duke of Gloucester. What do you think, Anne?"

The Countess gazed down at me, head on one side. "The poor child looks tired."

I tried to stand up straighter and look alert; I was bone-weary from the ride, my hips and back full of dull aches, but I did not want to be regarded as a helpless infant. I was a son of York...and brother to Towton's victor.

Countess Anne looked thoughtful. "Is the middle brother, Clarence, like this little one?"

"Not really," said Cousin Dick. "George is...George. Oh, he is bright when he puts his mind to it, very princely, very handsome already...but he lacks a certain control in his temperament. I do not know where he gets it from—certainly not the Nevilles! I think, though...that he can be moulded with the right guidance. He is young enough."

I did not understand why George was the topic of conversation when I was the guest and this talk, made before my face as if I was not present, made me feel rather uneasy. I was also horrifically hungry, having had only a mouthful of sops when I rose just after dawn. My belly let out a most unseemly rumble that echoed through the chamber.

Blood rushed to my face, burning-hot. Isabel let out a high-pitched titter and put her hand over her mouth. Wide-eyed, Anne stared from me to Isabel and then began to giggle herself, her cheeks growing rosy with mirth.

I was mortified. My body had betrayed me. (How little did I know that it would do so in much greater ways in the future!)

Fortunately, Duchess Anne saved me from further shame. She rose in a rush of rich cloth, the tall cone of her headdress towering over me. "His Grace the Duke needs meat and bread," she said, taking my hand in hers in a motherly way. "I would not want Duchess Cecily or the King to hear that we had starved the youngest of the family! Dick, we can continue our discussion in private—the best place for talk of matters of importance."

Lord Warwick bowed his head and nodded. His lips quirked; I could see the loud roiling of my belly amused him too. "I forgot how much young boys like to eat," he said. "Off to the kitchens we go then, young Richard."

A few hours later I lay in my guest bed, sated. Warwick's Master-Cook had made me *Tart de brymlent*, a succulent fish pie made of salmon mixed with apples and raisins, with damson plums lying just below the steaming golden crust.

Stomach full, I felt less tired and more at ease with this new environment. Clad just in my thin night-shirt, I wandered over to the unlatched window and stared out into the night. Dusk had fallen, and below the castle walls, the river was a dark blue ribbon of reflected stars. Torches lit the ornate bridge that led toward the town with its tall, elegant church-tower; armoured guards walked back and forth upon the bridge's central span, the clash of their feet making a comforting rhythm.

I felt happy and content. All was strange and new here—and yet I was beginning to have a sense of my place within the world.

Cousin Warwick had business to attend at Warwick guildhall, arbitrating a dispute between of his tenants, so we did not immediately continue north to Middleham. I had hoped he might take me with him to hear the complaints and grievances and learn how a good lord deals with such matters, but he shook his head and patted me on the arm. "Time enough for those sorts of lessons later. Enjoy yourself while you are able, Richard—for you will have much work at Middleham to keep you busy. No, I mentioned Guy's Cliffe to you on our ride hither, and that is where I would like you to go, with my wife and daughters. The girls are eager to show you the abode of Warwick's local hero."

As I left the castle with Countess Anne and her retinue, I was rather sullen, imagining I might have to suffer endless children's tales about rescued princesses and slain dragons...but, to my horror, it ended up much *worse*. Soon I began to pray for dragons. For some mysterious reason, Isabel would not keep quiet about my brother George. As we rode through the town gates and out into the countryside, she leaned out of the Countess' litter asking, "Richard...what colour is George's hair? Does he have blue eyes like you? Does he like music? Books? Is he pious?"

I could not help myself; an impish mood that would have been worthy of George himself overwhelmed me at this onslaught of unexpected and unwanted questions. "Lady Isabel," I said with mock soberness, "He would surely disappoint you. George is wall-eyed and his teeth protrude like a rabbit's. I swear he has never read a book that his tutors didn't force upon him and his idea of piety is picking his nose during mass."

"Oh!" She gasped in shock, taken in…

Until I grinned at her.

"*Oh*!" Another loud, theatrical gasp. "You're horrid!"

"Isabel, *enough*!" I heard the Countess' voice from inside the litter. "Get back in here at once; it's unseemly for you to hang outside where all can see you. Remember your manners!"

"But Cousin Richard…" Isabel whined.

"Is a royal Duke," Countess Anne cut her off sharply, "and he is rightfully fed up with your silly prattle. Now, be silent."

Mercifully Isabel decided on obedience and I rode on in peace, although her sulky face appeared amidst the curtains of the litter to glare at me every once in a while.

When we reached Guy's Cliffe, off the Coventry Road above the waters of the Avon, the Countess led us straight into the chapel of Mary Magdalene, recently rebuilt by Isabel and Anne's grandsire, Richard Beauchamp. There rose the statue of the fabled Guy of Warwick just as Cousin Dick had promised—and he was far more impressive than I had expected him to be. Carved from the living rock of the cliff, Guy stood near enough floor to ceiling, clad in armour of the last century, looking almost as if he held up the roof of the small chapel. Perhaps, if he was as brawny in real life, he had indeed fought that fearsome, supernatural cow…

As I stared in awe, one of the chantry priests emerged from the vestry, a man somewhat past the prime of life, yellowish, with had a small round head, rather like a ball that bobbed on a scrawny neck. Bookish-looking, he blinked a lot; I noted he had ink stains on his fingers and burns from pinching out candleflames. A long nose, like a dagger, its tip very red thrust out before him—in my head I could not help but name him 'needle-nose.'

His real name, as Countess Anne announced, was Father John Rous. He cast a quick, disinterred glance in my direction, then began to fawn over the Countess and her daughters, whom he appeared to know well and like. Isabel lit up like a lantern at his attention, smiling prettily.

Eventually, after he had given his greetings to the Earl's family, he worked his way around to me. I was still examining the statue of Guy with interest. "Welcome to St Mary Magdalene, your Grace," he said, bowing his head slightly. "I take it you are interested in our history?"

I wasn't particularly but was bound to show him politeness. "Yes, Father."

"Then come, come, children, all of you, my ladies Anne and Isabel too, come outside—if her Grace the Countess agrees, of course."

"I shall stay in the chapel and light some candles for my deceased parents and other ancestors, Father," said Countess Anne. "But the girls and Lord Richard may go. I know you enjoy being giving guidance to the young and you will doubtless further their education."

She turned away toward the altar where votive candles were burning, and Father Rous beckoned to Isabel, Anne and me to follow him. We tailed his swishing black robes as he took us back outside the little chapel. He smiled at the girls, still vaguely ignoring me. "I will give you lessons, dear children, for knowledge is a wonderful thing. Be careful, little Anne, full of Grace like her namesake St Anne—there is a puddle beyond the porch from last night's rain, and your Lady *maman* would not be happy if your shoes were ruined."

"What about my shoes?" Isabel butted in. "And what saint's name do *I* have? If Anne has one, so must I."

"Why, Elizabeth of course. Isabel comes from Elizabeth. Bound to God."

Isabel beamed again. "Bound to God. Yes. I am very good and say my prayers; God will surely favour me."

"I was named after a saint too," I said, and wished I'd kept silent even as the words left my mouth.

Rous was glaring at me. I deduced that he liked to do most of the talking and I was swiftly coming to the conclusion that he saw me as some kind of interloper.

"I've never heard of a Saint Richard," said Isabel with superiority.

"Richard of Colchester," I said.

"Oh yes, *him*. A rather…*modern* saint," said Rous sniffily. "Not like good St Dubricious, who founded an Oratory here on the rock. He later became the Bishop of Warwick. He lived many centuries ago when the legions of Rome were leaving England!"

"Did he fight any murderous cows like Sir Guy?" I asked, that spirit of devilment still in me.

Another glare. "These are serious matters, young sir. No, he did not. He…he crowned King Arthur!"

Father Rous was scowling; I noticed his brows were drawn together so that it looked like he had a single great eyebrow like a furry caterpillar. I had to look away before I laughed. I noticed so did Isabel, although little Anne was oblivious.

Afraid that my expression might further incense Father Rous, I stared out across the nearby countryside, fixing my gaze upon a prominent bush-covered hill. Clouds were bubbling up behind its rim, threatening more rain; hit by the sun, their edges were limned with gold.

I heard the swish of the priest's robes; suddenly he was beside me, leaning over, a threatening crow. "Do you know what you gaze upon, my young Lord of Gloucester?"

"No, Father, I do not." I shook my head.

"Blacklow Hill."

It was as if he expected me to immediately know the name but I did not. I shook my head. "I do not know the significance of that place, Father."

He sighed as if to let me know he found my lack of education annoying. "It was there the wicked Piers Gaveston was beheaded, young lord. You know who he was, do you not? One who got above his station. Who led astray King Edward, second of that name, and caused a rift between the King and his lords and even his Queen. Two Welshmen with swords beheaded him on that spot on the orders of the Earl of Warwick and the great lords of Lancaster, Hereford and Arundel. So it comes to all who reach beyond their lot and try with devious means for what is not rightfully theirs. It is a lesson that all men—and boys—should learn."

I was old enough to know some disloyal men whispered that my father the Duke had brought about his own demise by putting forth his rightful claim to the throne. I missed my sire and would hear no word that seemed to slander him, and although I was not certain, I suspected the priest was doing so in a devious manner. As wicked as it was, I was beginning to dislike this priest who seemed to have love only for the Earls of Warwick.

"I suppose this Piers was as monstrous as he was evil," I said, feigning childish innocence, and doing my best imitation of George, who frequently got away with such mummery. "That he was born with fangs and shaggy hair like a beast. I am surprised Guy of Warwick himself did not step out of the land of Faerie to smite the varlet himself."

George would have been proud of me.

John Rous sputtered and went red.

Isabel and Anne clutched each other, stifling their mirth with their hoods.

Rous stalked away toward the door of the chapel. "I fear my Lord Warwick will have his hands full with you, young lord. Duke though you may be, you are clearly insolent and untrained; I have no fear of telling the truth as I see it. Still, I am certain his lordship, with all his wisdom, will teach you what's what up in Middleham and make a great man of you, as would be expected of the King's brother."

I suspect I made an enemy at Guy's Cliffe that day. Still, as they say, one who makes no enemies makes nothing.

"Goodbye, Isabel. Goodbye, Anne."

I sat upon my horse, gazing down at the two girls as I readied to leave Warwick and travel with Cousin Dick to his castle of Middleham.

Small Anne was subdued; she gave a polite little curtsey and scuttled away behind her mother's skirts. Isabel, however, remained at my stirrup, the wind rippling her dark sleek curls. "We'll meet again soon, I'm sure," she said brightly. "We fare to Middleham to visit Father quite often. It is a good place to go riding; there are fine horses in the stable that Father buys from the abbey of Jervaulx."

My heart leapt at the thought. *Horses!* I loved to ride.

"Since you are at Middleham, maybe George will come to visit," said Isabel thoughtfully. "I would like to be there if he should come..."

A little frown crossed my brow. "Isabel, what is this all about? What is your interest in George? Why do you keep mentioning him?"

Standing near my stirrup, she gazed guilelessly up at me, wide eyes mirroring the blue of the sky. "Silly! Father hopes that one day I should marry him!"

"Isabel!" Countess Anne's voice was the lash of a whip. "I have told you before about your hasty tongue. Go find Anne and take yourself with no more malingering to the nursery—it is almost time for your dance lessons."

Isabel looked stricken by the Countess' harsh words but dared not argue and ran with her head bowed towards the castle door while nursemaids bustled about her.

Countess Anne smiled sweetly at me. "Pay no attention to Isabel's prattle, my lord of Gloucester. She lets her imagination run away sometimes. Hears things said in…in jest and imagines them as true."

"I-I understand!" I stammered, but I did not understand. Why would anyone jest about her marrying my brother?

However, her outburst certainly gave me something to think about on the arduous journey north. Who *would* George marry? Surely, not Isabel, even though Ned loved Cousin Dick as a brother or even a father. George, at present, was heir presumptive; an Earl's daughter, while adequate enough, would probably not be a preferred bride. Edward would want a stronger alliance, probably with a foreign princess, maybe some maiden from France or Spain. Oh, and not only for George but for himself. Already I had heard that Cousin Dick was making advances on Ned's behalf to the King of France for the hand of Louis' kinswoman, Bona of Savoy. Queen Bona—how strange that sounded to my English ears! Maybe, if she did wed Edward, she would change her name to something more suitable like Joan or Elizabeth.

Riding hard, our company veered north past Nottingham where the great royal castle towered on its dark conical rock that, Warwick told me, was honeycombed with hidden caves. He had no business at the castle but stopped briefly at Lenton priory; from there, he took me to the workshop of an alabaster-worker where he purchased a beautiful carving of the Virgin to send back to Warwick Castle. "The Countess has badgered me to buy some Nottingham alabaster for many a day," he told me with a smile. "It will keep her happy when we are apart. Remember that when you are older and have a wife of your own. Keep them happy, or your life may end up a misery."

Leaving Lenton, we headed into Sherwood Forest, which stretched across the midsection of England like a great dark belt, a primaeval tangle of oak, elder, alder and birch. The air smelt of leaf mulch and sap; unseen birds called in the gloom and rattled the branches; the wind in the boughs whispered tales of that famed outlaw of long ago, Robin Hood. Dreamily I imagined hooded robbers lurking in the ferns but was vaguely uncomfortable because, as much as I loved the tales of the old-time outlaws, I knew our party would be exactly who they'd want to rob!

Fortunately, no arrows flew at us from the green mirk; we spied nought but bounding deer, hooded journeymen, pilgrims heading south and east, and parties of monks marching to Nottingham from the monasteries at Rufford, Newstead and Worksop.

Eventually, we rode through Newark, guarded by the louring castle where King John had expired during a fierce storm that heralded the descent of his soul to Hell, and stopped for a time to change horses and gather supplies. I sat, saddle-sore, outside the castle gates, munching a greasy mutton pie one of Dick's squires had bought from the local pie-man and stared up at the broad, squat gatehouse where my ancestor had died. Then it was back to our steeds, following the Great North Road to Retford, Bawtry and finally Doncaster where Cousin Dick called a halt for the night. "We will stay in lodgings here, Dickon. There is a renowned shrine to Our Lady that we must visit so that we may have Her protection on the rest of our journey."

The shrine stood in the House of the Carmelites. John of Gaunt, my ancestor through my mother Cecily, was one of the founders, along with King Richard II, who had proclaimed throughout all England, '*This is your Dowry, O Pious Virgin Mary.*' Inside the priory, all was dark except for the flickering cresset lights. The shrine glinted dully amid the candle smoke and trails from burning incense; a crown lay upon it, gilded, and a girdle rich with jewels; above a painted statue of Our Lady smiled benignly down at her supplicants. Her hand was extended, white fingered, graceful, offering hope to those who visited.

I stared up upon that serene face with its rayed halo of gold, and it was as if she looked back at me. A warm feeling crept into my heart. I almost imagined the Virgin spoke, not with words but into my head, "Welcome, young Richard Plantagenet; be not afraid on your journey. This land in the north is where you will find your power."

A little strangled noise escaped my lips as the hair on the nape of my neck prickled.

"Are you well, Richard?" Cousin Dick was frowning over at me, from where he knelt before the shrine.

"Yes, sir," I whispered hoarsely. "I am just…tired."

Above me, the Virgin continued to smile her enigmatic smile, the tapers lighting the blue robes that were the hue of the endless northern sky.

Warwick's entourage departed Doncaster the next morning after Mass. The wind was sharp, the heavens streaked with thin white clouds as filmy as a woman's veil. North we rode and then further north still. My back ached and my buttocks were sore from the saddle but I made no complaint and soldiered on manfully. I noticed Warwick gazing over with something like approval in his eyes, and felt pleased. I set my jaw; I would not give in to pain or discomfort like a baby.

"Now we leave the main body of the Great North Road," Cousin Dick said at length, as the company reached a fork in the road, one arm, the lesser of the twain, running away into a misted green distance, the other heading straight up the country. "A minor branch runs on towards Middleham. We are not so far from our destination."

We journeyed onwards, as a thin rain began to fall, a curtain of silver touched by the sun as it sought to break through the thickening cloud cover. And then there it was, rising like a castle of King Arthur's time through the strands of that misted, sunlight pall—Middleham, its walls glimmering wet, jewel-like, its keep a stern fist punching up at the sky, almost as great as the White Tower or Windsor's keep, though bulkier and less in height.

Warwick drew in his steed and sat staring at it for a moment as if he, too, was overawed by its magnificence even after all his years of ownership. "There it is, boy," he said in a low voice. "There it is. Home."

Home.

At that moment, a screech sounded from above. We both peered heavenward. A large, red-tailed hawk soared above our party, wheeling and diving. The bird gave another piercing shriek, sped down toward the rain-soaked grass then ascended the heights once more, borne aloft on the ragged wind currents, before streaking off in the direction of the castle walls. At the same time, the clouds tore asunder as if hewn by the swords of angels, and the sun emerged in complete triumph, turning the raindrops from pale silver to molten gold and illuminating the stonework of the great ancient fortress.

And Cousin Dick tossed back his dark wild hair, shining with raindrops, and he laughed, an open, honest sound of pure pleasure. Then making a hand gesture signalling for me to follow, he struck spurs to his stallion's flanks and sped along the puddled track towards Middleham. Heart high, I leaned forward and whispered in the ear of my placid nag, "Go fast as you may, my sure-footed fellow. Let me follow my Lord of Warwick...*home!*"

The old beast pricked up its ears and began to trot and then, jerkily, to canter, his great thick hoofs thudding upon the wet ground. I trailed Dick by what seemed miles but no matter, the wind was in my hair and in my face and the rain jewelled on my lashes as I raced my cousin across the moorland with my heart high and my destiny lying before me, gold and green and splendorous in the burgeoning light of the sun.

Chapter Ten

"Harder, you young imp! Hit me harder! I am not made of glass!" The thunder of John Greene the Master of Arms' voice blasted into my ears, galvanising me into action.

Sweating, I swung my wooden blade at Greene, a gangling old veteran with a huge jagged scar running down his cheek that he had acquired fighting alongside Cousin Dick at St Albans. Nimbly he leapt away from my wild blow, dancing like a spider in a web, and he thrust back at me, smashing his makeshift weapon against my padded arm.

I grimaced with pain, saw his thin lips curve in a mocking sneer. "Bah! If I'd struck you with a real sword, your bloody arm would have been lying on the floor."

A flare of anger ripped through me, amplified by the stinging pain in my arm and shoulder. Without a moment's hesitation, I rushed at Greene, battering at him with my 'blade.' Like me, he was wearing a gambeson with a metal breastplate fastened over it, so most of my blows came to naught...but by chance one caught him on the hand, knocking his sword from his grip.

"Shite!" he yelped as the wooden practice sword he was using clattered to the ground. Around the bailey, other squires of the household stifled their titters. Greene was a stern taskmaster and not very popular in the Earl's household.

The old warrior held up his hand; already the fingers were swelling and purpling. I thought he might strike me but instead he laughed, a heavy huffing noise. "Well...well... the little lordling is certainly quick enough if nought else. Good. You may be a thin runt of a thing but that does not mean you cannot be a great fighter. You can, just like your kinsman, Little Fauconberg, who provided great assistance to his Grace the King at Towton."

"T-thank...thank you, sir," I stammered, surprised at the unexpected compliment. Old Greene seldom complimented anyone.

"Now get off with you," he said. "I've had enough of you pages and squires for the moment. Oh, and for Christ's sake, stand up properly! In the last few months, I've noticed you leaning to one side like the tower of a church made wrong—one with green wood that bends!"

Flushing, I tried to draw my shoulders back, to stand straighter. My shoulderblades hurt—especially on the side where Greene had struck me in our training session. Lately…there was always pain, not a lot usually, but always there even as I sat at my desk to do my schoolwork under my tutor's eyes. I did not speak about my discomfort to anyone, though—I did not want the friends I'd made at Middleham to think of me as weak or sickly. Nor did I want any preferential treatment because I was the King's brother— and indeed, Lord Warwick made sure I did not get any. I took my beatings for bad behaviour with the others, when warranted!

Leaving the fenced off training yard, I went to wash my face and take off the sticky, dirtied gambeson. In the room I shared with a clutch of other page boys was my newest friend, Francis Lovell.

Francis was younger than me by four years but he was rather tall so looked closer in age than that; we were eye to eye if we stood face to face when sparring in the yard. He had fairish sandy hair, a few shades lighter than mine, which had been a deep gold as a small child but was gradually turning earth-coloured with passing time. Francis was quiet and thoughtful; although he trained alongside the rest of us, he was not really a fighter, he had neither the stamina or the temperament. He told me he was a twin, born at the same time as his sister Joan, and it was miraculous that they had both survived their birthing—but there was a price for such unexpected good fortune. His chest was weak and he coughed and wheezed whenever the weather was cold. It was unseasonably cold now, as it often could be in Wensleydale, the mornings crisp and the nights full of ice-chip stars, and that had started a little rattle in his throat, so he was deep in Latin studies rather than joining the pages and squires in the yard.

"How goes it, Richard?" He put down the tome he was reading and glanced over. "I didn't expect you back so soon."

"My arm—old Greene hit me a good blow. I will be black and blue."

"The bastard."

"That is his job." I smiled wryly. "I gave him sore fingers in return."

"Good. I wish I had seen it." Francis grinned. "I am finished my lessons and Lord Warwick is away so we do not have to attend him—Do you want to go into the village?"

"Not to William's Hill, away from the other lads?" On a rise behind the stern walls of the castle was an earthwork—the foundations of an older fortress guarding the road into Coverdale. When we had finished our duties, Francis and I often escaped there to lie amidst the brambles and briars, the trees that sprouted through the lumps and bumps. Wild rabbits kicked ancient broken pottery out of warrens there, and once I found a battered coin of the reign of the Red King, William Rufus, who had died, struck by a stray arrow, in the New Forest. It was a secret, special place.

Francis shook his head. "I used to like it there...but I...I think it's haunted. Remember last time? The trees, the bushes...All grew still, even the birds stopped singing. A ghostly figure passed through the thorns and vanished into the earth mound...you saw it too!"

I remembered that day; two boys playing a game with dried rabbit bones from the only coney-warrens then scaring themselves senseless with tales of revenants. "That was no ghost, Francis; it was probably one of the squires playing a jest. Probably Rob Percy—you know he loved playing pranks when he can get away with it!" Robert Percy was another friend of mine; the first I had made at Middleham. He was nearly a full-grown man and had been ordered to take me in hand when I first arrived. I owed him much in those early days when half the boys were eager to take on a young royal Duke in some kind of juvenile challenge...

Francis said nothing but scuffled a shoe on the flagstones. I could tell truly he didn't want to go to William's Hill and I wasn't going to argue over the existence of wights and shades. Quarrelling over such a trifle was pointless. He was younger, after all, and the younger one was, I deduced, the more fanciful the imagination.

"The village is it, as you wish then," I said, draping a short cloak around my shoulders.

Together we left the castle through the postern gate, sneakily in case a tutor or the steward would spot us and summon us to do some errand. Once past the guards, we scampered down the rutted pathway into the higgledy-piggledy cluster of houses that comprised Middleham.

The town was busier than usual; it was market day and folk clustered around the two ancient crosses set up on either end of the cobbled square. The lower cross was the Swine Market where people drove herds of suckling pigs and sometimes goats and sheep in from the surrounding farms; further up, closer to the heart of things, was the main cross with its worn steps and ornately carved head depicting the Crucifixion. Lightning had struck it once long ago and half of Jesus' head was missing. A fat, red-faced monk who had trundled in from Coverham was preaching on the steps, his voice loud and obnoxious, while about him flowed pie-men and relic-sellers and old women with charms, ribbons and phials brimming with potions to make a girl fall in love with you, or to make you fall for a girl.

"Do you have a maiden you love, my pretty young man?" cackled one old crone, thrusting a little pot sealed with wax in my direction. It stunk even from a distance. "What pretty blue eyes you have! Here, a penny for this and no maid shall be able to resist those charms of yours…"

"I am but a young boy, old Mother with not the traces of beard on my chin—I have no interest in any maidens and the reek of that muck you are hawking would scare off a pig!" I stepped back from the crouched old creature, her red and rheumy eyes tearing in the wind. My nose was wrinkled in disgust not only from the reek of the unguent but the thought of using such a ploy to attract girls! I remembered Isabel Neville prattling away about George, her face all pink and flushed and shiny. Maidens were, frankly, annoying, even if one must honour them as a good knight.

The crone began to mutter and mumble darkly, casting us displeased glances, and Francis and I skittered away from her and her potions and lost ourselves in the crowd. Fruit and vegetable stalls ran down the slight slope, and men were rolling in and out of the town's small tavern, ale mugs in their hand as they haggled for bargains alongside the town's goodwives in their white aprons and caps. We were getting jostled and pushed by the crowds, swollen by incomers from nearby villages, so we quickly brought two pastries from a pieman and then fought our way through the crush to the lich-gate of Saint Alkelda's church. In the relative quietude of the churchyard, we flung ourselves down by the holy well sacred to the saint and scoffed our pastries, licking the crumbs from our fingers to get every last bit of the rich, buttery taste.

"I wonder what will happen if I drank the water," said Francis, rolling onto his belly and staring into the weedy green depths of the well. Bubbles frothed up, breaking on the surface. "I am mightily thirsty after fighting my way through that crowd."

"You can't drink *that*!" Shocked, I pointed at the well water with the authority of one four years older. "It's holy, meant only those who are blind or have poor vision! The Saint might grow angry and...and dry up the well...or bring forty days of rain to Middleham!"

"I won't, then; it rains enough up here as it is." Francis stirred the water with a questing finger. "Richard, did Lord Warwick say when he might be back at Middleham?"

I shook my head, drawing my knees up to my chest and watching the long grasses wave over the heaped graves in the churchyard. "No. Last I heard he was going to France to try and finalise a marriage for Ned. To a kinswoman of King Louis. Bona."

"King Louis has a huge nose and looks like a jester rather than a ruler—or so men say," said Francis. "I wonder if Bona has a big nose too."

"Hopefully not—she's only related through his Queen anyway," I answered. "I don't think Edward would fancy a bride with a big nose. Edward likes pretty girls."

"But a Queen doesn't need to be pretty, does she? Just the right blood."

I nodded thoughtfully. "True enough, Francis." And Ned would find lovely women, married or no; I was old enough to know that. Since coming north, my young eyes had been opened to how it was between men and women. Castles were crowded places and it was not unusual to come across a pair of lovers. I'd stumbled on them in the loft in the stables and in the bushes atop William's hill; florid milkmaids straddled by spotty-faced youths with their hose tangled about their ankles. On a trip to York with Warwick, many of the squires were giggling as they passed a 'house of ill repute' and some boasted they had been inside. As for Ned, I knew my handsome brother always had eyes for both maids and matrons, and rumours of his conquests had even reached even my tender ears here in the north.

"Is Warwick finding you a wife too, Richard?" Francis said, still stirring the water.

I spluttered, not having thought of it. "Uh…don't know…"

My friend sat back and sighed. "I am getting married next year, Richard."

My eyes widened in surprise. "You kept that secret, Francis."

He nodded. "Warwick told me to…until all was finalised. The wedding shall be on St Valentine's Day. Of course, my wife and I won't live together for many, many years…but we will still be legally married." He sounded vaguely frightened.

"Who is it? Do you know?"

Slowly, he nodded. "Anne."

"Anne? Not Anne Neville?" Instantly my thought went to Cousin Dick's youngest daughter. I'd seen her, and Isabel, once or twice since our first meeting at Warwick Castle—and decided she was the more tolerable and sensible of the two sisters, young though she was. Isabel was still enamoured of George and when my brother had come to visit on a solitary occasion, he had spent no time with me as he was busily courting Isabel. I wondered if Ned knew. I supposed he did but was surprised he'd let things go this far, as I was sure he'd want a more beneficial match for the heir presumptive.

"No, not *that* Anne," said Francis. "Another Anne. Anne Fitz Hugh. Her mother is one of Warwick's sisters, so a cousin to you. They live at Ravensworth, not so far away."

"I know of them," I said, nodding. "It will be a good match. And I am sure Anne is very nice. She has brothers too, so you will have strong allies when you are older."

"Yes," he said, his voice a squeak.

"Ned offered me as a bridegroom to a Spanish princess just this year," I said, trying to give him comfort that I, too, would soon be in his predicament. "Isabella was her name."

"Truly?"

"Yes, but it was never going to happen. She wanted to marry Edward, not me. She was quite offended that a little brother nowhere near manhood was offered."

"Why did the King reject her? Would such a union not have made a good alliance?"

I shrugged. "I do not know, Francis, but he would not consider the match at all from what I have heard."

Suddenly a long shadow stretched over us; we both gasped and shrank back, feeling guilty and slothful, although we had done nothing wrong. We relaxed as we saw it was on Rob Percy, flushed and breathless from running, his unruly dark hair blowing into his eyes.

"You two little miscreants! I've been searching everywhere! A messenger has arrived at the castle and we must busy ourselves at once. Lord Warwick is set to arrive before Matins."

"Jesu!" I leapt to my feet. "That is sudden—and unexpected. He has not been away very long at all. What happened to negotiations with France? The marriage alliance for the King?"

Rob passed his hand over his sweating brow, pushing back his fringe. "I do not know the full story, Dickon, but something has gone horribly amiss. There will be no alliance. I dare say no more on the matter—it is all rumour at the moment anyway."

"What kind of rumour?" Nervously I clambered up, brushing grass from my hose.

Rob folded his arms over his chest. "I was in York, on the Earl's business...and I heard *things,* tales brought from the south by merchants and other travellers. I put these stories down to misheard rumours...or even outright lies that had gained purchase through long-time repetition. But then I heard the same tales in Richmond and even in little Leyburn and began to wonder!"

"I must know, Rob!" Imploringly I grasped his sleeve. "Please."

"I dare not, Dickon, forgive me. Warwick will tell you...and he'll have the truth of it all. Now come! You and Francis are both a fright with grass stains on your knees and knots in your hair! You'll end up with a beating rather than an explanation for the Earl if you don't get prepared!"

The Earl arrived later that afternoon, riding swiftly through the gatehouse on a grey destrier. Dismounting, he flung the reins to the stable boys and marched towards his apartments. He nodded toward the assembled henchmen, a curt, almost imperceptible motion of his head, and we all streamed after him, ready to serve our lord in any way we required.

In his private solar, he stood road-muddied and wind-blown, as we removed his soiled outer garments and replaced them with a rich red velvet gown with a pattern of running hunting dogs along the hem. I could tell my cousin was not himself; his shoulders were taut beneath the fabric of his robe, and a muscle twitched in his jaw. And his eyes! They were hot, burning, thunder-dark.

I dared not ask anything as I rushed about the room, taking up his goblet while Francis poured good Rhenish from the castle cellars into the cup. Bowing, I handed the goblet to Dick.

He took it and threw back its contents, downing them in one go. Red stained his lips like blood. His expression was taut, unnatural. Almost mad.

Fear ran through me. He was staring at me now with those hot, angry, raven eyes.

"You…henchmen…" his voice grated out, a slow, tired and frustrated rumble, "it's bloody cold—get the fire burning, Francis, Rob, Thom, shutter the windows. Hal, you go to the kitchen and have some bread and cheese sent up. Then make yourself scarce, all of you. I have many things on my mind and would fain not hear the roar of boys in my ears."

I assumed that with his final words he was dismissing all those not given a task and walked smartly towards the door. "No, Richard, you stay. I must speak with you."

Wheeling around, I returned to his seat. "Cousin Dick?" I said uneasily.

Warwick said nought but merely stared straight ahead as the fire was stoked, the windows sealed for the night and refreshments brought from Cook. Once the other henchmen had fled, he gripped a large chunk of demain bread, took one violent bite, then, gripped by an evil humour, began to tear it into pieces, throwing them down on the floor. His dog, a shaggy hound named Troy, lunged forward and gobbled them up, his teeth flashing in his long, grizzled muzzle.

I stared as the pieces dropped, not daring to guess what had brought on this extraordinary behaviour.

"I take it you have not heard the news, Richard," he said at length when the bread was thoroughly destroyed. "The good, joyous news from Edward."

"Sir?" Perplexed, I glanced up at him.

Breathing heavily, he leaned back in his seat; he reminded me of a bull about to charge. "You know that I was in France, negotiating for a fitting bride for your brother? Attempting to bind our kingdoms together with a meaningful alliance? Finding a royal virgin who will bear the King many healthy sons?"

I nodded.

"Well, your halfwit of a brother has ruined it all. The King has acted like a knave and humiliated me before the French—and all the other great lords of Europe. They are all laughing at me. At *me*, who helped put Edward upon the throne. How poorly have I been repaid by the King…it is a day of much wickedness and grievous insult."

I dared not ask what he meant least he tore me asunder like that demolished bread loaf, his strong hands rending my flesh and small bones apart. Whatever Edward had done, it must have seriously hurt Cousin Dick to speak words that were…well…nigh unto treason.

"Cat's got your tongue, then, eh, coz?" said Warwick mockingly.

I flinched, slightly resentful; I had done nothing to warrant his mockery. It seemed as if he was punishing me in some way merely because I was Edward's brother.

"You know what he has done, Richard? Well, no, no, clearly you don't—you are gawping at me like a brainless sheep. Well, I shall tell you. Now you can see him for the ungrateful bastard he is—your idol, the focus of your childish admiration. Richard, Edward has taken to him an Old Grey Mare." He laughed but his voice sounded strained, strangled.

"A mare? I blinked. "What's a horse got to do with it?"

Warwick slapped his thigh with a hand; it made a loud crack that made me jump. "This is a different kind of mount, my young innocent cousin. An old jade that has borne two colts already. Her name is Dame Elizabeth Grey and she is from the Woodville family—staunch Lancastrians all! She is a widow with two sons…and he has married her. Aye, he's wed this Woodville creature because he deems her beautiful. He has shamed me, caused tension with France and put a common woman on the throne."

My mouth fell open. "But…he…he never told…"

"You expected to attend his nuptials, Richard? To sit in glory near your brother at a great banquet attended by the lords of the land? So did we all…but Ned married this strumpet in secret, out in the wilds of Northampton, and has only just revealed the truth!"

With that, Warwick jumped out of his seat. "I feel in my bones and blood this mésalliance will not end well—but I will do my duty and see the wench crowned. What else can I do? What else?"

He stalked over to the fireplace and slammed his clenched fist against the carved mantle. Poor Troy gave a nervous whine and crouched down, ears flattened against his long skull. Dick seemed to have forgotten I was still standing there, in shock at Ned's unexpected wedding. I dared not say a word lest I unleash his wrath.

At length, he turned back towards me. "You're still here? Go…*go* Richard. You'll probably want to write to Ned…and congratulate him!"

Edward presented his new Queen to the lords at Reading Abbey on the Feast of Michaelmas. I was still considered too young to have a part to play but Warwick was there along with George, both raising unsheathed blades to hail the new Queen, who stepped forward holding Ned's hand with such demure beauty that no man could take his eyes off her, no matter how he felt about the unorthodox manner of her wedding to the King. Cousin Dick kept his feelings to himself, as was prudent, playing the part of the perfect courtier. George, of course, revelled in the attention he received, calling out acclamation for Dame Grey—our new Queen Elizabeth—in the loudest voice of all.

Although I had not been invited to the presentation of the Queen, I was summoned to court to attend her Coronation early the next year, although only as an honoured onlooker. It was a grand affair lasting several days and even though I had not yet had a formal introduction to Elizabeth, my heart was soaring as I observed the celebration. I felt quite favoured to have joined the wedding party, even if not in a high position; Warwick was away on a diplomatic errand (where intentionally or not, I could not say) but rather than have me miss out on the occasion, which would have been frowned upon by Ned, he sent me to London in the company of his brother, George Neville, newly returned from negotiations with the Scots and angling for a new bishopric—York.

Newly-made Knights of the Bath escorted Elizabeth in an open-horse litter from the Tower through the teeming streets to Westminster, and it was there I had the first view of my brother's chosen bride, the widow he had wed to the shock of all the nobility—especially Warwick. She was the ideal beauty, I could see that even in my youthful naivety—her hair silver-gold, flowing free as only Queens were permitted, her forehead high and shining pale, her face smooth and uncannily serene. Yet there was a certain cold cast to that white, immobile face with its pale green eyes and sleepy, heavy eyelids that filled me with an instant childish dislike. I chided myself for such unworthy thoughts—she was my Queen after all, and by marriage my sister, and I, as a young knight, should attempt to be more chivalrous.

Elizabeth was taken into the Palace of Westminster and I was free for a while and eager to see my family after long absence. Hurriedly I went to find them amongst the commotion.

I bumped into George first. He was wearing a high, fancy hat with a plume and his shoes were long and capped with gold. A huge glittering chain hung around his neck—he was to take the role of Lord High Steward for the Coronation. He seemed in a happier mood than usual, enjoying the attention and the deference of the crowd, and he even forgot his new-found manly dignity and captured me in a hearty embrace as I entered the Palace.

"God's teeth, Dickon, you've grown a foot!" he said.

"But I won't ever catch up to you or Ned, I fear!" I laughed, hugging him back with surprising affection. "How is it, George? You never write."

"Pah, I am not made for writing—I'll leave that to bookish sorts such as my little brother." He glanced at me, blinked, and suddenly said with wonder. "And what else is different, since I saw you? Your hair—it's gone all brown."

"Yes." I touched my hair, newly shorn to just below my ears as was the current fashion amongst noble-born youths. The last cut made with the barber's shears took away the last of the fair curls of childhood.

"Odd! Your face…you remind me of Father, but with darker hair. Edmund too…" He halted for a moment, remembering our murdered brother, and I stared at the elaborate floor tiles, feeling a sharp pang of remembered loss. It should have been Mother crowned at Westminster, not Dame Grey.

As quick as George's melancholy gripped him, it vanished. He was always mercurial, emotions flitting one way then another, laughing one moment, ranting the next. "How is Isabel? Have you seen her?"

"I have. She and Anne stayed at Middleham all through the winter. She asked about you all the time."

"Did she?" He puffed up like a proud peacock. "Well, that's only natural I suppose."

The old pompous George was back.

"What is it between you and Isabel? She said once…"

"Hush!" He loomed, a conspiratorial shadow, overwhelming me. "Say nothing, Richard. It's all secret between me and Cousin Dick, you understand, and Isabel."

"Why have you not spoken of it to the King?"

"No, Richard, no! He would forbid it; Dick and I know that. Ned wants a foreign princess or heiress for me, probably some

Burgundian or Frenchie. *I* want Isabel." Familiar petulance shone from his features as he glowered. "Edward married whom he wanted, even though he is King and should have thought about alliances! Why should he have a choice while I get foisted off with a garlicky princess with a hairy lip!"

"But you hardly know her."

I met her at Middleham, don't you remember? One visit...and I knew. She was the one I would wed."

"What is the new Queen like?" I asked hastily, changing the subject, regretting that I had ever brought up Isabel's name. I had never thought capricious, shallow George would play the part of a lovestruck swain. "When shall I be introduced to her?"

George's deep blue eyes narrowed. "You'll find out what she's like soon enough. Might have you earmarked for one of her sisters..."

My eyes must have bulged in startlement for George let out an amused hoot of mirth. "Your face, Richard! But I do not lie; it could happen. It is the fate of young Buckingham. He has already been married off to one of Elizabeth's endless, tiresome sisters."

"Has he, indeed?" I remembered Harry Stafford from our stay with Aunt Anne after the disaster at Ludford Bridge. It was not an altogether pleasant memory.

"Yes, and he was most put out, and I can't say I blame him." George leaned in conspiratorially. "The Woodville brood are full of thoughts and actions far above their station. You'll find out."

At that moment, a page skidded into the hall calling for George to attend to some matter in his temporary capacity as High Steward. "I must go," he said, straightening the heavy chain of office around his neck. "I am sure Mother and Meg will be glad to see you. Our older sisters Anne and Elizabeth are here too."

He hurried away and I managed to catch a passing squire to lead me to my family whom I had only seen from a distance, for I had walked with Warwick's retinue in the procession. They were gathered in a large ante-chamber at the side of the Hall. Mother, sitting on a high-backed red chair, wore a rather sour expression, more apt for a funeral than a Coronation; I had heard how she had reacted with fury about Ned's marriage to Widow Grey—I mean, our new Queen—berating him and even calling him a bastard. This was a most shocking thing to say for she was making herself out as an adulteress, something she truly could never have been, tirelessly travelling at my father's side. I guessed it was a way of trying to control her son, threatening to bring him down with lies if he did not bend to her will—but her ruse did not work. Edward was as stubborn and hot-tempered as she and had temporarily sent her from court to the partly derelict castle of Berkhamsted, where she had stewed angrily for many months. She was in London now though, so had come round to the idea of Ned's marriage, at least to a degree.

Meg was at her side, by far the tallest lady in all the room, with her huge, spire-like headdress making her seem even taller. My other sister Elizabeth was there too, sitting near Mother; she was the wife of the Duke of Suffolk and was much older than me, so much so that we had spent no time together as children—she was already married. She resembled Meg but shorter in stature and with slightly darker hair revealed at the front of her headdress. The only sibling missing was Anne, my eldest sister whom I knew even less than Elizabeth, for she had visited my parents very rarely. Married to Henry Holland, an ardent Lancastrian and from what I'd been told a faithless, violent creature, she had recently separated from her husband and sought an annulment.

It was Meg who spotted me first and came rushing towards me, the veil from her hat waving like the tail of a happy hound as she approached. She bent to kiss my forehead, which was a little embarrassing—I was twelve, after all. "Meg, be careful. You could put my eye out with that!" I gestured to the tall, pointed cone bound on her head.

"Oh, what? Ah, that!" She adjusted her headgear. "I had to do something; you know—to stand out. You would think the Woodvilles were the royalty and our family common, the way they are parading about. The Queen, her mother Jacquetta and her sisters are dripping in jewels and silks—supplied by Ned, of course."

"You don't like the Woodvilles?" I whispered. "Tell me truly, Meg."

"I do not, in all honesty. But Neddie has made his bed so he must lie in it—although I have no doubt he will lie in many others as well!"

"Meg!" My jaw fell open. I had not expected such frankness from my sister, an unwed maiden. But Meg was intelligent and not like most other girls. Where so many gawped in expensive looking-glasses, Meg observed and listened and thought deeply on things.

"Richard, you will catch flies in your mouth if you do not shut it." Meg's eyes twinkled. "We will say no more on this matter. You may find it different, and who knows? Maybe after time passes, even I will warm to the Queen. I doubt Mother ever will, though. Look… she is staring our direction and seems displeased. She is probably peeved that you have not greeted her yet."

I swallowed. Where were my manners? Leaving Meg, I hurried towards my mother the Duchess and reverently went down on my knees before her chair with my head bowed. She was like a Queen, and so she styled herself Queen by Right "My Lady Mother…"

"Richard, come, get up; let me look at my youngest son."

I stood, trying to hold myself proudly and properly so as to escape any criticism. My shoes were polished, my clothes clean and my hair new-trimmed—I hope that would do.

I seem to have passed muster. A sigh escaped her lips and an expression of sadness flitted over her features. "So like your father in so many ways; more so, it seems, the older you get. I trust my nephew Warwick is happy with your progress in his service?"

"I believe so, my Lady Mother but it might be best if you asked him yourself."

"I shall when he returns to England," she said, "though I would not burden him with any new cares." Her lips pressed into a straight line. "What's done is done. I just pray Edward is not as dismissive of Warwick's counsel on matters of state as he has been on matters of...*love.* Such rashness could bring far greater problems that this lowly marriage."

I flushed. I could feel the anger towards my brother within her and it unnerved me.

"But we shall see. Fortune's Wheel is always turning. Today and tomorrow we will celebrate the crowning of a new Queen and we will do so with dignity and grace. Richard, attend upon me now, and for the rest of the evening. Let me see what you have learnt in Warwick's service."

The next morn all of London, or so it seemed, was out in the hazy sunlight to view the Queen on her way from Westminster Hall to Westminster Abbey. The Bishops of Salisbury and Durham processed before her, mitres rising up like the spires on the Abbey's tower, while Elizabeth glided along in complete calmness as if she had always known this was her destiny. She was clad in an ermine-lined purple cloak that trailed on the ground and a coronet glittered upon the unbound glory of her hair; in one hand she bore the sceptre of St Edmund, in the other the sceptre of the realm. Aunt Anne, the dowager Duchess of Buckingham, attended upon her, carrying her heavy train with dignity and grace. My sisters, Elizabeth and Meg, followed directly after, along with the Queen's mother, Jacquetta Woodville, whose spangled blood-red raiment and bejewelled headdress outshone even the elaborate scarlet gowns of my sisters with their trimmings of Baltic fur. Jacquetta was an attractive woman, but her expression was self-congratulatory—the cat that got the cream. Of the noble House of Luxembourg, she had married below her station for love, secretly wedding Richard Woodville when left a widow by the death of her first husband, the Duke of Bedford—but now she had redeemed herself through her daughter, now the highest and most revered in the land.

The procession continued out through the hall towards the open doors of the Abbey. Glimmering in blue cloth-of-gold and sarcenet, George was barging people out of the way as Elizabeth Woodville daintily walked barefoot on a long carpet of cloth up the small stone steps into the confines of the church where the Archbishop of Canterbury awaited her.

"Out of the way, lout!" I heard George bellow, pushing a fat merchant who had strayed too close to the edge of the carpet while trying to get a better view of the Queen. The man stumbled into a hastily-set up stand for onlookers, causing the women seated there to shriek and shout. The male occupants shoved the unfortunate fellow back again, and there was a fracas as he stepped on some dignity's best poulaines. Fists flew, as I heard George yelling pompously, "Be still, sirrah! You have offended the eyes of your Queen! You will be dealt with."

Inside the Abbey, the vast nave was lit by hundreds of expensive tallow candles, wax streaming like waterfalls down their sides. The tombs of Kings rose around me, my ancestors encased in lead and stone; I held my breath, feeling as if they were present, watching over the congregation. Watching over *me*, blood of blood, bone of bone.

My spine prickled at the thought, and more and more I felt the sensation of being watched. And then, as the lords and bishops and my family and the Queen's kin took their places near the high altar, I saw *it*—an eye pressed to a hole in the panel of a decorative screen, observing the proceedings.

A gasp escaped my lips. Standing at my side, Lord John Howard, one of Edward's most loyal supporters and cousin to the Duke of Norfolk, overheard my dismayed intake of air. Sir John had always shown a fatherly kindness whenever I'd seen him, and he glanced down at me with frown lines creeping between his eyes. "Are you well, young Gloucester?"

"Sir, there's an *eye...*" I whispered hoarsely, nodding as unobtrusively as possible in the direction of the offending orb, which was, disconcertingly, still pressed to the chink in the painted board, right above a depiction of a devil ramming a trident into a sinner's naked bottom. I did not want to alert the spy, whoever he might be, and perhaps have him leap from hiding to attack the wedding party.

Sir John followed the path of my gaze. To my surprise, he began to smirk...and then to grin, although he was trying to suppress the expression.

I blinked, big-eyed in the candlelight. He did not seem concerned at all. "Sir? Did you not see?"

"You must pretend you have witnessed nothing."

"But I have. You admit you saw it too, Sir. I do not understand..."

His dark brown eyes, deep set in his weathered face, were twinkling. "Fear not, you know the watcher well. Very well."

"Assuredly, sir, I beg your pardon, but I do not..."

"Richard, it is the King! *The King*! It is not permitted for the monarch to attend the separate Coronation of his Queen, and so he is observing the ceremony from behind a screen!"

"Oh!" I tried not to look over at the eye. *Ned*! I wagered he was laughing at me...

Up ahead, Elizabeth Woodville had prostrated herself before the altar on the beautiful whorls of Cosmati tiles placed there centuries ago by King Henry III. The Archbishop of Canterbury was praying over her prostrate form.

I shuffled, all too aware of my brother's presence in the gloom behind me. A laugh began to bubble up inside, and I had to bite hard on my lip and think all sorts of sad thoughts to keep it under control. John Howard side-eyed me and shook his head, a little grin still lingering under his heavy moustache.

I manage to control myself as Elizabeth rose and the Archbishop anointed her with the Holy Chrism. That was the sacred moment which made her more than just a mere woman, which made her a true Queen in the eyes of God. I peered through the candle smoke, seeing if she had visibly changed at the touch of the blessed oil, but she appeared just the same—fair, haughty and cold. As the crown came down on her white brow, I reckoned a brief look of triumph crossed her features—but I was not sure in the flicker of the candelabrum set all around.

She then sat upon the throne, regal and upright, her hair falling in a silver-gold rush over her coronation robes, so beautiful she might have been Queen Guinevere from legend. But...*cold*.

At my side, it was Jockey Howard's turn to shuffle. He glanced at me surreptitiously. "Now, lad," he said in a whisper, "comes the best part..."

"What is that, sir?" I frowned. The Ta Deum was being sung; I thought the ceremony was all but over.

He grinned. "The feast, young Richard! The feast!"

The Coronation Banquet went by in a blur. Wearing a purple surcoat, the Queen swept into the Hall and was ushered to the high table, where she reclined on a gilt chair beneath a regal canopy threaded with silvered roses. Whenever Elizabeth partook of her food, she removed the crown from her head and set it on a tasselled velvet cushion; when she had finished chewing, she set it gracefully on her head again.

I had, to my startlement, been seated next to Harry Buckingham, who seemed to have forgotten the unpleasantness of his family's enforced stay in his grandparents' castle. Harry, married to one of the Queen's sisters, a pretty blonde girl named Katherine, had been carried into the feast on a squire's shoulder, along with his little bride. I was glad I had not suffered what I would have seen as an indignity, but he was quite proud. "It is because I am the Duke of Buckingham," he said. "It is to make sure all men see me and know me before I have even gained a man's stature."

Unable to meet his eyes, I nodded and poked a portion of lamprey around my trencher with my eating knife. "Of course."

"I am surprised you are not wed to a Woodville too, Richard," said Harry. "There are so damn many of them..." A frown crossed his chubby, flushed face. "I must admit, I am not that impressed by my marriage. Katherine is...decent enough, but I am of royal blood. It is a bit of an insult."

I was just raising a speared piece of eel to my lips and spluttered. It fell onto the trencher, splashing sauce onto my tunic. Hastily I rubbed the spots in. "Harry, don't let anyone hear you say such things. The Queen is...well, the Queen now; you can't say bad things about her sister. Especially when she's your wife"

"Oh, don't worry, everyone knows how I feel," said Harry breezily.

And no one cares, I thought. I glanced at little Katherine Woodville, curtseying before her sister the Queen. I feared Harry would make the poor girl's life a misery.

Buckingham was nudging my ribs with his elbow. "She's doing it *again*! The Queen! That's the tenth time she's removed her crown to eat. Shall we play a game, Richard? Let us guess how many more times she will do it before the night is over."

"And what's the prize for the winner?"

Harry yanked a small gold ring with a leaf-patterned bezel from his finger. "If you win, you get this..."

"So be it." I removed a ring from my own hand; it had a blue stone to signify the Virgin. "You win, and this is yours. But have a care, I somehow do not think our game would go down well with our elders...."

We played and I won, but I did not get Harry's ring, for he pouted so much and looked fit to explode with wrath, so I backed off from claiming my prize and said that the competition was a draw. "I must have miscounted," I said.

"Yes, I think you did," said Harry. "You must have."

At the top of the Hall, on the dais, Elizabeth Woodville was rising in splendour, my sisters Meg and Elizabeth likewise getting up to attend her. She was leaving. The banquet was over.

Harry scrambled from his seat, rushing over to Katherine, who was waiting with some of the other Woodville sisters. A pair of squires hastened to their sides and lifted the children onto their shoulders, and they were carted off into the depths of the palace, Buckingham puffed out like a peacock, unaware that he looked faintly ridiculous rather than stately, as the red-faced, straining squire laboured under his weight. Harry was certainly portlier than I remembered.

A hand descended on my shoulder, making me leap in startlement. Turning, I gazed into the craggy, perennially grinning visage of Ned's close friend, Will Hastings.

"It was a splendid ceremony, was it, not, my Lord of Gloucester? Even George played his part well, with few dramatics."

"Ah…yes," I said breathlessly, surprised but secretly a little pleased that he had seen through George, who was good at charming folk to get what he wanted.

"You will be coming to the joust tomorrow?"

I made a little face. Most boys my age loved nothing more than a good joust but, truth be told, I found jousting exceedingly dull and rather pointless. Real battle for one's King, for one's country—that was a different matter. Combatants knocking each other off horses, breaking bones and even heads, sometimes with fatal consequences…such antics were not for me, although like all other noble boys, I had my own spills in the tiltyard. Yes, the first, the first thunderous charge, the roar from the crowd and splinter of lance on armour brought a brief, fleeting thrill. After that, for me…tedium.

Hastings looked quizzically at me. "Ah…you must come, young Dickon. Ned wants you to attend."

"Does he?" My eyes brightened.

"Yes, of course. He wants to introduce you properly to her Grace the Queen, as is only right and proper. I am sure you'd find the day amusing—the Queen's brother, Anthony Woodville, is going to participate. He's supposedly an excellent jouster…" He nodded toward a tall, handsome, man lounging beside the chamber door, deep in conversation with other members of the huge Woodville clan. "That's on top of being an esteemed scholar and a poet!"

I detected a tinge of mockery in Hastings' words and knew with sudden instinct—he did not like the suave Anthony Rivers. Jealous? Who knew?

"I shall come if Ned wishes it," I said.

Hastings clapped me on the shoulder. "Good lad; I'll expect to see you there."

He hurried away and I sighed. No getting out of it now.

The day of the joust was clear and sunny, drawing the crowds who clustered around Smithfield, climbing trees in an attempt to get a better view of the participants. I was seated in the box with the other members of the King's family. Higher than the rest of us on the stand, Ned was lounging on a carved throne, clad in a purple, furred robe and jewelled coronet. A platter lay before him filled with cheeses, sweetmeats and mince pies; he was taking handfuls and devouring them as if he had not eaten for days. His muscles strained against his skin-tight violet hose; the links on his golden belt strained a little too. And yet…there was no doubt he was the most handsome prince in Europe—all who beheld him said so. Broad as an oak, taller than the common man, fair featured with a shining glossy cap of gold-streaked brown hair.

I could never compare but there was no jealousy in my heart—just a burning desire to serve that perfect prince as best I could. I looked at him, King with a common touch, speaking to lesser men as if there were equals, even laying a royal arm around men's shoulders in a friendly gesture. I could never emulate him, never had such an easy manner with others…but I swore to myself I'd try and win my peers over in other ways.

My gaze drifted across to Ned's Queen, seated at his side in a confection of silver-blue veils and long taffeta skirts; her lips gleamed cherry-red and her lashes cast dark shadows on her cheeks. Although she'd borne two children to Sir John Grey, a Lancastrian knight killed at the second battle of St Albans, she remained as slim as a young girl. The two boys in question stood behind her seat—the elder, Thomas, appeared near in age to me while Richard was a few years younger. Both had tousled yellow hair and were fidgeting about in their formal clothes. Thomas wore a pompous expression nearly a match to that of Harry Stafford. Clearly, he was enjoying his new elevation in the world if not hours of standing about.

I turned my head away as the crowd roared. Some fellow with a gaudy yellow feather on his helm had been unhorsed in the joust and lay on his back on the ground, legs feebly kicking the air. His squires dashed to assist him, pulling off his helm. His head lolled back as he fell into unconsciousness.

Edward peered over the railing of the royal box. "Unlucky," he said, grabbing some wafers from a wooden tray proffered by a page.

"Wait till my dearest Antony joins the lists," Elizabeth murmured, taking a delicate sip of wine from her goblet. A jewel of red liquid glistened on her lip; she licked it away with a tongue small and neat as a cat's. "He never disappoints."

"Nor do you, my dearest Queen." Edward reached out a finger to gently stroke the wetness from her mouth. His eyes were deep, intense, his hand drifting down to her thigh. She did not move a muscle, merely smiled, cat-like, almost purring.

An embarrassed flush rose to my ears and I hastily turned my attention to the tiltyard. Trumpets were blowing wildly, heralding the arrival of two new combatants. Antony Woodville was riding into the field, mounted upon a great, prancing bay. His armour gleamed like the sun and he wore a tabard bearing the Woodville arms: *Argent, a fesse* and a *canton conjoined gules*. His horse was draped in fine cloths that bore the words of his motto—*Nulle le Vault*. Nothing is Worth It. A strange-sounding motto to my ears but the night before I overheard Hastings laughing with some courtier and saying that Antony meant that nothing in life was worth anything save his sister. Hastings seemed to be making some private, slightly distasteful joke that I did not understand.

Anthony cantered up to the stand and removed his helm, bowing his head before the King and Queen. Elizabeth stepped forward gracefully and wrapped a kerchief around the tip of her brother's lance. "Do me proud, Antony," she said. For one of such lithesome aspect, her voice was surprisingly deep, smoky, alluring. I saw Ned's eyes follow her every move and his expression was hungry as if he wished to devour her like the candied violets another squire had thrust toward him in a glass bowl.

"I will, my Queen." Anthony smiled and at that moment, the cloud burst through the clouds above, making a halo of his neat silver-gold hair, so like his sister's but of a deeper, richer hue. He truly looked an Arthurian knight, and I noticed both my sisters Elizabeth and Anne goggling at him, impressed. It made me feel inexplicably cross.

Mercifully, Anthony put his helmet back on and closed the visor, before giving Queen Elizabeth a salute and riding out to meet his adversary, Sir John Pilkington. I wriggled around in my seat, seeking comfort on the hard bench, and called a page to bring me a candied plum. I hoped it might sweeten my declining mood.

As it turned out, Anthony did not win the joust, much to the chagrin of the Queen and most of the female onlookers. He unseated Pilkington without much difficulty but fell before the gigantic John Cheyney, a gigantic Midlander who stood even a few inches taller than Ned. He had charged onto the field like Goliath from the Bible, clad all in black, wearing a great helm from another age adorned with battered raven wings that flapped in the wind of his steed. Without any preamble, he struck spurs to his mount and barrelled straight at Anthony Woodville, who tried to avert a collision at the last moment by wrenching his steed away—but was struck hard on his right gardbrace, tipping him from the saddle onto the ground.

I heard the Queen gasp; her ladies and her sisters fluttered around her like agitated butterflies. Even the King appeared concerned, pausing in the midst of consuming a honeyed tart.

But Anthony was up on his feet in a flash, although somewhat wobbly. He removed his helm again; held it under his arm. "I concede," he said to the hulking Cheyney, who answered with a grunt.

The bets were on as to whether John Cheyney would win the entire joust, his huge size and swift steed a definite advantage, but as it happened, he lost. To Lord Stanley of all people. I'd not heard of Stanley's prowess as a jouster and thought of him as rather an old man, more devious than valorous, but he unseated Cheyney after several passes and left him half-conscious on the ground. Cheyney's straining squires had to drag him by the legs from the tourney yard while the crowd booed.

Stanley appeared at the stand, unhelmed, fawning over the Queen's outstretched hand as she rewarded him with a great golden ring bearing a ruby as large as a pigeon's egg. Stanley held the gewgaw up so that the sunlight swelled thought it, casting bloody fire onto his long, sallow face with its thin pointed beard, and making him look devilish. A cloud swept over the sun; the red light faded. Stanley pocketed his prize and trotted back to his pavilion to a chorus of cheers.

I made to rise and leave as the stand began to empty out but the King called me back. I had not realised he was even aware of my presence, so involved with his lady-wife—and his food—was he.

"Ah, I cannot let you slip away, Richard," he said, beckoning me close. "I must present you to her Grace, the Queen. She is your sister now."

Clumsily I went down on my knees before Elizabeth Woodville. Silence fell. I would break protocol if I spoke first or even glance up at her face, so I remained kneeling, sweat starting under my collar. Was she deliberately making me wait?

"Rise." The deep, smoky voice sounded at last.

I clambered up to stare into a pair of deep, hooded green eyes. Unreadable eyes.

"So, you are the young Duke of Gloucester." Small, pearl white teeth flashed. "Let me have a look at you." Elizabeth peered at me, gazing up and down; I felt like an animal in the marketplace under the scrutiny of those long-lashed, sleepy emerald eyes.

She turned to Edward. "How strange it is, Ned! Your family are all so very different in appearance. I would never have guessed you and Gloucester are kin."

I reddened. Was that meant to be insulting? Instantly I became aware of my posture, my thinness, my lack of height.

Edward reached to a platter, took an apple and bit a chunk from it. "It is the way of things, sometimes. Dickon has my father's face, as did my brother Edmund, God assoil him. His smallness is from my Lady Mother's side though I pray you not tell her that! My uncle, William Neville, Little Fauconberg, who helped me greatly at Towton, was of Richard's build. I inherit my height from my ancestor Lionel of Clarence as does my sister, Margaret."

"How interesting," said Elizabeth, sounding like she was anything but interested. Her nimble fingers toyed with her veil. "My lord King, may I be guided to my brother Anthony's tent now? I am so concerned for his welfare…"

"Bess, bless you—he only took a little tumble!" said Edward, reaching out a hand to lift her to her feet. Her ladies clustered around her, primping and pulling at her dress, holding up her long train, making sure she could walk with dignity.

The King lingered a few seconds after her departure. "I must go, Richard but let me say this, I have my eye on you…" He laughed. "Just as I did in Westminster!"

"I thought you were a demon, sire."

A loud natural laugh burst from Ned's lips and of a sudden, he no longer seemed the King, but my brave, handsome older brother who had always shielded me when he could. He put his arm around my shoulders, almost overwhelming me with his bulk. "A demon! Well, some might claim I am. But jesting aside, I have watched you and am pleased with what I see."

"I do not think her Grace was impressed," I said, both honest and rueful.

"You must not mind Bess. She is new to all this pageantry and glamour! She will learn. You may have had a narrow escape there anyway, Richard. She might well have wanted you to marry one of her numerous sisters or cousins."

I grimaced.

"Not that I'd have permitted it. One of them has got Buckingham, another one the Earl of Kent, one is soon set to marry Arundel…and Bess is considering Bourchier for another. That's enough! I will deal with your marriage in time, Dickon, but not right now. Finish up your training with Warwick first…" He frowned, hooking his thumbs into his great jewelled belt. "Learn all you can while you can, for it is in my mind to soon have you return to London. I'd rather you were in my household, not Dick's…but we shall see how he acquits himself upon his return to court. You will not object, will you, Dickon?"

"Of course not, your Grace!" I yelped, although my mind was reeling. Did he want me at his side because he desired to involve me with his court? Or because he no longer trusted Warwick?

His attention was no longer on me. Elizabeth stood like a frozen angel, the wings of her headdress sailing above her head. "Ned…" She held out her graceful hand. "Anthony."

The King turned and left me without a backwards glance. It was indeed as if he had fallen under a spell, one I was still a little too young to understand.

I returned to Middleham and the Earl's household, and my duties there resumed. Cousin Dick returned from business abroad then set off again for Sherriff Hutton but left the Countess and Isabel and Anne in residence. Isabel continued to ask about George, and I continued to evade her questions, or, if the mood took me, teased her with accounts of George's flaws. I did not want to be cruel but wanted to discourage her. If Edward had ever for one moment considered letting George marry one of his girls, he never would now, I was certain. I hoped the Earl would find someone else to take her mind off my brother; she would doubtless have many suitors being joint heiress along with little Anne.

Francis and I spent long days in arms training and lengthening evenings sitting against the sun-warmed castle walls just watching the sun descend, a red ball of fire, over the lip of the dale. Francis was a married man now, having wed Anne Fitzhugh back in February; I marvelled at that, as I was still firmly unwed, though I was grateful not to have been parcelled off to a Woodville like Harry Buckingham.

Regretfully I told him that I might soon leave Middleham on the King's orders. "I will stay in touch as best I can," I said. "With you and Percy."

Francis nodded. "We must. I-I-you may think me mad for saying this, Richard, but I feel…there is a bond between us. Some destiny the three of us all will share. You, me and Rob."

Flinging back my head, I laughed. "So you are a soothsayer now, my friend?"

Hurt, he stared at me; I felt guilty and clapped him on the shoulder. "We will remain friends, I swear it."

"It will be strange to leave this place." Francis gazed up at the high walls behind us; the dying sun had stained them vivid scarlet. "It has been good here. I missed my sisters and mother at first, but my father…he was not a good man. I fear I was a disappointment to him, not strong enough, fierce enough, too bookish for his taste. Warwick was as much a father as he." He dropped his gaze, circled his knees with his arms. He seldom spoke of his younger days or his family, save for his sisters, Joan, who was his twin, and Frideswide, whose name I stumbled over. She was named for a famous saint in Oxfordshire where Francis' family held many lands.

"The Earl is like a father to me, too…well, sometimes," I murmured. I tried to think of my own Father; his image was like a spectre, fading away in my memory. Soon, I deemed, when I had departed Middleham, it would be the same with Warwick. Since Edward's unexpected marriage, everything had changed.

Both suddenly pensive, we sat in silence as the blue cloak of twilight descended and the warmth went out of the stonework behind us. Stars came out above and the wind was rushing over the moor and tickling the tops of the trees on William's Hill.

"We had best go inside." I pulled on my friends' arm. "We've been long away without a care in the world for our tasks. If we are missed, we may well both get a beating."

We made to rise but even as we stumbled to our feet, a pair of familiar yet oddly furtive figures came creeping through the shadows in our direction.

"Is that who I think it is?" I hissed in Francis' ear.

His eyes were big and round. "It is. What by God's Toes are they doing? They should not wander out after dark."

"Come, don't let them see us." Still dragging on his sleeve, I hauled him round the edge of the wall and into a crevice under the stone stairs leading to the walkways above. I could hear the tramp of the guard's boots against stone; surely, they, ever keen-eyed, had not missed the newcomers? Mind you, the pair were well-furled in dark garments; nonetheless, it was a real risk for them if some spotty-faced new guardsman, eager to earn respect from his betters, fired off an arrow into the dark, imagining he'd seen a wandering wolf or a bloodthirsty Scot who had strayed over the borders.

My heart began to beat with sudden concern. What had made them behave so foolishly? Yes, Francis and me were out, but we…we…were…

"Richard!" I heard Anne's voice before I saw her face.

Muffled in her dove-grey cloak, hood drawn up, she stumbled towards me and Francis.

"Anne, look what you've done, you've given us away." Isabel, beside her, gave her sister a hard shove; she sounded angry, shrewish.

"Isabel, do not treat your sister so!" I stretched out my arm to keep small Anne from smacking her face against the castle wall. She glanced up at me, grateful, like a puppy. "What are you doing here anyway? Where are your nurses? Does the Countess know the pair of you are running about like hoydens in the dark? Anything could happen! The curfew bell has not yet been rung; some passing foreign rogue could sweep you both up and carry you off from the castle."

"You're exaggerating, Richard," said Isabel, but her cheeks were fiery red.

"No, I am not," I said seriously. "You are now the perfect age for some miscreant to abduct and force into marriage!"

Isabel's face grew even brighter crimson and her eyes were brimming with what I imagined were tears of rage. "How dare you say such foul things! You...you're not my father!"

"No, but I'm your kinsman and he's not here, so I am taking his place. Anne..." I glanced over at the smaller girl, huddled in her cloak. "I can trust you. You won't lie to me, will you..."

Solemnly she shook her head.

"What are you doing out here, wrapped up as if you intend to run away."

"We weren't running away," Anne blurted. "Isabel's received a letter. She was afraid the nurses would find it—they're so nosy, they poke into everything we own. So she wanted to read it behind the stables—and promised if I'd go with her as company, she'd let me know what was in it."

"Anne! Isabel wailed, stomping one slippered foot. "How could you tell...Richard, of all people? Of all people."

In that instant, I guessed who the letter was from. My heart sank. "Where is it…the letter?" I said in a low voice.

"Here…but I shan't let you read it." Isabel pulled out a crumpled parchment from under her cloak. A messy red seal bled wax all over the back. I managed to get a glimpse of it and my fears were correct—George.

"A secret messenger brought it," she said breathlessly. "He left it with the old herbalist who makes the lotions and potions for mama's aches and pains. As I'd told George to tell him to do."

"So, this is not the first letter he's sent."

"No." The dusk was shadowing her eyes, filling them with stars. "Richard, we want to marry. Not just me, before you go thinking that I am some addle-pated goose—George wants this, too. My father approves."

"But the King…you'd have to ask permission from the King to marry, Isabel. I do not tell you this to show cruelty, but I doubt he'd say 'yes.' Especially now that things are strained between him and your sire."

"What better to make things right once more?" said Isabel in desperation. "Our houses joined, as it should be. Father helped Edward to the throne, after all. He's done so much for Edward; the King's so ungrateful."

"Isabel!" Francis interjected. "Remember to whom you speak…."

Her lip trembled. "I am sorry—I did not mean to speak ill of the King. But I truly want to marry George and he me. If the King could wed for love…"

"But he's the King…" I said softly, pitying her. I pitied too that she should be so enamoured of George!

"We would be his strongest supporters," Isabel continued to argue. "You could marry Anne, Richard—Father has thought about that too, did you know?"

It was my turn to blush now; at my ear, Francis gasped in surprise and, hanging on my left arm, Anne made an embarrassed little mewling sound.

"No, I did not know," I said dully. "This is…madness. All of it."

"I will tell you something else, if you promise not to tell!" Isabel swirled over to me, her hair flying in a cloud, looking like some kind of elf-woman escaped from one of the burial howes on the moors. "Do you swear?"

I hesitated. Francis nudged me with an elbow. "You might need to know," he said quietly.

"And you…you must swear too, Francis Lovell!" Isabel's tone was fierce. "Do you?"

"I—I do swear…on my life," Francis stammered. He made the sign of the cross above his heart.

"And you, Richard. Will you follow Francis' suit?"

My stomach felt sick and sour. "Oh…yes…yes…I swear by the Blessed Virgin. I shan't tell a living soul."

Isabel sidled up to me until we were almost touching. I was not used to having a female, especially a young and pretty one, so close, and found it both embarrassing…and exhilarating.

"So what is this secret?" I said gruffly, half dreading what I would hear next.

Isabel took a deep breath. "As you know, we are cousins. Your mother Lady Cecily was sister to my late grandfather, the Earl of Salisbury. If I were to wed George and you Anne, we would need dispensations due to our closeness of blood. Well…Father…Father has written to the Pope asking for such dispensations, to hold in readiness…"

"Christ!" The disrespectful oath burst unbidden from my mouth. I would have punched the castle wall with my free hand, but Francis grabbed my arm.

"You won't tell, will you? You swore!"

"I won't tell," I said heavily. "Jesu, Isabel, I am at a loss for words! I think your Father has gone mad!" *Or he's desperate…* I could only pray the Pope would deny the dispensations or that the messenger to Rome would never reach the Holy City. Even better would be for Edward to recall me to London as soon as possible. I loved it here, but I would not be drawn into Warwick's schemes—not against my own brother's royal will!

"It will come out all right in the end. You'll see!" Isabel cried, unnerved by my anger.

I said nothing. The night fell over us. In the distance, dogs barked and suddenly there was a commotion and a hubbub of voices calling out the girls' names.

"Your nurses are looking for you," I said with sour countenance. "The very least you can let me do is call them over; I do not want anyone to think I had any involvement in your mischief."

Isabel nodded. "So be it." She thrust George's letter back under her cloak.

"Over here!" I called out, dislodging Anne and stepping out from the wall. "Over here! Lady Isabel and Anne are here—I have them safe!"

The nurses descended, guards and lanthorn-bearing servants at their heels, scolding and reprimanding Isabel and Anne for their foolishness; they then started on Francis and I for reasons we could not fathom even though we were guiltless.

"When his lordship is home, there'll be trouble!" shrieked one enormous beldame, waggling her finger, the white wings of her crisp headdress sailing up into the dark. "Mark my words."

I feared that what she said would indeed prove true—but not in the way the nurse expected.

Chapter Eleven

Summer continued, sweet and lush and deep. Lord Warwick returned, his mood somewhat happier—and there were no further mentions of dispensations or of Isabel marrying George. In my free time, I visited the kennels or the mews; occasionally I was allowed to hawk or hunt alongside the Earl. How beautiful it was to gallop across the moorland, the long grasses rushing beneath the horses' hooves, the wind cool in my hair and the hills beyond a misty-blue haze. Released from their jesses, the hawks would rise up, shrieking, masters of the skies, their wings casting black shadows as they dived for their prey.

Once Warwick took me to Jervaulx Abbey, which was not so far away, the nearest monastery to Middleham after Coverham and a much richer foundation. The Abbot there, John Brompton, bred fine horses, and Cousin Dick knew I loved to ride and had some aptitude in the saddle.

A House of the Cistercian brothers, Jervaulx was dedicated to St Mary. Besides breeding horses, they made cheese which was imported far and wide across England. Cousin Dick nearly always had the monks' cheese on his table—it was mixed with ewe's milk as well as that of a cow, which changed its texture and hastened the growth of blue moulds upon it.

As we arrived, the monks were carrying out cheeses wrapped in cloth for distribution to families in the local village. Carefully they stacked the blue-veined truckles in waiting carts, making sure none could be damaged in transport. The cheese's pungent aroma reached into my nostrils, making my mouth water. It seemed hours ago that I had broken my fast with sops.

Upon seeing the Earl and his party riding through the gate with its statue of the Virgin and brass bell, one of the monks hiked up his long skirts, revealing fat, hairy ankles, and ran to tell the Abbot.

Shortly, Abbot John appeared, a cherubic man with great round red cheeks like apples, a necklace of wobbling chins and a ring of flyaway white hair. "My Lord Warwick!" he cried. "What brings you here today? It is long—too long—since I had the pleasure of your presence! Have you come to sample some of my delectable cheeses?" He gestured to the carts and their odoriferous burdens.

"I would not mind a few to take home for the table," Cousin Dick said with a grin. "You have tempted me, Abbot!"

Abbot John threw up his chubby hands. "My cheeses are as tempting as Eve's apples clearly!"

Warwick started to climb down from his mount. "They are indeed...however, they are not the real reason for my visit. I have come to purchase a horse—for my young cousin here, the Duke of Gloucester."

The Abbot nodded in my direction. "Your Grace. I hardly recognised you. You've grown like a weed since last our acquaintance if you pardon me saying so."

"Which is exactly why my kinsman Richard needs a new horse. The old tame ones he first trained on when he came to Middleham he's long outgrown. He needs a beast of greater stamina and spirit—a challenge though not evil-tempered or vicious. Have you anything in your stables that you deem suitable?"

The Abbot thought for a moment, scratching one of his chins. "I think I may...Would his Grace like to come and have a look?"

The Abbot led us through the abbey outbuildings to the paddocks set out at the rear of the cloister. Several young horses swept to and fro as if eager to leap the fences and stream away across the dales. One was chestnut, shining warm red in the sun, another was bay with a white streak like a lightning bolt down its face. The third, though, was the one that caught my eye. He was dappled grey and white, with a dark smoky face and a pale mane and tail that flowing out behind him as he paced back and forth, nostrils wide, head thrown back.

"That one!" I pointed. "He would be my choice, I think."

"A good choice." Abbot John folded his arms over his immense belly. "He is of mixed Andalusian stock, hence his distinctive appearance. Were he purebred, he would be worth his weight in gold. His dam came from a house of Carthusian monks in Spain who are dedicated to furthering the breed."

"Look closely before you make your choice final," instructed Warwick. "Make sure the beast's beauty has not dazzled your eyes. Check him over for suitability in the way I have taught you."

I approached the pen. The three horses shied away, running in circles, their hooves kicking up soil, their manes and tails flying. One of the monks who worked in the stable, a thin young man with a ginger tonsure and a face of freckles, entered the corral at a signal from the Abbot and managed to get a bridle onto the head of the grey.

"He has been broken, my lords," said the young monk, as he brought the stallion over, pulling against him, "but only newly so; he still has much to learn."

"As does my young ward," laughed Warwick, clapping me on the shoulder in a way that seemed very fatherly. "What do you think, Richard?"

I leapt the fence, uncaring if it was not terribly seemly for a Duke, even a twelve-year-old one. Trying to remember what I'd been taught about decent horseflesh, I ran my hands over the grey's flanks, knelt to look at his fetlocks, although I dared not touch them. I did not want my young brains dashed out by an angry hoof. The horse had a broad, sound chest, a good coat, an intelligent eye and a grace of movement—he was superb in both conformation and collection as far as I could see. I cast cursory glances at the other two horses to please my cousin of Warwick but my heart was still set on the crossbred Andalusian.

"He is the one," I said, stepping back with my inspection complete. "All are fine beasts, Abbot, but the grey appeals to me most in every way."

"He will be yours then," said Warwick, satisfied, his arms folded.

"Can I ride him home?" I asked, filled with excitement at the thought.

"No! You heard the Abbot; the beast's training is incomplete. Your brother the King would not be best pleased if I let you ride a half-wild horse and you ended up dead in a ditch somewhere in Yorkshire with your neck broken. The horse will go back to Middleham with the entourage and I will put him in the hands of my personal horse-trainers. You will liaise with them in his training—and yours."

I bowed my head. "So be it, Cousin. I am grateful indeed. This is a rich gift."

"As I said before, having this beast at such a young age will be a challenge—one that will improve your skills as a horseman…and as a knight who may well go to war in the future. Have you thought of a name for him?"

I grinned. "A challenge you say, my lord? Well, I shall call him Challenger then. Is that fitting?"

"Fitting enough."

I went home on the dull old hobelar I was used to riding, with Challenger at the rear of the party, tugging on his lead and rolling his eyes. Every now and then I turned my head to gaze at him, entranced—he was beautiful and he was mine.

I was not so young and foolish that unease did not overwhelm me too, and when not admiring Challenger, I furtively glanced over at the sword-straight profile of my Cousin. His gift was a great one indeed, but was it done for the love of a kinsman…or because he was trying to bind me to his cause?

Days passed, slow, humid and dreaming—the remnants of one last happy summer. The moor turned yellow and the waters in the bathing pool in the river known as Black Dub ran low and turgid. St Alkelda's well had almost dried out and the lanes of

Middleham were dusty where horses and mules passed by. When the market was held, the farmers bringing their livestock in were brown as berries despite wearing great, broad-brimmed hats; their tunics were off and their shirt sleeves rolled to the elbows.

I continued my training in the Warwick household, and now it included dancing, of all things. It sounded unmanly but the dance-master, a foreign fellow with a coiled black moustache, worked us as hard as the Master of Arms, striking our legs with a long stick if we shuffled our feet or performed the wrong steps. "Many of you will be in the King's Court someday," he admonished in a thickly-accented voice. "You must learn the arts of gentlemen or make fools of yourselves!"

At first the squires had to dance with each other, the smaller boys taking the parts of the women, leaving them open to all sorts of taunts and japery. I had feared I might also have to play a girl because of my lack of height and girth, but the master saw fit to allow me a man's role. Perhaps he would not put a royal Duke into a humiliating position, or perhaps he thought I showed some skill and was rewarding me for such. Certainly I did not receive the lash of his stick on my calves more than once or twice.

Then came the Feast of St John, Midsummer's Eve. Cousin Warwick held a small banquet for some of the local gentry such as Scrope of Bolton and the Metcalfes of Nappa Hall. The castle's Great Hall was decked out in green boughs of birches, bunches of fennel and St John's Wort, and the high table was decked in bouquets of white lilies. Glass lamps stood on the table also, one on each end; they would remain burning throughout the entire night. Behind the seats of the Earl and Countess was an ironwork screen fashioned to resemble a tree branch, and it was hung with many smaller lanterns.

I attended Warwick in my expected role as a page, but as the feast progressed, he called me over to his side with the crook of a finger. "I wish to see how well you've learned to dance," he said "and my daughters are eager to practice their own skills with lads of similar age. You will dance a carol with Isabel and then a Basse dance with Anne."

"My Lord." I bowed my head to indicate my willingness, although I was quite nervous with all eyes upon me.

It went well enough, however, even when Isabel sighed, "I wish George were here." I found Anne a better dancer than her sister, truth be told, even though she was but small—she tried harder, her face solemn with concentration. Isabel got all the attention, though, for she had begun to mature and hence received admiration from the men within the chamber. I could not help gawking at her myself, although I didn't particularly like Isabel, with her fixation about my brother.

After the banquet's end, with all food cleaned into the voiders and the Hall emptied, some of the older henchmen went out into the town. By all the usual rules, we should have been in our beds, but Cousin Dick did not always keep a tight rein on us. He knew we did not dare get into trouble in Middleham itself where everyone knew everyone else.

With Francis at my side, we left the castle sallyport and hurried into town. The air was pungent with the scent of bonfires and wake fires, one filled with dry bones, the other with clean dry wood. Sparks and smoke hung in the air. Passing into the heart of the village, people were dancing around a crackling pyre, singing and kicking their heels high in the air, while a Giant and a Hobby-Horse lumbered through the streets asking for pennies and cake. A trestle table stood in front of the blacksmith's forge, where the baker and the innkeeper were handing out sweet bread, slices of cheese and good ale to all-comers.

"Welcome, young lords," cried one of the village elders, a man called Mathew, who had no fair on his head at all but a long trundling beard to his waist. Tonight, it was plaited with bright ribbons. "Come join us. We are about to have a Marching Watch to the church!"

Flaming torches were thrust into our hands. We paraded along the cobbled street, the locals clustered around us, in the direction of St Alkelda's Church. Once within the churchyard enclosure, the villagers gathered around the saints' Holy Well, dry and rank though it had become, and prayed on its edge, dropping wreaths of St John's Wort into the murky trickle, to honour St John, whose night it was. The well-water stood in for the waters of the Jordan where St John had been baptised.

The Rector, John Cartmell, emerged from the church porch and a Cross wrought of fresh-cut masterwort and goatsbeard was brought forth to receive his blessing as he extolled the virtues of "St John, he who is a bright and shining light…"

As the ceremony concluded, the villagers doused their torches in the muddied waters of the well and went back toward the market square to continue their celebrations. Many would get no sleep that night; in the gloom, we saw couples cut away from the throng and vanish into the drifting smoke-wreaths.

"We had best get back to the castle," said Francis. "Too late out, and they'll search for us, whether we have leave or no."

I nodded. I was weary after the day's work anyway, my back a red-hot ache. Ashes were stuck in my hair and settling on my lashes; I fancied I smelt of smoke and sweat.

Together we hurried back toward the sallyport where the night-watchman would allow us entry despite the lateness of the hour, curfew being suspended for the Saint's Eve. As we crossed through an unlit lane between two cottages, an old woman approached. We did not recognise her, which was not surprising, because all the nearby crofters piled into Middleham for the St John's celebration, swelling the population for that night.

She was bent, leaning on a hawthorn stick—a bad omen, for the hawthorn was thought by locals to be a fairy tree. When its white blossoms were out, they smelt of death, the odour of decaying flesh…

"What have we here?" she said, the odour of drink and unwashed flesh hanging about her.

Francis and I glanced nervously at each other. My friend took a deep breath and tried for politeness, "Old Mother, I ask that you stand aside and let us pass. We are henchmen of the Lord Warwick's household."

She squealed as if in delight; rags of verminous grey hair blew about the pocked mask of her face. Leaning heavily on her stick, she closed one eye and squinted at us through the other, which made her appearance vaguely comical but also sinister as if she was giving us the Evil Eye.

"Tonight is a night when futures may be divined," she whispered and she began to intone in a slurred voice,

> *"The Mad Saint has fallen but Where Dwell he now?*
> *Out in the wet wilds, with wolf and with crow!*
> *But what is hidden by folly may one day be found*
> *And then most unlikely shall surely be Crowned...*
> *The One Who Makes Kings shall soon Make Another,*
> *But who Shall Wear the Crown at Time's End?*
> *Son of Sun or Birth Brother?"*

"She's mad," whispered Francis in my ear. "And maybe a sorceress! What shall we do?"

I should have shown courage or maybe pity for the crone's affliction, but I was not yet thirteen summers old and, foolish or no, her near-treasonous prophecies affrighted me with some deep, dark fear I could not name. Grabbing Francis, I propelled him past the crone, while the woman stumbled back against the wall, coughing and wheezing with drunken laughter.

"You don't think she was a witch, do you?" Francis asked, wide-eyed with dismay, as we raced through the dark toward the safety of the postern gate. "She might have cursed us! You know what they say about Midsummers's Eve..."

"No, she's not a witch," I said more snappishly than I intended. "Mad, yes...but nothing more."

And yet, as we entered the comforting ring of lantern-light at the castle's back gate and the wooden door with its iron bands banged shut safely behind us, I felt a sudden rush of utter relief.

The woman was mad and her 'prophecies' born of drink but her words reverberated through my mind— "Who shall wear the Crown... *Birth Brother*..."

I thought of Cousin Dick's falling out with the King, and his secret desire to marry Isabel to George.

George! Warwick could not possibly be thinking of raising him to a King's dignity!

Could he?

Despite standing near the guardroom's hearth, a shiver ran down my spine. Change was coming, I could feel it like a living entity, an ominous presence. Dame Fortune was most surely spinning her endless Wheel, which threw the mightiest to the ground and raised others to great heights.

Mood darkened, I bade a hasty goodnight to Francis and hurried to the stables where I began to curry Challenger despite the lateness of the hour. Eyes closed, I leaned into his flank and buried my face in his long mane, savouring the familiar horsey-scent of him. He nuzzled my hand, hoping for treats, his breath warm on my skin.

Even he could not cheer me tonight, although I appreciated his sturdy presence.

Change was coming.

Night on a month later there was a great change indeed. An event of significance that rippled through England. Good Yorkists all, the lads of Middleham cheered and chattered excitedly into the night after the news was delivered to the castle. Even Warwick, vexed and dour for months, managed a triumphant smile.

After roaming around the wilds since the Battle of Hexham, King Henry VI was apprehended at last. When his army was defeated and the treacherous, false Henry Beaufort lost his head, the old mad King had fled west into Cumbria, staying at Muncaster Castle, Bolton Hall, and finally Waddington Hall. It was at Waddington, the foolish old soul grew overbold. He invited Doctor

Manning, the Dean of Windsor, to dine with him, just as if Henry still wore a crown upon his brow. The arrival in the north of Manning alerted the local Yorkist faction—Sir James Harrington, Sir John Tempest and members of the Talbot family. As Henry sat at the table, sipping his wine with Manning, these stout men burst through the hall door. Henry fled as Manning shrieked and hurled himself in front of the men who confronted him, swords drawn. As no one dared harm a churchman, Henry managed to slip away through a secret passageway which led to the river—he crossed by the Hipping Stones and hid in a thorny wood on the far side. However, the Talbots had brought their hounds, and they chased the former ruler and brought him to heel, his flight ended. He was returned to London tied to his saddle.

"What will Ned—I mean, the King, do with, well, the other King?" Francis asked me, somewhat uncomfortably. We were sitting in the buttery, where it was cool amidst the vast wine casks, having not long finished our day's training. Both of us were winded and bruised, our hair lank with sweat.

I shrugged. I really did not know; I had not thought about it. "Maybe…maybe pack him off to a remote monastery?" I said. "Many think he'd be happier there than on a throne."

Francis licked his dry lips, leaned his hot forehead against a chill barrel. "But he'd always be a danger, wouldn't he? And his son and the Queen are out there still, trying to drum up support for his cause."

"Surely the damn Lancastrians can see it is no use," I said irritably. Sweat was making my collar itch. "Edward is the rightful King and…and a hundred times better than weak, stupid Henry!"

Francis stared down. "I heard Warwick talking to his brother John. He was saying it would be for the better if Edward…if…he…" His voice trailed off.

"If he what?"

"If he finished it."

"If he finished what?" I was uneasy now, not liking where this conversation was going.

"You know…if he got rid of old Henry."

"You mean killed him."

"Yes, that's exactly what I mean, Dickon. That's what Warwick said to John. The King must die"

I leaned back against the casks, stunned.

"You know…it rather makes sense," said Francis tentatively. "A death for peace…"

I reacted with fury. "You should not be talking of such things, not here. Not anywhere, Francis! How old are you? You're just a child! Just cease!"

He immediately shut his mouth, looking hurt.

I scowled into the gloom. No, no, what they were suggesting seemed all wrong. Henry was defeated, in bonds—it was not the same as if Edward had fought him on the field, man to man. To kill him as a prisoner, an anointed king, no less, in cold blood… *No!* But then I thought of Father who had died humiliated, a paper crown placed upon his head, and Edmund, poor Edmund, given no mercy despite his surrender…. Groaning, I put my head in my hands.

Francis moved in the shadows, placed his hand on my shoulder. "Sometimes a king must perform "unpleasant acts for the betterment of all," he said quietly. "Well, that's what I've heard anyway."

He was old beyond his years, Francis Lovell. Quiet of voice and watchful, less inclined to storms of emotion, be it despair or joy, than I.

And he was right. But still, I did not want to think of my brother executing his rival.

But nothing happened to the Mad King, not then. He languished in the Tower of London, well-cared for but unfree, while Edward ruled England strongly with his glittering, dragon-eyed Woodville wife at his side. The Queen was now with child and the King and his counsellors prayed she would be delivered of a healthy son to assure the success of Ned's fledgeling Yorkist dynasty.

George Neville was made Archbishop of York, as he had long wished, and a great feast held in his honour at Cawood Castle. Cousin Dick's good humour returned and I had the honour of an invitation—not to attend as a mere page but as a member of his own family.

Cawood Castle stood a few miles outside of York close to Bishop Woods, where much good hunting took place. It was a long, low castle, built more for comfort than defence, but had a sturdy, towered gatehouse and a banqueting hall beyond. The Ouse slid through its weedy bed beyond the walls, its ferry bringing in more revenue to the Archbishops and its many wharves used for the unloading of stone meant for the great Minster in York and other church buildings.

"We shall be here a week, Dickon," said Warwick cheerily to me as we rode under the gatehouse arch and into the bailey. "There is enough food to feed two thousand! Are you hungry, boy? You always look as if you could use a good feed—although I hardly starve you at Middleham."

I blushed a little but answered him back, with a wry little smile. "I am as God made me, sir. Like Uncle Faulconberg."

"And I dare say you shall be as fierce as Fauconberg in battle." He clapped me on the shoulder, supportive, paternal.

The Great Hall of Cawood was decorated with ornamental shields and huge wooden figures of Biblical figures made by the artisans of York—the Patriarch, Noah's Ark, a voluptuous Eve holding up a carved apple, a terrifying Goliath with a huge black beard. Michaelmas daisies and other flowers of late summer such as Betony and Cornflowers decorated the tables with their starched linen cloths; bunches of sage, hyssop, rue and camomile hung from the rafters to help sweeten the air.

Cousin George, the new Archbishop of York, sat enthroned at the head of the room under a canopy emblazoned with the

Neville Saltire. Other bishops were clustered around him and rich abbots and most of the gentry of northern England.

Warwick, acting as steward for his brother, ushered me to one of the trestle tables set apart from the others under a canopy bearing traceries of suns and roses; the benches nearby were already filled by my sister Elizabeth, Duchess of Suffolk, the Countess of Westmoreland, the Countess of Northumberland and Isabel and little Anne in red and green gowns with their hair loose top their waists. Elizabeth sat on my right, and the girls were near my left. I was slightly peeved about being seated with all females, especially two excited and giggly young girls, but then realised why Warwick had done it. By positioning me thus, he was stating our family relationship and its importance—and perhaps even suggesting that I wed one of his daughters. My gaze slid to Anne's shining head with its sleek tresses of fairish hair touched by a hint of fire that bloomed in the light of the flambeaux set about the chamber.

Would it be such a bad thing? Anne was not so terrible for a girl…and she probably would improve with age. That's what Rob Percy told me, that girls get more interesting when they turned thirteen or fourteen… He certainly seemed engrossed with his new wife, a winsome creature called Eleanor, who was sixteen, dark-haired and dark eyes with pearlescent skin. Indeed, as they now had started to live as man and wife, his duties were changing, and he seemed more like an uncle to Francis and me than a friend.

Clarions sounded, and the buzz of excited voices in the Hall faded away. The food was on the way! Expectantly I watched as servants brought water and napkins to wash the hands of the Archbishop. Then they came round to our table and I laved my hands first, then my sister Elizabeth, then the other countesses who were not princesses, and then Anne and Isabel. I noticed Isabel flick a bit of water from her fingernail into Anne's eye; she squinted and I cast Isabel an exasperated look. She did not notice, though, for Warwick was also looking in her direction with a frown, and she was pretending she was a fine, grown-up lady.

The trumpeters ceased their strident fanfare and a party of minstrels in bright yellow began to play and sing a song decidedly secular considering that the feast was in honour of George's appointment as Archbishop—

Gentle butler, belami,
Fill the bowl night and high,
That we may drink by and by,
With how, butler, how. Bevis a tout!
Fill the bowl, butler, and let the cup rout!

Here is meat for us all
Both for great and for small;
I trow we must the butler call.
With how, Butler, how Bevis a tout!
Fill the bowl, butler, and let the cup rout.

A drum was beaten, and in time to its rhythm the servers entered the room, stout lads in bright caps and short crimson jackets carrying carafes and jugs, platters and plates. The food was worthy of a royal coronation—wild bull, stag, mutton, lamb, suckling pigs, pikes, bream, cranes, quails, plovers, mallard, capons, partridges, woodcocks, venison pies, and hot tarts in custard. Most exotic were porpoises and seals from the far north coasts, their bodies fat as old men and dripping in rich sauce, and swans and peacocks complete with feathers and gilded beaks.

Assuming the role of steward with gusto, Cousin Warwick advised and ordered, seeing that the guests were all fed according to our status, and that the wine and ale never stopped flowing into our goblets—even us youngsters, although I dare say the hippocras and ale had been watered down slightly, taking our young ages into account…

"What is that thing?" Anne nudged Isabel with her elbow. She was pointing to the porpoise brought to our table on a huge silver tray. The cooks had boiled it in wheat and almond milk and its oily bulk was streaked with yellow saffron and cardamom.

"It's a porpoise," I said. I was eager to get away from my sister Elizabeth for a moment. From the moment I took my seat, she was sighing and straightening my collar and saying how much I resembled father and how her baby John was a fine lad and how Mother complained that I did not write enough to her comfort.

Anne wrinkled her nose. "I am not sure if I want to try it. Are you going to, Richard?"

"Of course," I said. "It is a great honour to have porpoise served. It is a royal fish, permitted only to grace the tables of the highest-ranking men in the land."

"Anne's a peasant," tittered Isabel, from behind her linen napkin.

"Am not!" said Anne furiously.

"Eat some porpoise then," said Isabel, eyes narrowed. "Show us your worth. Go on, I dare you."

Anne's little face was white but determined. "I-I will then. But…" she looked pleadingly at me, "will you go first, Richard? After all, you are entitled to the first cut, you being a Duke and a prince…"

My head was spinning from the wine and Elizabeth's chattering. "I gladly will!" I motioned to the waiting carver, a youth with a long pimply face and a bowl of black hair. "Cut me the lion's share, boy," I said with unaccustomed pompousness. I realised I was aping my brother, George. Despite myself, I began to giggle most improperly.

The carver's visage was one of affronted fury. I could tell I had ruined a night he had thought would be full of great honour with my silly posturing. He smacked down a slab of sauce-drenched porpoise onto my waiting trencher. A shower of yellow sauce made pungent lines on my good doublet. Isabel shrieked in dismay and fury as a small dollop hit her gown, then began to make strange mewing noises—she was on the verge of tears at having her dress ruined. Anne, ever more practical, dabbed at the bright blobs with a napkin, but only succeeded in smearing them the more, which made Isabel shove her sister away, "Leave me alone!".

"Watch me; I am about to attempt the porpoise!" I cried, trying to distract the girls, not wishing to see either of them weep—or come to blows. I brandished my knife, its blade glinting wickedly, and then plunged it into the rather fibrous meat. After a few moments of huffing and puffing, I managed to cut myself a decent lump that would fit into my mouth. The sauce was now everywhere; on my hands, my garments and the tablecloth. My sister Elizabeth was giving me a stern, purse-lipped look which made her look just like Mother; I ignored her—I was too busy impressing Warwick's daughters. Or so I thought in my youthful folly.

The speared chunk of porpoise landed in my mouth. It was tough and sinewy and made my teeth and jaw ache as I tried to chew. Its taste was not particularly pleasant, either, for all that I enjoyed the fish that was frequently delivered to Middleham, brought in from the sea at Whitby and Scarborough.

My face must have shown my distaste for Isabel, forgetting her spoilt dress, leaned over, mocking. "That was only a little morsel, Richard of Gloucester! You must eat all that you've been given or I shall call you craven and a baby. If you don't eat every last bit, it will be a great affront to Uncle George—porpoises are not easy to come by."

Feigning gusto, I hacked off another portion of porpoise. And then another. And another. In between, I washed the taste from my mouth with draughts of sweet hippocras. My head began to reel—and my belly to object.

A horrible cramp snaked across my midriff, making me clutch my stomach in despair. The torches flickered in my eyesight and my ears rang. I pushed myself away from the bench on which I sat, intending to run for the nearest privy, but my legs would not hold my weight. I fell on my knees on the rushes and was sick.

"Oh Richard," said my sister Elizabeth, softly and disapprovingly. I knew instantly the tale of my greed with George Neville's porpoise would go straight to Mother…

Isabel looked both triumphant and disgusted. It was little Anne who came to me, with her table napkin and wiped my face and mouth as I struggled to rise.

"Richard…have you imbibed too much drink?"

With a groan, I stared up into the sun-bronzed face of my Cousin of Warwick, standing peacock-bright in his steward's robes, his hands firmly planted on his hips. "N-no, sir…"

"You little liar, Dickon!" he laughed and dragging me up, gave me an affectionate clout on the shoulder that both hurt and felt oddly good at the same time. "Well, there's no shame in that. All men must learn to hold their drink sooner or later!"

Anne was smiling shyly, Isabel goggling at me and her father in amazement. A nearby squire was glancing over at her, ogling a patch of bare white skin revealed by the square neckline of her gown. Warwick, who saw *everything* even when he was engaged in another activity, deposited me on my bench and with a lazy backward swing of his arm, clouted the lecherous oaf who fell to the floor with a loud '*oof.*' "Keep your eyes ahead, knave, and away from ladies far above your station."

Everyone laughed at the mortified youth sprawled on the rushes; Isabel, realising what the squire had been doing, went red, and Anne, mouse-like, curled up next to me and said in a whisper, "My father likes you, you know. He may not always show it but he does. You are like a son to him, the son he never had."

Now it was my turn to flush crimson. "You are kind to say so, Anne. I won't forget it."

The banquet finished with the arrival of a huge, sugared subtlety shaped like St George killing the dragon. The entire horde of feasters craned their necks and made approving noises as it was paraded about the banqueting chamber.

Cousin George Neville beamed from his chair of estate.

A singer appeared on the dais and a musician began to pluck on a lyre. "*Omnes gentes plaudit!*

I saw many birds sitting in a tree,
They took their flight and flew away
With Ego dixi, have a good day!
Many white feathers has the magpie—
I may sing no more for my lips are so dry!
Many white feathers has the swan—
The more that I drink, the less good I can.
Lay sticks on the fire, well may it burn!
Give us one last drink ere we go home!"

I reached for my half-finished hippocras to toast my cousin's elevation to Archbishop but could not reach it. My fingers seemed numb. My head slumped on the table.

Vaguely I remember being carried from the chamber, I am not sure who by—I half-dreamed Warwick himself, although that seemed unlikely. All I remember is that despite my sick belly, I felt strangely content. Strangely *happy.*

When we departed for Middleham a few days later, the happiness, if dimmed a little, was still with me.

Of course, like so much in my life that I held dear, it was not to last….

The day was muggy, one of those September days still clinging to summer when the sky was blue and the breeze warm. Soon winter would come, though, and winter was harsh in the Dales. Soul-caking in October would die away to November bleakness with only Christmas to look forward to.

Francis and I had been exercising Warwick's hounds and running errands to the town; by the time late afternoon came and we were dismissed from our duties, we were both sweaty and dusty.

"Let's go to Black Dub," suggested Francis. "We won't be able to swim there for much longer, I'd wager. Within the next week or two, the rains and grey skies will come, and the water will be deathly cold."

I nodded; sweat stained my shirt below my arms and my face felt gritty with dust from the bailey. "Aye, let's go. I reckon you're right—within a month or two we'll be able to skate on the Dub instead of swim. I wisely kept my bone skates from last year."

Off up the drover track behind the castle we wandered, stolen sweet tarts in our pockets, passing the mound of William's Castle which loomed like a black boil overlooking the road to Coverham. On its summit, the overgrown bushes were swaying, a green haze of knotted hair on the head of the hillock.

Then the hill lay behind us, dwindling in our peripheral vision, and there was only open countryside, with rippled grasses snarling round our ankles and a distant dark line of trees marching away on the horizon. No one was around which gladdened our young hearts, for when the village children played in the Dub, rambunctiousness often turned to brawling—they mimicked our accents, goaded us to fight and tried to steal our clothes as we swam in the river.

Cresting a verdant rise and pushing past a couple of stray, baa-ing sheep, we entered Black Dub, a secret stronghold of the River Ure, where lines of tall thin trees surrounded a deep swimming-hole filled with water of a midnight hue. The heart of the Dub was surrounded by slatey flat slabs of stone where we would lie out in the summer sun after plunging into the eternally chill waters.

There were dark legends about Black Dub—tales of water-witches with streaming weed-hair, of drowned maidens' shades that moaned from the treetops, of ugly knuckers, dark-scaled monsters with eyes like beacons, that crawled at the bottom of the hole—seeking to grasp young boys' ankles and draw them under to their doom.

We were not afraid though—well, not very. It was broad daylight; the sun was dancing in the leaves above, and we did not know of a single person in Middleham who had ever been eaten by a knucker.

Hastily we doffed our garments after a quick check round that we were not being spied upon by hostile village lads. Seeing that we were safe, we dived off the flat rocks into the water, screeching as the coldness bit into our skin. After the initial shock, we began to do as all the youths did when swimming in the Dub— we splashed each other, wrestled in the shallows, pretended to drown then burst up in a haze of spray and a shout of childish triumph.

At length, as we tussled in the weeds, Francis waved his arms. "Enough!" His breath sounded raspy and I wondered if the water had been too cold for him despite the sun-splashed afternoon. I was feeling oddly tired myself; my back was aching dully, like a toothache. It had given me pain often the past few months, making my nights sleepless and uncomfortable. I'd hope the water might soothe the pain—but no. It was worse.

"If you wish, we will finish for the day, but you must cede the last wrestling content to me!" I said and I swam strongly to the shore, climbing out and swiftly bending over to retrieve my clothes.

Behind me, I heard a splash and then a loud exclamation. "What's wrong. Has a knucker bitten your…" I began, teasing.

"R—Richard!" He called to me, his voice grown oddly shaky. He was splashing, fighting the current, trying to gain footing and run to my side.

I stared, wondering if I needed to rescue him—but he seemed fine although distressed. "What, by Christ's Toes, is it? You're frightening me, Frank!" I was hopping one-footed, trying to get my hose on and make myself decent. My bare shoulders and back were a mass of goosebumps; the sun had moved and the Dub was darker and chillier than before. A north-eastern wind was rising, making eddies on the water's surface.

"Richard, you need to see the Lord Warwick as soon as we return to the castle," he panted, gaining the bank and scrabbling at his own clothes. "Get him to call the physician—At once!"

"Why? What's the matter with you?" I frowned, whirling on my bare heel. "Are you hurt? Tell me!"

"N-not me, Richard. Y-you!" he stammered. His eyes were dark with distress.

"Me? But I am fine." I looked down my whipcord-thin body, my wiry legs, my delicate but surprisingly strong arms. Everything there and intact, as it should be, though a little blue from the cold water of the Dub.

"It…it is *here*, Richard." Francis came up to me and lightly pressed a finger against my spine. His trembling fingertip traced the length of the column of bone, and as he reached a spot just below my right shoulder blade, I could feel his hand veer to the side, almost as if my backbone was not where a backbone should be. As if…as if it was twisted.

I gave a sharp gasp and stumbled forward, grasping my shirt and thrusting it over my head. My heart raced, thudding against my ribs. It could not be…*could not be*! I was the King's brother, blood kin to handsome, perfect Ned Plantagenet. I could not be…damaged. And yet, I knew. Everything became clear. The Master at Arms telling me to straighten my stance, the ache as I sat at my studies, the wearying pain that ofttimes made me toss in my sleep.

I…I was a crookback.

God had punished me for some terrible sin.

I must have looked dreadful, white as a linen shroud, shocked and dismayed by this dreadful revelation. Haphazardly flinging on his garments, Francis grabbed hold of my arm, steadying me as I reeled about on the slippery rocks. "*Please*…Come, Dickon, the doctor will know what to do. Warwick will know what to do!"

I stood in Cousin Dick's solar, stripped to the waist, trembling like a leaf on a windswept tree. Dick's visage was dark, expressionless as his personal physician, a dour greybeard in a long black robe, shuffled into the chamber. "My Lord Warwick, how may I help you."

"My cousin, the Duke of Gloucester. It has come to my attention that he may have an injury…or irregularity…on his back. It must be examined right away, and the King must be notified if aught is amiss."

"I see." The ancient doctor stroked the stringy beard that hung from his chin almost to his waist. "Young sir, would you turn away from me and lean forward?"

Sick with shame, I did as I was told, bending forward until my fingers skimmed the floorboards. I heard a rasp of indrawn breath from Cousin Dick.

"*Hmmmm.*" The doctor made a noncommittal noise that set my teeth on edge. "Stand up again, my Lord."

I stood as he took a measuring rod from the dark bag he carried and measured my shoulders. Once, and then again.

"Well?" asked Warwick, filled with impatience. "What do you think, man."

The doctor licked his thin, faded lips. "I am afraid…his Grace's right shoulder is higher than the left. The spine curves below it in a form that is…incorrect."

Warwick's brows lowered. "Is there anything that can be done for it? Can he be stretched?"

I began to sweat, imagining what tortures they might devise to restore my normalcy.

The physician shook his head. "It is sometimes done upon request, but in my estimation, stretching solves nothing."

"Then it would be a waste of time."

"In my opinion, yes, my lord Warwick. This condition, alas, can only be endured by the sufferer, never cured. Perhaps the young lord has a calling to the Church?"

"No!" I shouted, breaking my silence. The Church brought up again!

I flailed at the air, thin, white, exposed, ashamed—and furious all at once. "I…I am a Knight of the Garter, a Knight of the Bath. A *knight*, not a monk. Lord Warwick, you know how hard I train—not one boy or man in Middleham can say I do not have aptitude with weapons. I can turn cartwheels in armour. I ride better than most of the household! I will *not* become a monk…"

"Calm yourself," said Cousin Dick sharply. "Stop this foolish rambling about monks. You will be a soldier and, one day, a great magnate—you are the King's own brother. But you must work twice as hard as the other lads due to your difference. Do not expect preferential treatment, Richard—for you will not get it."

He lifted my fallen undershirt and tossed it to me, then, as I dragged it over my head, he slapped me on the back as if to show me that my deformity was nothing, a trifle, an inconvenience to be overcome. "Be not so serious, Dickon," he said. "You won't break. You will attain all that you desire one day, I promise you."

As we left the chamber, Warwick sidled over to me. His visage seemed kinder, with that same brief fatherliness I had noted at Cawood Castle. I thought of my own sire and felt an uncomfortable pricking in my eyes. I glanced down; I could not let Dick see my grief. He put a hand on my shoulder, gentler now; a great blood-red ruby winked on his finger.

"I must tell Edward of what we have discovered," he said. "And then I will see that special doublets are tailored to hide your small problem. No one need know. No one need ever know, Richard, save those closest to you. You can trust me—we are blood."

The next year Edward made me a Knight of the Garter. He was in a cheerful mood ever since in February the Queen had borne their first child, a daughter called Elizabeth. He must have felt disappointed that the babe was not a son, but he showed no outward signs of it and showered his little daughter with gifts and affection.

George was quite pleased; however, for the lack of a son meant he was still Edward's heir presumptive. "It was ever so amusing, Richard," he said to me when I arrived in Windsor for my induction as a Garter Knight. "When the Queen was in the throes of her travail, Master Dominic the physician was hovering outside of the door, predicting to all and sundry that by the way the babe lay in its mother's womb he was certain that it was a boy. He kept calling out to the midwives to give him the good news the moment it happened. Suddenly one old dame stuck her head out of the birthing-chamber and faced him angrily, saying, "Whatever her Grace has borne in here, sure it is a fool that stands without." Dominic turned white, hiked up his robes and fled the palace."

Even I had to smile at that image.

After the Garter ceremony the King spoke to me in private as I stood proudly in my rich dark purple mantle, the Cross of St George blazing on my shoulder, the collar of gold heavy round my neck, the sky-blue garter circling my thigh.

"Now that you have joined the twenty-four Garter Knights, you must come to dwell with me soon, Richard," he said, almost distractedly. "It will be for the best; it is your destiny."

But no arrangements were made and I returned to Middleham and the year dragged on. I was not entirely displeased to return to the Dales, although I knew my ultimate fate was bound with that of my royal brother. I liked my life n the north, especially now that, aged thirteen, I was given more duties in Ned's service—such as sitting in on commissions of oyez and terminer with Cousin Dick and his brother John Montagu.

In their company, though, I became privy to the fact that things were still not well between Warwick and Edward. In fact, they appeared worse. Dick loathed the Woodvilles, calling them jumped up upstarts; he was sore peeved that he had not been the 'mighty earl' who sat in the King's place at Elizabeth Woodville's churching after little Elizabeth's birth. "He gave the position to

Arundel!" he stormed. "It was meant as a slap in the face. How dare he!"

Of even greater worry, he disapproved violently of Edward's foreign policy. Warwick had been involved in negotiations with the King of France, the ugly but devious little man known as the Universal Spider. A plan was afoot, devised by Cousin Dick, to have Edward renounce any claims on the throne of France and invite Louis to become his brother-in-arms, which would assure a lasting peace. England and France united in brotherhood against the world....

My surprise knew no bounds when Warwick himself took me aside and spoke to me of these plans, not only because he was spilling them to an untried youth but because I was the brother of the King whose own plans he scorned. Truth be told, I agreed with Ned on the matter. To my mind, the idea of an unbreakable bond with scheming Louis seemed dishonourable; wars had been fought and blood spilt over England's rightful claim to France. The sacrifices of countless Englishmen should not have been made in vain. And what would Louis *really* give Edward in exchange for such an alliance?

"Peace, lasting peace," said Warwick gravely as we sat in his closet, bathed in thin candlelight. "Think of it—the united power of England and France. United against the Scots instead of the Scottish King invoking the 'Auld Alliance.'" I must have looked dubious for he lowered his voice and muttered, "And you will play a part in bringing peace…maybe."

"Me? "I blinked. "You teach me well, my lord, but I am not old enough to treat with wily lords and kings yet!"

He threw back his head and laughed. "I did not mean that you would. It is not your diplomatic skills that are needed, young Dickon."

I raised an inquisitive eyebrow and sat forward on the edge of my chair.

"King Louis has a daughter…"

I fell back, trying to keep my expression neutral. So…it was *that* time, when a wife might be chosen for me. I was strangely terrified. I had almost begun to think that one day I would be able to choose my own bride just as the King did. He had no pushed a woman on George not on me thus far. "Tell me of her, Cousin."

"Louis' second-born daughter, Princess Jeanne. She is but two."

"Two!" I said in dismay. "But…but that would mean we would not truly live together as man and wife for many years."

"That might not be such a bad thing for a young man," grinned Warwick. "It would give you plenty of time to gain experience in the world if you follow my meaning." I did, a boy going on fourteen summers was vastly different to innocent twelve …and I flushed a dark red.

"But she is so young, I would almost be an old man before I had any sons of my own!" I blurted bitterly after a moment or two.

"The match may be sweeter than you think. There is more involved than just a royal alliance. The Spider King is offering Burgundy and the lands of the Duke of Charolais as Jeanne's dowry."

I snorted and folded my arms defensively over my chest. I was no fool of a boy, thinking only of games, hawks and hounds. I listened carefully to the tales of what went on in the wider world. "Do you truly think those lands would ever materialise, my lord? After all, they are not truly Louis' to give. An army would have to wrest them from their present owners. And is not Charles of Burgundy attempting to obtain my sister Meg's hand in marriage?"

Surprised, Warwick stared at me. "You seem to know a lot, my young friend."

"I am not so young now, Dick, and I make it my business to know as much as I can about what is going on. Meg writes to me as frequently as she may; she is bored to tears. She's well past the age most girls marry and is eager to wed."

Warwick's brow furrowed and I cursed myself inwardly for being too open; I could now expect any missives from my sister to be carefully perused before I received them.

"I will have you know I do not like Charles," said Warwick. "A man of folly—men call him the rash or the bold. Whichever is correct, I find him unsuitable for a princess of York."

"If he is unsuitable, someone else must be found and soon," I found myself saying, despite my better judgment. "It is unfair to my sister."

"As you know, I had hoped for Edward to espouse Bona, the Spider King's sister-in-law, but he chose the Grey Mare instead," said Warwick grimly. "But all may not be lost on that front. Philip of Savoy is interested in Margaret's hand. I shall do all I can to see that she marries Phillip and not Charles. In fact, I will leave for France soon to begin negotiations. I just hope Edward will reconsider Phillip's suit instead of Rash Charles'"

"Tell me more of this possible marriage for me with this princess Jeanne." Sulkily I stared out of the narrow window with its views out over the courtyard. Rain was sluicing down, as dismal as my mood.

Warwick narrowed his eyes. "You are truly not enamoured of the idea, I see. Well, you did make a fair point against wedding Jeanne—you would long be a man grown before having an heir. Look, Dickon, although I pray you will do your duty for England as Edward did not, I would not burden you—especially as I will admit, I have heard the girl was born deformed…"

I cringed, thinking of my own shortcomings—my ruined spine, the curse of which lay heavy on my uneven shoulders.

Dick's visage grew softer as if he guessed the subject of my self-conscious thoughts. "I am sure there is another bride out there who may be more to your liking and still of acceptable stature to wed a royal Duke…Richard, did you know I informed the French king that George was no longer available as a marriageable prince?"

I shook my head.

"Well, I have. And I suspect you know why. My girls are, like most maidens, overly quick to chatter and gossip. It is a folly common to nearly all women, and Isabel, in particular, is no exception. Anne is fortunately a little more circumspect."

If my face had reddened earlier with all this talk of marriage, now it was truly aflame. I did not want to deny what Isabel had told me and lie to a man I respected, yet it was a dangerous thing to admit. If Edward were ever to find out I had known Warwick's intention to wed his eldest daughter to George and said nothing, it would lie perilously close to treason.

Warwick smiled, his lips long and thin in the fluttering candlelight. "I will not press you, Richard—it would be unfair on one so young. But just let me say, if George should marry Isabel, why should you not..." He shrugged, leaving his thoughts unsaid...but obvious.

"It is best we do not talk about it, my lord Warwick," I croaked. I knew of what, or who, he spoke.

"So be it," said Cousin Dick, "but do not forget what I can offer. You like it here at Middleham, don't you?"

I sat in silence but the truth must have shown in my eyes. He laughed, the sound strangely loud and unsettling in that small, close room.

Then he picked up his cloak, slung it over his arm, and rose, our meeting clearly over. "I return to King Louis' court soon," he said. "We will see how the die falls. "

"Whatever takes place, I remain loyal to Edward." My throat was dry.

"Ah...Loyalty." Warwick's voice was a taunting murmur in the darkness. The candle had gone out. My heart felt heavy, beating hard against my ribs. The room reeked of wax, candesmoke...my fear? "*Carpe diem, quam minimum credula postero*, Richard of Gloucester."

Words from Horace; I had learnt them from my tutors long ago.

Seize the day, put very little trust in tomorrow.

Chapter Twelve

In June of 1467, Edward held a joust at Smithfields in which Anthony Woodville, dressed in the costume of a hermit, jousted against the Bastard of Burgundy. I did not attend since Warwick was away on business again and Edward did not command me to London. I was just as glad to ride Challenger on the moor and attend my daily lessons and duties with the other henchmen. I was growing taller and stronger all the time, despite the curve in my back, and even managed to tip the Master of Henchmen on his arse, which made him look at me with a satisfying mixture of hate and pride.

During the tourney, news reached England that Phillip of Burgundy had expired. The joust was cut short and the Bastard fared home on the next ship, but the court was filled with excitement for it meant Charles the Bold was now Duke of Burgundy, which made him an even more attractive groom for Meg. A widower, he had a young daughter, Mary, and seemed keen to have a wife to run his household.

Warwick returned home, a foul aspect upon him. He spoke to none except the Countess, who tried to soothe his cares away with gentle words and calm manner, but all ploys she tried failed, and her brow was creased with worry. The rest of us, from low to high, were glared at by the Earl, and we moved in frightened silence under his stony gaze.

In the relative privacy of the stables, Rob Percy caught me as I groomed Challenger. His visage was grave in a way unusual for one who liked to jest and tease. "Richard, I must speak with you." He placed his hand on my arm and guided me into the tack room, shooing out the stable boys who were oiling leather and cleaning bits and stirrups.

"I know you like to keep abreast of things," he said. "As you may have guessed, Lord Warwick's quest to make a French alliance has come to nought—yet again. Edward has decided to proceed with a match for your sister, Lady Margaret, with Charles of Burgundy. As for that ridiculous idea of Edward forgoing claims to France—it is dead and buried."

"I thought that would happen," I said. "Edward clearly favoured Charles for Meg. And why should he give up ancestral claims? Cousin Dick should not push him. As he is King, he must have the final say."

"Indeed," said Rob, "but Christ's teeth, the Earl seems to have forgotten it. Richard, Warwick and the King are at loggerheads with each other in a manner never seen before, even when he secretly married the Queen at Grafton Regis. The King sneers at the efforts of his former friend and Warwick rails that Edward is ungrateful…and no statesman. King Louis, it seems, has given up on Warwick and bemoans his lack of action in brokering deals that will benefit France—which further humiliates and enrages the Earl. Rumours have even spread that his lordship is gathering men."

"I have not seen anything to indicate such action!" Shocked to my very core, I dropped the curry-comb I had been using on Challenger. Dick gathering men against Ned? That would be treason! Cold sweat broke out on the back of my neck.

"I have seen no signs of it either," said Rob, soothingly "but the Earl's lands and resources are many. None of us knows what may take place elsewhere. I mean, he's hardly going to do aught amiss in front of you, the…."

"The King's brother," I said, heartsick, leaning against Challengers broad flank.

"I just thought you should know how it stands. It does well to be prepared."

"Yes. I thank you, Rob."

Stiffly I exited Challenger's stall and walked to the stable door; Rob did not follow. Wraith-like, I approached the stone stairs leading to the wall-walk of the castle and motioned for the guard stationed at the foot to let me pass. "Yes, my lord of Gloucester."

He peered at me curiously from under the rim of his helmet but he dared not turn me away.

In silence, I stood on the height, buffeted by the ever-soughing breeze, inhaling the pungent wood-smoke smoke from the fire-braziers that burnt throughout the night. Longingly I gazed into the gathering dusk beyond the walls. Nightbirds had begun to sing in the trees on William's Hill; the moor was darkly purple like fine wine. I drowned myself in the sight, taking it all in as if for the last time.

I knew my time here was at an end

In less than a fortnight, Edward sent a Lord Hastings with a small but heavily armed retinue to inform Warwick that the King wished his most entirely beloved brother to resume residence in London and begin the duties expected of one of his station. My presence at court was expected as soon as possible; there would be no time for long farewells.

I stood in my chamber, watching bleakly as my paltry possessions were placed in chests and carried out to waiting wains. Equally miserable, Francis sat in the window embrasure. "I know it is not manly to say so, but I will miss your company here."

"You don't have to be manly yet," I said, attempting levity. "You are only eleven in September. Even though you seem older." He did, even more so than before. He had grown even lankier and was of such serious bent, though with a sly wit, that many thought him of similar age to me.

"I will write…if it is permissible," he faltered, looking down at the book he was clutching. I had given it to him on his last birthday; a collection of tales of Gawain.

"I, too," I said, though I rather doubted it would be often. His family had been firm Lancastrians, and although Francis was in wardship and allegiances had changed, including that of his widowed mother who married Sir William Stanley, Slippery Stanley's younger brother, Ned never showed any of the Lovells any kind of preferment. "Maybe Ned will give me a position in the north in a few years. I will ask him. With luck, and God willing, we will meet again then."

I began to move around the castle to say my last goodbyes to all and sundry. Rob gave me a brief, hard hug. "You come back north some time, Richard. There will always be a place for you, I'll wager. As long as you don't become one of those popinjay dukes strutting around with huge feathers in your hat."

"I will try to keep myself from such a hideous fate," I said. "I promise, Rob."

Then it was on through the rest of the henchmen, then the steward, the Marshal, the cooks, the men in the armoury, the archers, washerwomen, chambermaids, falconers, huntsmen, dog-handlers, grooms and stable lads. Last of all, I was called to Countess Anne's solar where she was seated on a cushioned stool, with Anne kneeling on one side of her and Isabel on the other.

"We are truly sorry to see you depart, Richard," said the Countess. "Dick was very...*fond* of you. May God go with you and grant you safety upon the long road south."

I bowed in my most courtly manner. "My thanks, my lady Countess. I will remember you to the King and Queen, and also pray for you and my Lord of Warwick, and the Ladies Anne and Isabel."

I headed for the door but was stopped as the girls ran after me in a flurry of skirts, ignoring their mother's admonishment. "Richard, send my greetings to George, I beg you," breathed Isabel into my ear, but I hardly noticed her. Anne was staring up at me with luminous, intent eyes.

"I will miss you, Richard. You were kind to me and you were the best dancer amongst all the henchmen."

"You were kind to me too," I blurted back, embarrassed, "when I played the fool at Cousin George's feast."

She looked pleased with my compliment, paltry though it was; and her cheeks grew rosy. Suddenly she leaned forward and thrust an object into my hand. "A gift, Dickon."

I looked. On my palm lay a shiny pebble with a natural hole through the centre—a hag-stone. It hung on a simple thread of red ribbon twined with a sprig of heather, dark purple-brown. "The old goodwives say such stones bring luck and the heather…it's to help you remember Middleham—and us."

"Oh, I will not ever forget Middleham," I said, as I slipped the stone into my doublet and slid toward the door. "Or you."

Will Hastings was waiting for me in the castle bailey, wearing his usual grin that always savoured of lechery, although I knew not that name for it back then. "Are you ready, Duke Richard?" he asked. "Ned is eager to see you again. I am sure you are anxious to get away from this backwater, to all the wine, women and song of the great city of London! Oh, well, maybe not the women…not just yet, although I could be wrong, one never knows." He peered down at me, his beady eyes glimmering.

"And you will never know if I have any say in it, Lord Hastings," I said with a supercilious smile.

He roared with laughter and slapped his thigh with a gloved hand; not quite the reaction I was expecting. "You're not like your kingly brother in that respect, that I can see! Never mind! Each must find his own way; some find joy in praying on their knees, others in lying on their backs…"

"I must find my horse, Challenger," I interrupted. "And see that he is properly saddled for the journey. Do you mind?"

Without waiting for an answer, I ran to the stable. Challenger awaited, pawing in the hands of a groom, eager to go. I took the reins, mounted. I wondered where the Earl of Warwick was. I had not seen him since Hastings arrived with the letter from Ned demanding my return to the York family fold. He had said nothing at the news, but stalked away to his private apartments, agitated and radiating ill-concealed anger.

But there was no more time to worry. Hastings was fretting, mounted on the back of his great, heavy-hoofed bay, his grey hood pulled up with his rather large nose poking beyond the rim. "We need to be upon the road, young Richard," he said. "The journey is long, taking many days, and we must arrive at suitable lodgings by nightfall. Many outlaws dwell on the lonelier roads here in the north and even with my band of stout fellows, I would rather not risk a fray."

I nodded my acceptance and the company passed below the gatehouse in a fanfare of horns. Above, I sensed the presence of the ever-vigilant archers, stern and motionless as statues against the harsh northern winds, hardly distinguishable from the weather-worn stone defenders carved upon the battlements by earlier lords of Middleham.

And then I noticed my cousin, the Earl of Warwick, standing there atop the gatehouse, the breeze lifting his hair, his red cloak a flame in a grey world. Briefly his gaze pierced me, sharp as a sword blade, and he did not smile. Then he raised his hand in brief farewell, a mere second, before vanishing back into the belly of his stronghold.

I was left with Will Hastings and his men. Will, ever merry, began to sing a song—a bawdy one about a jester and a noble-born maiden, which was no surprise.

"There was a jolly jester who rode afore a lady's gate,
She thought he was an angel that had come for her sake!
He rode and he pranced into that lady's fragrant bower,
She thought he was an angel come from heaven's tower
A fine prancer was he!

"Where be ye, my merry maidens, that ye come not to me?
The windows of my bower must you open so I can see
The hero in mine arms, a fine duke or else an earl—"
But when she looked upon him… he was a blear-eyed churl!
"Alas!" said she…"

I blocked out his rather tuneless singing and thought only of my waiting family whom I had not seen for far too long. And I realised how much I had missed them. Even George.

My life with the Earl of Warwick was over. It was my duty to return to Ned's side where my true loyalties lay. I touched the small collar of jewelled suns and roses that I wore around my neck, symbols of my House. Symbols of the destiny that bound me.

In the distance the road twisted, veering down into a hollow masked by cloud-capped trees, then it rose again beyond the greenwood, running along a high ridge where a faded beam of sunlight turned its length to a ribbon of gold.

Roads. They could bring one to so many places, to joy or to endless sorrow. A man might ride upon them to war, to death in bloody battle—or to his heart's ease, to wealth and happiness. My road from my childhood home of Fotheringhay had been a tortuous one, beset with many sorrows, many tears, many losses. It had taken me across the sea and back, and to the north which I had grown to love for its harsh beauty and forthright people with little artifice.

Where would my path lead next, after I had rejoined the King and all my kin?

Only God in his Heaven knew; it was not for mortal man to question, or seek to divine his ultimate fate.

"Come on, Challenger!" I suddenly struck my spurs into my steed's smooth grey flanks. With a whinny, he galloped past a surprised Lord Hastings and then outstripped all his men, eager to be away, to be free.

"My Lord?" Over my shoulder, I saw one soldier turn to his master, raising his visor, questioning.

"Let him go," I heard Will say. "He's headstrong, like the King. Maybe the only thing about them that's similar but you won't stop him. He'll come back when he's ready. Let him go on alone for a time. He will find his own way."

I would find my own way indeed.

Ahead of Challenger's hooves, the road rose, rain-washed and silvered and smelling of wet earth, leading me on, leading me to my destiny.

AUTHOR'S NOTES.

I hadn't intended to write a book about Richard's childhood and earliest youth, hence starting my 2015 book I RICHARD PLANTAGENET: TANTE LE DESIREE at the Battle of Barnet. What could I do with a kid, I thought…but within a year or two I began to have doubts. Richard's story was not really complete without those formative years.

So I decided to write the prequel, and it actually grew into two books, the first of which you have here. THE ROAD FROM FOTHERINGHAY STARTS AT THE DEATH OF Richard's small sister Ursula and finishes when Richard leaves Warwick's household. Needless to say, Richard's whereabout in this period are not always clear in the record, so I have had to guess or reconstruct what may have happened at the time.

You will note I have placed him at Ludlow earlier and for longer than most accounts, fictional and otherwise, have it. I have based that on the teeth isotopes taken from his remains, which showed his East Midland birth then a change to the west sometime after the age of 4/5 or so. To acquire such clear isotopic changes would require a period of time drinking the water from that region, not just a few weeks or months. I never quite could buy the idea of the Duke of York having his family travel over the middle of England to Ludlow when he knew there was trouble brewing in that region. Of course, there were also other castles in the general area of the Borders where the York children may have been. Usk, for instance, has an interesting local legend that Richard was born there. Could it be a folk memory of a stay at the castle, which was indeed held by his father? I decided to use that unusual setting because I found the idea so intriguing.

There is no evidence that Richard was at Elizabeth Woodville's Coronation, and likewise no evidence that his mother Cecily was there either but absence from the record, does not mean one or both couldn't have been there. Many records are not complete and Richard at that time may have been seen as too young and unimportant to get a mention.

I also made mention of a visit to Warwick Castle. This is invented but it WAS one of Warwick's finest holdings and it is not so improbable Richard's party may have stopped there on its journey from London to Middleham.

As I mentioned in my first I, Richard novel, we don't really know how Richard became friends with Francis Lovell but, following other authors, I made their friendship blossom at Middleham. Of course, really Richard would be leaving around the time Francis was settling in, and Francis was also four years younger—that is not to say, they couldn't have found common ground! Anyway, for continuity, Middleham it remains.

Thank you all for your support and please, if you can, leave a review. The next book of the Prequels, AVOUS ME LIE, which covers Richard's youthful feud with the Stanleys and his exile with Edward, should be out later in the year.

For further updated reading, I'd recommend Matthew Lewis's new book, RICHARD III, and Michele's Schindler's LOVELL OUR DOGGE on Francis Lovell.

OTHER WORKS BY J.P. REEDMAN

MEDIEVAL BABES SERIES:

MY FAIR LADY: ELEANOR OF PROVENCE, HENRY III'S LOST QUEEN

MISTRESS OF THE MAZE: Rosamund Clifford, Mistress of Henry II

THE CAPTIVE PRINCESS: Eleanor of Brittany, sister of the murdered Arthur, a prisoner of King John.

THE WHITE ROSE RENT: The short life of Katherine, illegitimate daughter of Richard III

THE PRINCESS NUN. Mary of Woodstock, Daughter of Edward I, the nun who liked fun!

MY FATHER, MY ENEMY. Juliane, illegitimate daughter of Henry I, seeks to kill her father with a crossbow.

RICHARD III and THE WARS OF THE ROSES:

I, RICHARD PLANTAGENET I: TANTE LE DESIREE. Richard in his own first-person perspective, as Duke of Gloucester

I, RICHARD PLANTAGENET II: LOYAULTE ME LIE. Second part of Richard's story, told in 1st person. The mystery of the Princes, the tragedy of Bosworth

A MAN WHO WOULD BE KING. First person account of Henry Stafford, Duke of Buckingham suspect in the murder of the Princes

SACRED KING—Historical fantasy in which Richard III enters a fantastical afterlife and is 'returned to the world' in a Leicester carpark

WHITE ROSES, GOLDEN SUNNES. Collection of short stories about Richard III and his family.

SECRET MARRIAGES. Edward IV's romantic entanglements with Eleanor Talbot and Elizabeth Woodville

BLOOD OF ROSES. Edward IV defeats the Lancastrians at Mortimer's Cross and Towton.

RING OF WHITE ROSES. Two short stories featuring Richard III, including a time-travel tale about a lost traveller in the town of Bridport.

THE MISTLETOE BRIDE OF MINSTER LOVELL. Retelling of the folkloric tale featuring Francis Lovell, his wife and his friend the Duke of Gloucester.

COMING SOON—AVOUS ME LIE. The youth of Richard III part 2 told from his first-person perspective.

ROBIN HOOD:

THE HOOD GAME: RISE OF THE GREENWOOD KING. Robyn wins the Hood in an ancient midwinter rite and goes to fight the Sheriff and Sir Guy.

THE HOOD GAME; SHADOW OF THE BRAZEN HEAD. The Sheriff hunts Robyn and the outlaws using an animated prophetic brass head. And there's a new girl in the forest…

STONEHENGE:

THE STONEHENGE SAGA. Huge epic of the Bronze Age. Ritual, war, love and death. A prehistoric GAME OF STONES.

OTHER:

MY NAME IS NOT MIDNIGHT. Dystopian fantasy about a young girl in an alternate world Canada striving against the evil Sestren.

A DANCE THROUGH TIME. Time travel romance. Isabella falls through a decayed stage into Victorian times.

THE IRISH IMMIGRANT GIRL. Based on a true story. Young Mary leaves Ireland to seek work…but things don't go as expected.

ENDELIENTA, KINSWOMAN OF KING ARTHUR. Life story of the mysterious Cornish Saint and her magical White Cow.

Printed in Poland
by Amazon Fulfillment
Poland Sp. z o.o., Wrocław

58519014R00136